A FLICKER OF MOTION DREW CHEKOV'S ATTENTION TO HIS NAVIGATION CONSOLE.

The short-range scanner had picked up an object leaving the sunlit face of the planet under heavy acceleration—and heading straight for the *Enterprise*. The intense brightness of the missile left no doubt as to its identity: someone had launched a photon torpedo.

Instinct, or academy training, instantly took over. "Incoming!" Chekov shouted, and he jabbed at the switch that activated the defensive shields.

"Red alert!" Kirk said. "Lock phasers on that tor—"

But there was no time to shoot it down. The ship rocked as the intense matter-antimatter detonation knocked the *Enterprise* off course . . .

Look for STAR TREK Fiction from Pocket Books

Star Trek: The Original Series

Star Trek: The Next Generation

Star Trek: Deep Space Nine

Star Trek: Voyager

STAR TREK®

TWILIGHT'S END

JERRY OLTION

POCKET BOOKS
New York   London   Toronto   Sydney   Tokyo   Singapore

An *Original* Publication of POCKET BOOKS

POCKET BOOKS, a division of Simon & Schuster Inc.
1230 Avenue of the Americas, New York, NY 10020

ISBN: 0-671-53873-X

First Pocket Books printing January 1996

10 9 8 7 6 5 4 3 2 1

For Kent Patterson
who helped brainstorm many a wild yarn

Acknowledgments

I'd like to thank a few people for their help and support while I wrote this book:

Steve York and Dave Bischoff for urging me to try it in the first place. Dean Smith and Kris Rusch for the inspiration and peer pressure that helped me finish it in time. John Ordover for the fun we had with titles (I still like *The Spin Doctors),* and for the 7:30 wake-up call every time he had good news. Marybeth O'Halloran for the tapes (research!). Steve Gillett for chort and the sulfides. Philip Stockstad for the brainstorming on the Edge, and the reminder two years later when I needed it. Jerry Jolley for his alter ego and the beer. And Sylvia Shapiro for the creative atmosphere and refuge from phones.

TWILIGHT'S END

Chapter One

"DAMMIT, JIM, they can't keep doing this to us!" Leonard McCoy, chief medical officer for the Federation *Starship Enterprise,* slapped his hand on the vacant diagnostic table that separated him from his captain. The sound echoed in the conspicuously empty sickbay; Nurse Chapel had already fled from the doctor's wrath, taking the room's single patient with her, ostensibly for physical therapy.

McCoy didn't care. He was getting tired of holding back his frustrations, and now that he'd finally let himself blow up, it felt good to clear the room as well as the air. He pointed a finger at Kirk and said, "If we keep missing supply ships, pretty soon I won't have enough equipment to treat a skinned knuckle. My portable protoplaser is down to its last emitter coil, and my genetic scanner is off-line more often than it's on. Even my tricorder has a flicker in the display. We need to take on new supplies, and we need to do it now, not when Starfleet finally gets around to letting us off the hook."

Captain Kirk held his hands out, palms toward McCoy. "I know, Bones, and I argued hard with Admiral York to let us make our supply rendezvous first, but he couldn't do it. Rimillia needs our help *now*. They've got a major terraforming project that's stalled at the most crucial time. Their chief scientist has been kidnapped by extremists, and some of the equipment has been sabotaged. They're on the verge of civil war over it. They need our help now, not next week."

McCoy turned away and faced the blank monitor over the head of the diagnostic table. Its flat, dark surface reflected the rest of sickbay, with its neat rows of surgical instruments lined up for use and its test equipment waiting, pilot lights blinking on standby. He could hear the ever-present chorus of beeps and whirs that the machinery made, too. It gave a false sense of readiness to someone who didn't have to count on it all to function at the right moment, but McCoy knew the real situation. In a crisis, he could be up to his neck in alligators in no time. "And just what kind of help can we give them with a poorly supplied ship?" he demanded.

"We can rescue their scientist. Repair the sabotage. Maybe even negotiate a settlement between the pro-terraforming and the anti-terraforming factions."

"Don't count on it," McCoy said sourly. He looked back at Kirk. "You're always so eager to charge straight into every new situation and set things straight, but I'm the guy who has to sew up all the people who get hurt in the process. And now you're taking us right into the middle of a war. I don't like it one bit, even if we were fresh out of spacedock, but especially not now."

Kirk sighed. "Bones, we're a little short on a few things; we're not a derelict. And it's not a war—yet. That's why we need to go there now, to prevent it from becoming one. If we do our job right, we can prevent hostilities, and there won't be so much as a snuffle for you to treat."

"I'll believe that when I see it," said McCoy. He glared at Jim for a moment, but the captain just glared right back. Finally McCoy said, "If you're waiting for me to say, 'Oh, I understand, don't worry about me, I'll make do somehow,' then you're going to have a long wait. You've given me my orders, and I'll carry them out, but don't push your luck. I've been patient long enough."

Kirk smiled. "I know you've been patient, Bones. That's why I made Admiral York promise us a full week of R and R just as soon as we're done on Rimillia."

McCoy's spirits improved considerably at the mention of R and R, but he wasn't about to let Jim know it. He crossed his arms over his chest and said, "Hah. I'll believe that when I see it, too."

"You will, don't worry." Kirk nodded to McCoy and stepped toward the door, but he turned just as it opened and said, "And if you *stay* patient, the mint juleps will be on me."

"I'll remember that," McCoy said, smiling slightly. But as the door slid shut behind the captain, his smile slowly faded.

* * *

Kirk sighed long and deep as he walked back to the turbolift. He hated wrangling with Bones over situations like this. If there'd been any option of meeting their resupply rendezvous, he would have taken it, and they both knew that, but Bones just wasn't the sort to accept the inevitable without a fight. That was one of the things Kirk admired about his chief medical officer, but it was also one characteristic he hated finding himself at odds with.

Actually, it had gone better than he'd expected with McCoy. The old carrot-on-the-stick ploy had worked once again, and he hadn't had to promise anything he hadn't planned to deliver anyway. And now that the doctor had had his say, he would do everything he could to keep his department running smoothly despite the hardship. He would even come to Kirk's defense if anyone else complained; that, too, was his way.

Yes, the meeting with McCoy had gone better than Kirk had expected. But how was he going to break the news to Scotty?

He considered his options while he rode the turbolift down to engineering. *I've got good news and bad news.* Trouble was, there wasn't any good news, at least from Scotty's perspective. He needed new supplies just as badly as McCoy did. *There's been a little change in plans* sounded better, but Scotty had been around long enough to know what was coming next. Not that it mattered, of course; Scotty was every bit as professional as McCoy, and would do whatever was required of him without complaint, but Kirk wanted to soften the blow if he could. After all, good morale started with the senior officers, and the happier he could make Scotty feel about their new mission, the happier the rest of engineering would be.

Maybe he was looking at it from the wrong angle. Sure, the missed rendezvous would be an inconvenience, and the job that now faced the *Enterprise* was mind-boggling when you thought about it, but there was also the technical challenge to consider. Scotty always loved a challenge.

Yes, that would do it. Focus on the incredible opportunity to participate in an engineering marvel. Get him interested first. Then drop the bomb.

When the turbolift deposited him outside engineering, he found his chief engineer on his back beneath the tractor-beam control console, only his black service boots sticking out from the access panel. The rest of the staff were busy monitoring the engines and the power-distribution and environmental subsystems throughout the ship, doing the routine jobs that kept the mechanical heart of the *Enterprise* beating.

Kirk cleared his throat. "Mr. Scott."

He heard a thump from within the control console, and a muffled curse. Then Scotty's familiar brogue: "Aye, Captain. Just a moment." The legs began to wiggle, and soon the entire Montgomery Scott slid into view. His red tunic was rumpled, and he held a scuffed cylindrical circuit probe in his right hand. "Yes, sir?" he asked.

"I've got a job for you," Kirk replied, suppressing a grin as he reached out and helped the engineer to his feet.

Scotty rubbed the top of his head where he'd banged it when he'd been startled. No lump—yet.

"What sort of job?" he asked, hoping it didn't have anything to do with tractor beams. He'd been working on them all morning, trying to lock down a phase shift in the graviton collimator, and he was having no luck at it.

"A big one," the captain replied. "But it's right up your alley."

"Is it, now? And what alley might that be?"

"Propulsion systems. Specifically impulse engines."

"Aye," Scotty admitted, relieved at the news. "I do know a wee bit about that."

"More than just a wee bit, Mr. Scott." Kirk smiled, and Scotty felt himself blushing. He was always uncomfortable when people called attention to his abilities. Besides which, he hadn't been born yesterday; he knew something was up. He'd noticed the course change a few minutes ago, and he'd heard the engines change pitch when they shifted to warp eight. He'd already known the *Enterprise* was off to yet another exotic new spot in the galaxy, probably someplace dangerous as well, and having Kirk show up in person to tell him about it just confirmed that.

"You said 'big,'" he asked. "How big?"

Kirk pursed his lips and glanced at the ceiling, then looked back at Scotty. "Well, pretty big."

"Pretty big?" Scotty echoed.

"Very big, actually." A hint of a grin was struggling to break through the captain's straight face.

"I see. And just how 'very' is it?"

"Quite. You might even say enormous. But it's a fascinating project, and most of the work is already done."

Scotty laughed. "I know where you're leadin' me,

Captain. Why don't we just cut to the chase and be done with it? What have you got us into this time?"

Kirk laughed, too. He leaned back against the edge of a computer systems monitor station and said, "All right. Have you ever heard of a planet called Rimillia?"

Scotty leaned against the tractor-beam console. "No, sir. I can't say as I have."

"It's a small planet, class L, tidally locked to its primary."

"Class L?" Scotty frowned. Class L planets were considered marginally habitable without artificial life-support. Not as habitable as the Earthlike class M's, but people could usually live on them, if they didn't mind a harsh environment. Scotty rubbed his hands on his pants to wipe off the dust and asked, "How can a tidally locked planet be class L? One face would be hot enough to melt rock, and the other would be cold enough to freeze oxygen. The entire atmosphere would freeze out on the dark side. There'd be nothing to breathe."

Kirk nodded. "Normally that's the case, but Rimillia doesn't *have* a dark side, technically speaking. It's part of a binary star system, and though the secondary star is a red dwarf in a long elliptical orbit, it still provides enough heat to keep the atmosphere from freezing."

Scotty pictured the situation in his mind. A world with one hemisphere perpetually facing its sun, the way Earth's moon faced Earth, with a second sun orbiting farther out, say Jupiter's distance, or Saturn's. The second sun wouldn't provide much heat, but it might be enough to vaporize oxygen and nitrogen on the dark side. That would give the planet an atmosphere, but it still wouldn't do anything to mitigate the outrageous extremes of temperature between the day and night sides. There would be only one environment on the whole world where people could live in the open: along the narrow band of shadow where day and night met.

"They live on the terminator?" Scotty asked incredulously.

"They do." Kirk shrugged as if to say he could hardly believe it, either.

"Why, it'd always be dawn there."

"More like dusk," replied Kirk. "They're dying out. They've overtaxed the ecology in their narrow biosphere, and it's rapidly declining to class K."

Class K worlds were only habitable with some kind of active life-support, like environment suits or domes over the cities. For a whole planet to switch over to artificial environments—even a planet with as low a population as Rimillia must have—would be an incredible task. It would take years. Could that be what they wanted assistance with? But no, the captain had said it had something to do with impulse engines.

"They're going to evacuate?" Scotty asked, puzzled. "With *impulse* engines? Besides needin' thousands of ships, at subwarp speed it'd take 'em generations to get anywhere!"

Kirk crossed his arms over his chest. "No, that's how their ancestors got there in the first place, about five hundred years ago, in a generation-style colony ship, and they're not willing to do it again. They've got more ambitious plans this time." Kirk's eyes twinkled the way they did when he was about to tell a particularly good joke.

"What then?" Scotty asked, his patience growing thin.

"They've decided to increase their living space."

"And how do they plan to do that?"

Kirk shrugged, as if he were discussing an abstract theoretical concept instead of the fate of an entire planet's population. "They've installed about thirty thousand impulse engines all over the planet's surface, and they're going to spin it back up to speed."

Scotty saw a brief image of a planet with thousands of engines sticking up from its surface like hair on an unshaven chin; then he burst out laughing. It was too ridiculous for words. "Hah, that's a good one, Captain. Now tell me, what are they really going to do?"

Kirk looked directly into Scotty's eyes. "They're really going to use impulse engines to spin it up to speed. Except the scientist in charge of the project has been kidnapped and the control systems have been sabotaged. They're up against the wall now, and time is running out. That's where you come in. They need someone to take over the project."

Scotty slowly set his circuit probe down on the tractor-beam console. Suddenly a phase shift in a graviton collimator didn't seem like so big a deal anymore. These people had gambled the fate of their entire population on a single plan? A single *outrageous* plan? And then they had let someone sabotage it? Scotty shook his head in disbelief. "Aye, Captain. It sounds like they do need my help, at that."

Chapter Two

SCIENCE OFFICER SPOCK found the whole situation fascinating. Big engineering projects did not impress him by their sheer magnitude, but what those projects said about the minds of the people who built them was often more intriguing than the projects themselves. What kind of people would try to rotate a tidally locked planet? And what kind of people would try to stop that from happening?

He sat at his science console on the upper level of the *Enterprise*'s bridge, reading through the computer's files on Rimillia. Nominally in charge of the ship while the captain was off the bridge, he paid little attention to the monitors or to Chekov or Sulu or Uhura or any of the other bridge personnel at their duty stations. They needed no supervision for the routine task of directing the ship from point A to point B. The bleeps and pings of the ship's controls were no distraction either; in fact, they helped Spock focus. He would know by auditory stimulus if anything required his attention, so until then he could apply himself completely to the task at hand.

Unfortunately, the computer files held very little data. Rimillia wasn't yet a Federation planet, so the only information was in the report filed by the survey ship that had discovered them nearly thirty years earlier. At that time, the planet had been classified as late-industrial-age in its development, with limited spaceflight capability. Curiously, in this case the term "limited" resulted not from an inability to produce warp-driven spacecraft, but rather from a lack of desire to do so. The Rimillians were descended from space travelers who had made the long crossing from their homeworld the hard way, through normal space, and now that they had found a place to call home they were not eager to strike out again, even in exploration.

Spock knew the danger in saying "the people" wish this or that. Too often major decisions like the development of spacecraft were made by a relatively small group of individuals who held the actual power. But in this case the government seemed to be a true republic, with representatives who answered to their constituents in regular elections. Presumably if they did not follow the will of the people, they would soon be thrown out of office.

That would seem to indicate that the majority of the Rimillians were in fact not interested in spaceflight. Yet when their home became threatened by ecological collapse they were willing to attempt an engineering project of even greater magnitude to repair it. On the surface, that seemed to be a contradiction in temperament, but Spock was sure a good explanation could be found if he looked hard enough. He looked forward to answering the puzzle. Unfortunately, that solution would have to wait until he arrived at Rimillia and could examine the situation himself.

The turbolift doors swished open, and Spock looked up to see Captain Kirk enter the bridge. As usual, his timing was impeccable: only moments after he sat in his command chair, Sulu announced, "Approaching Rimillia, Captain."

Kirk leaned back in his chair. "Very good, Mr. Sulu. Bring us out of warp. Mr. Chekov, establish a polar orbit over the terminator. Lieutenant Uhura, put the planet on the main viewer, please."

The main screen at the front of the bridge flickered, then steadied out with the view from the forward optical telescope. The *Enterprise* was approaching from out-system, so consequently most of the hemisphere facing them was dark, but a narrow crescent of bright white reflected sunlight from the primary.

Spock looked to the computer readout for its local name: the Torch. Or simply Torch. Appropriate. It was a G-0 star, only slightly brighter than Sol, and actually somewhat dimmer than Vulcan's primary, but for anyone on the planet's sunward face it would indeed seem like a torch aimed directly at them.

The secondary sun, a dim M-3 star called the Spark, was not visible on the viewer. Spock checked its location on the long-range sensor grid and saw that it was currently on the far side of the Torch. That meant Rimillia's dark face was now at its coldest. The atmosphere would be slowly condensing there in great rainstorms of liquid nitrogen and oxygen, pooling in shallow seas until the Spark came around in its orbit to vaporize it again. Fortunately the Spark's orbit around the Torch had a period of only sixteen years—far too short to allow more than a fraction of the planet's atmosphere to rain out.

A ragged cluster of other points on the sensor grid drew Spock's attention. Curious. All six of the system's planets were also on the opposite side of the sun, approaching that rare state of conjunction known as syzygy when they all lined up in a straight procession outward from the primary. In another four days, they would line up nearly exactly.

Rimillia alone marred the perfection of the syzygy. Instead of joining its planetary brethren in their stately procession, in a week it would be directly opposite them in its orbit, as far away from them as it could possibly get. If Spock were an animist, he would say that the other planets were hiding out against the possibility that Rimillia would blow up when its inhabitants activated their impulse engines to begin its rotation, but he wasn't an animist, and he understood planetary motion perfectly well without resorting to untested hypotheses. Multiple planetary conjunctions were rare, but not impossible. Given the number of star systems he had visited in his years with Starfleet, he was bound to see one sooner or later.

He bent over the sensor display for a closer look. Fascinating.

When the captain asked for a polar orbit, Chekov cursed himself for a fool. He'd been about to set up a standard synchronous orbit around the equator, which on this planet would have meant a period of exactly a year, at a distance of over a hundred million kilometers. Not exactly within transporter range . . .

The captain was absolutely right; a faster, closer orbit was required here, and as long as they couldn't keep station with any point on the surface anyway, a polar orbit at least gave them the opportunity to overfly the narrow strip of habitable land along the terminator. That would keep them in contact with every populated spot on the planet once per orbit. He quickly calculated the proper course and fed it to Sulu, then watched the viewer as Sulu flew the massive starship smoothly into position.

The planet grew in size until it nearly filled the screen, the dark half an inky black semicircle against the stars, the sunlit half so blindingly bright that all detail was washed out. The fuzzy line separating them was the only feature that the eye could fix on, but without magnification it showed no sign of habitation. Uhura made an adjustment and the contrast lessened, revealing cloud patterns in great streaks across both faces of the planet. Without Coriolis force to bend air currents into curves, the storm systems crossed directly from high- to low-pressure zones. Most of them clustered across the shadow line, where the steep energy gradient pumped them up to hurricane force.

"What a hellhole," Chekov muttered. "Compared to this, Siberia is paradise. No wonder they want to rotate it."

As Sulu stabilized their orbit with a final course correction, he said, "I still don't understand why they're going to the trouble. There are plenty of habitable planets in this sector; why don't they just evacuate this one and start over?"

14

From behind them, Spock's even voice said, "That would be impractical." Chekov turned to look at him as he addressed Sulu: "At their current population of one-point-seven-eight billion, it would take the *Enterprise* four million, one hundred and thirty-nine thousand, five hundred and thirty-five trips to carry them all to safety. That is assuming a birth rate of zero during the evacuation. If the Rimillians continue to procreate, as humanoids are wont to do even in times of crisis, then the evacuation would take considerably longer."

"Considerably, Mr. Spock?" Captain Kirk asked playfully, but the science officer didn't rise to the bait.

In a stunned voice, Uhura asked, "One-point-seven billion? All squeezed onto that tiny little strip of land?"

" 'Squeezed' would not be the term I would choose," Spock replied. "Even at their admittedly high population density, there are only six hundred and fifty-nine people per square kilometer. Less than in some of the nations on your own home planet."

"Oh, well, only six hundred and fifty-nine," Chekov said sarcastically, waving his hands in dismissal. "That would almost give you room to swing a cat without hitting anyone."

Spock looked from Uhura to Chekov, a puzzled frown on his face. "What purpose would swinging a cat achieve, Mr. Chekov?"

Deadpan, Chekov replied, "It's an old Russian custom, started by an ancestor of mine named Anton Pavlovich. He claimed it would—"

"We're being hailed," Uhura interrupted him.

"On screen," Kirk said, then in a quick aside to

Chekov before Uhura could make the transfer, he said, "I didn't think Anton Pavlovich liked cats, Mr. Chekov."

"That's why he swung them, sir," Chekov replied softly.

The viewer came to life with the image of a woman. She looked to be in her mid-thirties, and near the Terran end of the spectrum for humanoid body shape. Her head was oval, her forehead smooth and high, her cheekbones and jawline prominent but not alarmingly so. Her eyes were her most unusual feature; they were larger than normal by about half, and their pupils extended out into violet irises in six-sided starbursts. Her ears were set high on her head, and they rose to graceful points, but unlike Spock's they were rimmed with a fine line of silvery fur. Her hair was also silver, and hung down to her shoulders in thick curls.

She wore a dark blue bodysuit, sleeveless on one side and plunging well below her bare arm. From what Chekov could see, she looked pretty Terran all the way down to her navel, also exposed, just above the heavy wooden desk behind which she sat.

"I am Nashira Joray, world coordinator of Rimillia," she said. Her voice was low, but deeply inflected, with an accent that seemed to place most of the emphasis in her words on the vowels. It reminded Chekov a little of Scandinavian.

Kirk smiled, plainly appreciating what he saw. "James Kirk, captain of the Federation *Starship Enterprise.*"

"We are honored by your presence, Captain. We have prepared a complete briefing for you. Would you care to beam down to our meeting hall to receive it?"

"Of course, Coordinator."

All business, eh? Chekov had known women like that. Cold as ice at first, but once the ice thawed, look out.

A flicker of motion drew his attention to his navigation console, where the short-range scanner had picked up an object leaving the sunlit face of the planet under heavy acceleration. Straight for the *Enterprise.* The intense brightness of the missile left no doubt as to its identity: someone had launched a photon torpedo.

Instinct, or academy training, instantly took over. "Incoming!" Chekov shouted, and he jabbed at the switch that activated the defensive shields.

"Red alert!" Kirk said. "Lock phasers on to that tor—"

But there was no time to shoot it down. There had barely been time enough to raise the shields. The energy field was still powering up when the torpedo hit, but it had stabilized enough to absorb the brunt of the explosion. The ship rocked as its internal gravity generators struggled to compensate for the sudden blow. Chekov hung on to his navigation console until it steadied out, then immediately checked for more danger. No one had launched a second shot, but the intense matter-antimatter detonation had knocked the *Enterprise* off course. Struggling to keep his hands steady under the sudden adrenaline rush, Chekov plotted a return to their previous orbit and fed the coordinates to Sulu.

Ignoring the world coordinator for the moment, Kirk turned to Spock and said, "Sensors on constant sweep for more launches. Report?" he asked Uhura.

"Minor damage to decks nine and ten," she replied, cocking her head and listening to her ear receiver. "No injuries yet reported."

"Good." To the entire bridge crew he said, "Continue red alert. Do not return fire—yet." He turned back to Coordinator Joray. "Quite a welcome you've prepared for us. Do you have an explanation?"

Her starburst eyes had narrowed to tiny slits. "The Denialists," she said, almost snarling the word. "The same outlaws who sabotaged our project. It has to be them."

Kirk punched the intercom button on his command chair. "Transporter room, get a lock on anyone you can find at the launch location, and prepare to beam them directly to security."

The ensign on duty said, "They're heavily shielded, sir. Sensors won't penetrate ... wait a minute. Shields are down."

"So is the facility," said Spock. "There has been an explosion at the launch site. From the lack of organic debris, I surmise it was an automated station, set to attack when we identified ourselves, and to self-destruct when scanned."

Kirk sighed. "Leaving no trace, and no evidence. Clever. Very well, stand down to yellow alert. Coordinator, my chief engineer and medical officer and I will beam down to your meeting hall. You will understand if we bring our own security team?"

If she was insulted by his bluntness, she didn't show it. She merely said, "Of course, Captain. You will be welcomed properly when you arrive."

"I look forward to it. Kirk out."

The screen switched back to the orbital view. Kirk stood up and said, "Mr. Spock, you have the conn."

With no further instructions, he entered the turbolift, leaving the crew to deal with the situation however they saw fit.

Chekov swallowed to wet his dry mouth, and took a couple of deep breaths. "I'm not sure I care for Rimillian hospitality," he muttered to Sulu.

"Get used to it," the helmsman replied. "By the looks of things, we might be here awhile."

Chapter Three

THE RIMILLIAN GOVERNMENT buildings were an exercise in opulence. They were built of quarried stone that had been polished until its swirling gray-and-amber surfaces gleamed like mirrors. The ceilings were at least a dozen meters high, and long windows ran the entire height. Prisms in the windows cast sunlight into all corners of the rooms, highlighting countless sculptures, paintings, and cultural displays along the walls.

They could set it up so intricately, Kirk realized, only because the sun never moved. But that would change once they spun the planet up to speed. It was already changing, in fact, as people removed the valuable artifacts for storage while the rotation was under way. That was no doubt a good plan; there would probably be earthquakes from the tidal stress and maybe from the engines themselves, and there would be periods of intense heat and cold before the speed built up enough to even that out.

There was still plenty to gawk at. Even the floors were works of art. Multicolored mosaic tiles—all soft hues, so they wouldn't jar the eye—depicted scenes from life on Rimillia. Forests of strangely twisted trees, people farming beneath banks of mirrors that reflected the low-angled sunlight down on their crops, buildings under construction, and so on. Kirk took them in quickly while he and Scotty and McCoy followed Coordinator Joray from the anteroom where they had met into the actual meeting hall where they would be filled in on the current situation.

Government officials as well as packing people moved back and forth through the great halls. Few of them even paused to look at the star travelers in their midst. Most were dressed in much simpler attire than Joray: loose blouses, simple pants, the occasional skirt. Most of the building's occupants were female, Kirk noted. What few men he saw were as a rule hurrying faster than their female counterparts, and carrying more paper. Minor functionaries, by the looks of things.

The side corridors were less crowded, but no less ornate. The place looked like a museum. Kirk expected buildings like this one to smell old and musty, but there was a different aroma to the air, a chemical odor that caught in his throat and made him feel constantly short of breath. He wondered if it was some kind of cleaning solvent the custodians had used in preparation for their guests, or if the smell came from the general atmosphere. He hoped it was the former; it would take a while to get used to this if the smell was worldwide. He would have to find a good moment to ask McCoy for an analysis, but it wouldn't do to simply ask "Bones, what's that smell?" in front of the world coordinator.

His and McCoy's and Scotty's footsteps, and those of the two security officers who followed behind them, made no echoes even among all the stone. The floors felt as solid as the planet itself, and thick tapestries on the walls absorbed what little sound their boots made. Joray made no noise as she walked, either, save when she spoke to point out a particularly spectacular or historically significant work of art.

"This mural," she said, stopping in a circular chamber at least ten meters across, whose walls were covered all the way around with scenes of a class-M planet in space, "depicts the destruction of our home planet, Duma, over five hundred years ago."

Kirk and Scotty and McCoy peered at the mural, startled. "Destroyed?" Scotty asked. "How?"

Joray laughed, and waved her right hand toward the walls. "Let us see if our artists were worth their commission. You tell me."

It seemed to Kirk like a waste of valuable time, but he reminded himself that he was the guest here, and Joray obviously wanted to impress him with her palace. He and Scotty and McCoy stepped closer to the walls, starting near the archway they had entered by. The security officers stayed put, back-to-back in the center of the chamber.

The mural was done in colored glass, painstakingly fused to the wall in shards no larger than a fingernail, which together portrayed surprisingly realistic images to an observer standing a meter or two away. It took only a moment to see the order of progression. The first scene showed just the planet itself, glowing warmly in the light of its sun, its blue oceans and brown landmasses showing through the veil of fleecy white cloud.

The next scene, moving right to left, showed the same planet with a space station in orbit around it. A much larger space station was still under construction, its toroidal shape only a third complete. Bare girders roughed in the rest of its outline, but there was clearly a lot of work yet to go.

The next image, however, did not show it complete. It didn't even show the planet, except as a tiny speck in the background. Instead, this image showed a large asteroid—Kirk estimated it to be ninety or a hundred kilometers across, by the size of the craters on its surface—being colonized instead.

No, that wasn't it. The next two images showed the asteroid in flight, propelled by enormous detonations in a single crater on the side facing away from the home planet. Mining was already under way in the second view; it was clear that they were bringing the asteroid in for raw material to finish their space station, and smelting ore on the way. With a growing sense of horror, Kirk followed the progression: steering rockets fired along the asteroid's rim as it drew closer to the planet, then a spectacular explosion as one of the engines malfunctioned.

The next scene showed the asteroid only a few tens of kilometers from the planet. The planet still looked warm and pristine, but the asteroid's shadow already blotted out a tiny section of the surface. A deceptively small speck of shadow, but Kirk knew how much energy even a small asteroid carried. He knew without looking what the next scene would be.

Sure enough: fiery impact, and a shock wave that had already engulfed half a hemisphere, leaving behind only molten lava and hurricanes of superheated steam. Huge blocks of ejecta speared out to crash ahead of the shock wave, wreaking more havoc where they struck.

Next, a pall of dirty yellow smoke surrounded the entire planet. Volcanoes spewed more clouds into the atmosphere. It must have been at least a day later, but the impact site still glowed angry red.

And finally, the first space colony was moving away from the devastated planet. Sunlight gleamed on its metal surfaces, giving it the same sense of warmth that had formerly belonged to the homeworld. The message was obvious: here were the survivors, heading into space to seek a new home.

It took Kirk a moment to find his voice. "I'd say your artists captured the . . . impact quite well."

McCoy nodded his agreement.

Scotty's voice was incredulous as he said, "I see no evidence here of a backup guidance system. Did you nae have any?"

Joray shook her head. Silver curls danced over her shoulders. "It was all our engineers could do to build the motors we had. Our economy was faltering, our planetary resources were drying up. The government was afraid that if the Dumada didn't establish a permanent presence in space, and do it soon, we might fall back to the ground and never reach the stars. A single asteroid in close orbit would have been riches beyond imagining. So they gambled. And they lost."

"That they did," Scott said, shuddering. He turned away from the murals.

Joray looked directly at Kirk with her captivating eyes. "I show you this so you will understand the opposition to our current project. Many of our people feel we are about to repeat our earlier folly, and wipe out the last of our race."

"But you don't," Kirk said.

"No. We have studied the situation carefully. It is dangerous, but we can do it. We aren't depending on everything functioning perfectly this time. We have over thirty thousand separate impulse engines; if some malfunction, they will hardly be missed."

"I don't know about that," Scotty said. "Impulse engines aren't just big rockets. They interact with subspace, with the very fabric of the universe itself. The fluctuations from that many engines distorting the continuum at once will be incredible. They'd all have to fire in perfect synchronization, or you could generate feedback loops and standing waves that could rip the planet apart."

"Very perceptive," a new voice said. "You've spotted the flaw in the plan immediately."

Kirk turned to see another woman in the archway that led farther into the building. She was dressed similarly to Joray, but in green, and her hair was shorter, darker, and straight. All Kirk's defenses rose to high alert the moment he saw her, for she carried herself like a tiger stalking prey.

Joray betrayed no surprise at the interruption. She nodded to the other woman, and said, "This is our minority advocate, Migina Haidar." She leaned heavily on the word "minority."

"Think of me as the loyal opposition," Haidar said,

stepping closer. One of the two security men eyed her carefully, while the other scanned the rest of the chamber, in case she was a decoy.

"She's the opposition, at any rate," Joray said.

"Do you accuse me of treason?" Haidar demanded, her voice suddenly harsh.

"Of course not. Not until I can prove it. But someone fired a photon torpedo at our guests only moments after they arrived. That means whoever did it had to know they were coming, and the only people who knew that were the inner council."

"There are fifteen of us on that council." Haidar walked slowly around behind Joray, making the world coordinator turn to follow her. "And seven of us are opposed to your insane project. Any of them could have leaked that information to the Denialists. Or you could have done it yourself, to discredit us."

"That's ridiculous," snapped Joray.

Kirk shifted uncomfortably. "Please, ladies," he said. "The damage was minimal. I'm willing to disregard it in the interest of peace. There's a greater issue at stake here, don't you think, than who threw the first punch?"

Haidar said, "How true. Our very existence hangs in the balance. And you, it seems, can tip the scale either way." She turned to Joray. "How kind of you to invite me to this briefing. Shall we proceed?"

Without waiting for a response, she set off the way she had come, leaving Joray and the others to follow her.

Kirk couldn't keep from grinning at her obvious ploy, but he had to admit that it had achieved its purpose. All eyes were on Haidar now, and where Joray had merely walked the halls, she swept through them, ignoring the splendor around her with the haughty disdain of someone long familiar with riches. She was putting on a show, and its meaning couldn't be made more clear. Her party might be in the minority at the moment, but she was no stranger to power.

She led them to a smaller, more functional room, which had been set up like a theater with three rows of chairs facing a podium and viewscreen. Before Joray could speak, she said, "Would you like refreshments?" and without waiting for an answer she began pouring shallow mugs full of something steaming hot and blue from a silver decanter near the podium. She passed them out to the visitors one by one.

McCoy unobtrusively passed his medical scanner over his, then nodded to Kirk and Scotty. Kirk took a mug and tasted the contents; it was some sort of strong tea. Drinkable, and the mug warmed the hands, which was a good thing. The air temperature here was a few degrees below what he was used to.

Haidar didn't offer Joray a mug, nor the security guards. When she had poured one for herself, she nodded toward the chairs and said, "Please be seated."

Kirk and Scotty and McCoy did so, taking the middle chairs in the front row. The two security officers remained standing by the door. It looked as if Haidar had completely taken over the meeting, but Joray simply walked over to the podium and said to her, "You may be seated as well. You are the minority advocate; I am the coordinator, and I will direct the discussion."

Her methods seemed blunt and crude compared to Haidar's, but Kirk realized he found that refreshing.

Joray had the legal authority to call the shots; she
didn't need to rely on subterfuge, so she didn't bother.
She was direct and open, and if she was somewhat
rough around the edges then at least it was an honest
roughness. Kirk admired that in a woman.

Careful, he warned himself as she activated the
viewscreen. Don't get involved in the local politics.
Especially not with these two politicians. Either one
of them could be dangerous as an enraged mugato if
they thought he could be manipulated through personal means.

Scotty had been itching to get to the specifics all
afternoon. At least it had been afternoon for him
when he'd left the *Enterprise*. Here it was perpetually
twilight, and already his sense of time was failing him.

Whatever; that wasn't the problem. The problem
was, thirty thousand impulse engines was such an
abstract figure that it didn't carry any real signifi-
cance, even for him, an engineer. He needed some
other sense of scale, some indication of how these
Rimillian people actually intended this incredible
project of theirs to *work*.

For instance, there was the issue of control he had
raised earlier. How did they plan to coordinate all
those engines, and monitor their subspace interactions? How did they intend to dampen the inevitable
oscillations that would occur with that many field
generators working at once? What kind of backup
system had they designed, and what were *its* failure
modes? He needed to know all these things if he was
to step in and see the project to completion.

Unfortunately, the briefing material began with an

overview of the ecological problem. Scotty leaned back in his chair and waited impatiently for it to be over, but before long he found himself interested despite the subject matter.

Simply stated, Rimillia's ecosystem was on the verge of collapse. The Dumadan vegetation that the colonists had brought with them from their homeworld had never adapted well to the lack of a diurnal cycle, and the native plant life—mostly immense, twisted, branching towers called cyclone trees —had been so severely disrupted by encroaching civilization that there was hardly enough of it left to even call a biome.

Animal life was even less successful. Only the least useful of the Dumadan species—the vermin, in other words—seemed to thrive in the perpetual twilight. Food animals survived if pampered, but keeping one healthy to maturity cost more in time and energy than it was worth. A few native species could be eaten, but they fared poorly in captivity and the natural population had been hunted nearly to extinction.

And as if that wasn't trouble enough, the atmosphere was slowly becoming unbreathable. It had taken a decade for the Rimillians to even notice the subtle shift in composition, but a graph of the accelerating rate of change showed it going asymptotic within a year. No one knew for sure what had caused it, but the result was perfectly clear: oxygen was disappearing somewhere, and was not being replaced. Most of the local ecologists blamed the destruction of the cyclone forests, which were the major oxygen-producing organisms on the planet, while others insisted it was a chemical reaction in the crust on the hot face, where robot mining equipment had exposed oxygen-hungry layers of sulfide-rich soil.

And some people, Scotty realized with a start when Haidar interrupted the briefing, didn't believe that it was happening at all.

"Propaganda and lies!" she shouted when the atmospheric composition chart appeared on the screen. "There's not enough data to support that conclusion. This interpretation of the data is the most extreme one possible. It's far more likely that we're experiencing a normal fluctuation in atmospheric makeup, which will reverse itself naturally."

"Through what mechanism?" Coordinator Joray demanded hotly from the front of the room, where she paused the viewscreen and turned to face Haidar. She had never sat down with the others, evidently preferring to retain their attention at the expense of her own comfort.

"Through whatever mechanism has kept the oxygen balance stable for millennia," Haidar replied, pounding on her armrest. "It is absolute arrogance to assume that we Dumada, by our mere presence in one small area of the planet, could affect something as immense as the planetary atmosphere. There has to be some other global effect at work."

"'One small area of the planet.' Hah." Joray mocked her words. "Define 'small.' We've completely filled the only life-bearing zone, and the poor are being pushed farther and farther out into the hot and cold faces. The cyclone forest that used to encircle the planet is now completely gone; the only natural areas left to us are the naturally dead ones. If you think our salvation is going to come from some magical oxygen factory at the hot pole, you're a worse fool than I thought you were."

"You're the fool, if you think rotating the planet is the solution. How is *that* going to produce more oxygen?"

Scotty's head whipped back and forth between the two women like a hypnosis subject following a pendulum. Kirk followed their argument with interest as well, but Scotty noticed the faint hint of a smile at the corners of his mouth. He enjoyed this little drama, which was obviously being played out just for his benefit. The doctor appeared to be distracted, but Scotty knew him better than to believe that. He was no doubt taking in the whole situation with the precision of a tricorder.

Joray said, "In the short term, it will vaporize what has condensed on the cold face since the Spark was last on that side of the world. That will buy us a few years' time, long enough for the rotation to produce more habitable land, which we can then plant with Dumadan vegetation, which will in turn produce a steady supply of oxygen. That's how."

Haidar snorted. "Maybe in another generation, and at the cost of all we have now. Your plan would subject everything to the Torch, would scorch every square meter of Rimillia with slow fire and then freeze the ashes solid, before you spun it up to sufficient speed to even out the temperatures. We'll be living in underground shelters for years before we can go outside again. There are less drastic ways to expand our living space."

"Oh, yes," said Joray. "Like extending the warrens farther into the hot and cold faces. My people are already wearing life-support suits in their own homes. What more would you ask of them, so you and your rich friends can keep your twilight estates? Environment bubbles around the trees? Domes over the gardens? We might as well live in shelters anyway. Or in space." She was pacing back and forth now, as she said, "No, the time for gentle solutions passed a generation ago, when the last of the cyclone forests were cut to provide land for our out-of-control population. We have already killed all that we have, but people like you won't accept that until the corpse stops twitching."

Haidar jumped from her seat and advanced on Joray. She seemed about to attack, but whether or not that was her true intention Scott never learned, for Captain Kirk stood up as well and in one smooth motion interposed himself between the two legislators. "Ladies, ladies," he said, not bothering to hide his irritation, "this is all very fascinating, but rather pointless, don't you agree? If I understand the situation correctly, the elected government has already voted on the issue, and the majority has decided to go ahead with the rotation. Isn't that correct?"

"Absolutely," Joray said, crossing her arms below her breasts.

"And as I understand it, we have been called in to help complete that undertaking because of sabotage and the kidnapping of the project's chief scientist. Again at the request of the majority of your governing body, correct?"

"Correct," Haidar said, "But—"

Kirk cut her off. "No buts. You two can argue among yourselves all you want, but my duty is clear.

The rotation will happen according to plan, unless your governing body reverses its decision. As far as I'm concerned, that leaves only two questions: What exactly *is* that plan? And where is your scientist being held?"

"We were just getting to that," Joray said, practically oozing satisfaction. She unpaused the viewer and while Kirk and Haidar sat down again she advanced the picture until an elderly, balding Rimillian man with a thick gray mustache appeared on the screen. "His name is Kovari Kostas. He's a professor of physics and engineering at our foremost university. We don't know where he's being held, but we have received ransom demands from the Denialists." She looked at Haidar and said, "That is, *I* don't know where he's being held."

Haidar leaped up again. "I will not tolerate such accusations! What evidence do you have that I am involved?"

"A lifetime of experience in dealing with you and your kind," Joray told her coldly. "You always have to get your way, and if you can't buy it then you steal it."

Tendons stood out in Haidar's neck. "I have never stolen anything in my life!"

"No, of course not. You've just changed the laws to give it to you. But now that we outsiders are in power, you've been forced to show your true colors." Joray waved her away. "You weren't invited here. If you won't help us, then sit down and be quiet or I'll have you thrown from the room."

If looks could kill, both women would have died in that moment. Scotty readied himself to intervene if they started to fight, but after a moment Haidar merely said quietly, "I will remember those words," and sat down again.

"Good," Joray said. "Maybe you'll learn something from them." She turned back to the picture of Kostas and continued as if nothing had happened. "Of course, the Denialists will settle for nothing less than the complete dismantling of the rotation engines. They know that we will not do that, but they also know that we must begin the rotation in four days or not at all, so they merely have to hold him until that time has passed and they will have won by default."

"Why in four days?" Scotty asked. "Seems to me you've got plenty more time than that."

Joray shook her head. "It's the subspace interactions you spoke of earlier. They're going to be complicated enough just locally, but when you factor in the much larger distortions caused by our two suns and the other planets in our star system, the calculations become impossibly complex. Beyond a four-body problem, the system actually becomes chaotic—no amount of calculating power can predict the outcome."

"Of course," said Scotty, instantly seeing the situation. Multibody orbital problems were always chaotic, and the more interactions you added to the equations the faster things became unpredictable. The thousands of impulse engines on Rimillia would not be pushing on just one planet; their subspace fields would also interact with the rest of the star system, and simple Newtonian physics dictated that the star system would have an equal and opposite—and when added together, large and chaotic—reaction on the engines.

"So what happens in four days that will change any o' that?" he asked.

"Syzygy," Joray answered. She advanced the display to show a diagram of the solar system. "At that time, the Spark and all the embers—that's what we call the planets—will line up on the opposite side of the Torch. When that happens we can treat the entire rest of the system as a single body. Actually, we'll have a few hours before they drift far enough to destroy the effect, but we'll need all that time because we need to fire the engines at full power to force the tidal bulge past the libration point."

Once again the magnitude of what they were trying to accomplish washed over Scotty in a wave of disbelief. Of course, the very tidal force that had locked Rimillia into its present position would resist any effort to spin it again. It would be like trying to roll a football endwise across a floor; the first quarter-turn would be all uphill. After that, momentum would keep it going with just a minor addition of energy, but that first push would take all the engines could produce. And with that much stress applied to the planet's crust, there would be no room for random fluctuations caused by other subspace interactions. No wonder they had to do it while all the planets were at their maximum opposition.

"I see," said Scotty, shaking his head. Oh, yes, he saw the situation perfectly now. He had four days to repair and fine-tune a propulsion system that would have to operate at maximum power right from the start, without testing. At least impulse engines were fairly simple devices, when taken individually.

Joray took his statement as permission to continue

2023-06-01

Jerry Oltion

her briefing. She advanced the picture again until an intricate collection of pumps and coils and conduit appeared. "This," she said proudly, "is one of the impulse engines Professor Kostas has designed."

Scotty leaned forward to study it, and slowly felt his heart slide into his boots. "Good God," he whispered, "it's a kludge!"

Chapter Four

ENSIGN TURNER didn't like this situation one bit. As he and Lieutenant Hughes flanked the captain and Dr. McCoy on their way back through the enormous government meeting hall, he could almost feel the searing heat of a phaser blast in his back. After that photon torpedo the moment they arrived in orbit, and after hearing the world coordinator and her minority advocate argue so bitterly before their guests—and after Captain Kirk's tone of finality in quashing that argument—he expected an ambush at any moment.

The only reassurance was that both Rimillian women still accompanied them. If there was to be an ambush, surely Haidar would have found some excuse to slip away first.

Provided she knew about it, of course. From what she had said earlier, there were at least six others in the High Council—or whatever they called it—who could just as easily arrange an attack.

And now they were going outside! Mr. Scott had excused himself to begin work on the impulse engines, but Kirk and McCoy had accepted Joray's invitation to see firsthand what Rimillia's habitable zone looked like. Inside a building Turner might actually have a chance to protect his captain, but outside he could do little besides track where the shots came from.

His mouth felt dry. He hadn't been offered any of the tea the others had received at the briefing, but tea wasn't what he wanted now anyway. He would much prefer a good beer. A bitter, probably, or a stout. Something with a little kick to it, to calm the nerves. Beer was his hobby, and he'd been planning to brew a batch this evening, before the *Enterprise* had been diverted and he'd been assigned to guard duty.

Maybe he'd still get the chance, if nobody started shooting. He vowed not to fire the first shot, but he kept his phaser ready to fire the second.

Joray led the group to another antechamber, the first normal-sized room they had seen in the building. It had massive wooden doors at both ends, and rows of heavy full-body suits on either side. They were all bright white, and looked almost like spacesuits, save that they were hooded rather than helmeted. The room was definitely an airlock just the same. Evidently conditions outside were harsher than Turner had been led to believe.

But Haidar breezed past the suits without a glance and palmed the ID plate beside the door at the far end of the room. Soundlessly, the ornately carved wood panel slid aside, revealing a calm, pleasant cityscape

38

beyond. The low-angled sun lit the buildings with golden light, and a soft breeze rustled the leaves on a line of trees that flanked the pathway leading away from the door. The trees were unusual. They had five or six trunks—it was hard to tell how many, because they wound around one another for the first two or three meters before branching out to support their leafy canopies. The sky above them was free of clouds. It was deep violet in hue, partly from the low sun angle, but from the difficulty he had in breathing Turner suspected there was simply less air there to scatter light, too. Rimillia had a thin atmosphere.

Dr. McCoy looked from the suits to the scene outside, clearly wondering the same thing that Turner did. "What are the suits for, if it's that temperate out there?" he asked.

Joray pulled one off the rack and handed it to him. It was thick and bulky, but lightweight by the way the doctor handled it. The sleeves and pant legs had tight cuffs to seal them against the elements, and the hood had a face mask. The smooth white outer surface crinkled as it moved; it was no doubt a heat retaining or reflecting surface. Turner had seen spacesuits that looked less substantial than that.

"We have a saying on Rimillia," Joray said. "If you don't like the weather, blink. It'll change." She glanced at a monitor set into the outer wall, then added, "But as Haidar already knew when she opened the door, you arrived during a relatively calm period. It looks like we have at least half an hour before the next storm hits. Should we take advantage of it?"

"By all means," the captain replied, stepping toward the door.

Dr. McCoy, however, interrupted to ask, "A half hour? Does it really change that fast?"

"Often faster," Joray said.

"So you need weather radar in all your buildings just so you'll know if it's safe to go outside?"

Joray shook her head. "Only people who can afford the service have it. The rich, who live near the median of the habitable zone. We call them insiders. The outsiders—the ones who live out in the fringes—don't have that luxury." She shrugged. "But then, out on the fringes the weather is always hostile, so radar would serve little purpose."

"Oh," said McCoy. "I see."

Hughes had taken the opportunity to step closer to the door, so he was the first one through. He looked quickly around, then nodded to Turner. No obvious danger, then. Turner glanced around the anteroom/airlock just in case someone had followed them; then, when he was sure they were alone, he followed the rest of the party outside. He felt a little paranoid, but right now that was his job.

They stood on a wide stone landing at the head of a shallow flight of steps. Across a wide courtyard filled with people, more stone buildings lurked in deep shadow. They were all low and massive, three stories high at most. Their surfaces were smooth, the edges rounded, as if they had been built for aerodynamic stability. The only break in their contours were the windows, and Turner noted deep notches along the sides of the frames where shutters could be fit.

Unlike the people inside, the crowd in the courtyard took immediate notice of the off-worlders. Only a few wore the white environment suits; the majority dressed casually, as if they were unaware that a storm was approaching in half an hour. A man in a light-weight suit no more substantial than Turner's own uniform shouted "There they are!" and a wave of noise spread among those gathered around him. Most of them remained where they were, but the one who had shouted advanced to the foot of the steps. Turner was relieved to see that four local policemen—at least that's what he assumed they were, by their identical black uniforms—immediately moved to block his progress. Standing before them, the first man shouted up the steps, "This is none of your business! Go back where you came from and leave this to the Rimillians!"

Someone farther back shouted, "Let us die in peace!"

Captain Kirk didn't reply. He looked to Joray, who shrugged and said, "We allow free speech here."

"Admirable," Kirk said. "But I'm not sure we have time to listen to more arguments. Unless you have some way past this little protest rally, I think our time would be better spent observing from orbit."

Joray said, "We will take a car. Come." She led the way around to the side of the building, where a large, wedge-shaped, repulsor-driven hovercar floated right at the top of the steps.

It held room enough for all of them, in two wide seats that faced one another. Captain Kirk and Coor-dinator Joray sat in the forward seat, while Dr. McCoy, Haidar, and Turner sat in the rear one. Hughes sat in the very front with the pilot. The interior was plush, covered with dark leather and padded so thickly that the occupants sank in as if in a cloud. There were straps to hold everyone in place, but Turner kept his loose so he could remain at alert on the edge of his seat next to the doctor.

The windows were tinted, so people couldn't see in. Once the car was in flight, cruising high above the heads of the crowds anyway, Turner relaxed and watched the scenery slide by below.

The city stretched out along the shadowy line of the planet's terminator without a break. Off to the sides, however, he could see evidence of its narrow width. The government buildings were near the median line; toward the horizon on either side of them the orderly progression of streets and buildings degenerated into a jumble of rough houses, jammed together with only the narrowest of lanes between them. Slums. Normally slums grew in the centers of cities, but not here. The middle of the terminator would be the choicest land, the playground of the rich and powerful. The less fortunate would be pushed outward, not inward.

The factories were pushed outward, too, mostly into the dayside, where solar energy could power them. All along the bright edge of horizon, tall stacks belched smoke into the violet sky. That was where the odd smell came from, no doubt.

Ensign Turner looked out at the graphic display of social stratification below him, and thought about the class struggles that such a system must engender. No wonder the poor, when they had finally gained control of the government through sheer power of numbers, had voted to wipe out the system forever.

And no wonder the rich were resisting. When the entire planet became habitable, their land would be no more valuable than any other. Their power base would vanish into the sunset.

Two separate groups, living literally side by side in a single strip city over thirty thousand kilometers long. One had nothing to lose; the other stood to lose everything. From a security standpoint, the situation was an antimatter bomb just waiting to explode.

The hovercar had its own air-purification system. McCoy noticed that immediately when his breathing slowed to normal and the chemical stench faded from his nostrils. He glanced at his tricorder and saw that the oxygen level had risen to fourteen percent; still low, but better than the ten it had been outside. Ten percent! At this pressure, that was just barely enough to keep normal humans going. It wouldn't be enough if they exerted themselves. Calling this planet class L was being generous, in his opinion.

All the same, the inhabitants' plan to turn it into class M seemed like sheer folly to him. As he looked out over the immense city, at its sprawling streets and factories and housing developments, and at the rows of stumps where the last of the forests had been clear-cut, a better solution to their problems seemed obvious to him.

He searched for a polite way to introduce the subject. "How much of the planet was forested before your people colonized it?" he asked Joray.

"The entire Edge," she replied. "That's what we call the shadow zone. Ninety kilometers wide, on the average, all the way around."

"That seems kind of narrow," McCoy said. "Doesn't twilight usually extend farther than that?"

The car bounced in an air pocket. Joray paid it no attention, saying, "Perhaps on a larger planet, or one with more atmosphere. Rimillia is a small world, and

43

has less air than most, so the temperature tends to vary dramatically in a very short range. That's especially apparent in places like the Steaming Sea."

"Steaming Sea?" Kirk asked.

"An impact crater," Haidar said, "that is filled with water. It boils on the sunlit side, and is covered with ice on the cold side."

"Do you have very many bodies of water along the Edge?" McCoy asked.

"There are a few, and some glaciers," said Joray, "but not many."

"That's too bad," McCoy said. "If a larger percentage of your surface were water, you might not have the problem you do now."

"How so?" she asked.

McCoy smiled. It wasn't the opening he'd hoped for, but it would do. "Well," he said, "plankton in the oceans can produce almost as much oxygen as trees can. It seems to me that the decline in atmospheric oxygen is almost certainly because of the loss of the planet's natural vegetation, so a couple of big oceans would have helped make up the difference. Course, you don't have oceans, so the trees are your only source of renewal. But you've cut all those down. That's your problem."

"Just as I've maintained all along." Joray glanced at Haidar as she said that, and McCoy knew he was dredging up an old argument. Maybe he could bring a new perspective to it, though.

"Right," he said. "But it seems to me it would be a much simpler fix to replant the forests, not destroy what few are left in some desperate gamble to force the entire planet into a completely new ecology."

Kirk shot him an irritated glance, but Haidar gave

him no chance to speak. "That's exactly what I suggest," she said.

Joray waved her arm out toward the city below them. "And where do you hope to plant these forests? It's all city now. Do you propose that we condemn the median ten kilometers or so and make parkland of it? Would you relinquish your holdings so we could do that?"

"I—I—" Haidar stammered.

Joray laughed. "Of course you wouldn't. Nor would anyone else without a fight. And even if they would, where would they all live? The Edge is already filled. There's no room anymore for both people and trees."

"There are the underground shelters we've built to hide from the Torch during spin-up," Haidar said. "The outsiders could live there."

"Oh, the *outsiders* could. Sure. While the rich take the entire Edge for themselves. No, we're tired of being pushed outward. We're not going to let you push us underground either."

McCoy nodded. This was the line he'd been waiting for. "Why not plant the *trees* farther out?" he asked.

"We tried that," said Joray. "They don't survive."

McCoy leaned forward in his seat. "Of course they wouldn't, unmodified. But I'll bet just a little genetic manipulation could harden them for a tougher environment. Why, I bet a good geneticist could design a strain that could grow another fifty kilometers in either direction. More than enough to repair your atmosphere."

"Excuse me, Doctor," Kirk said suddenly, his voice deceptively calm, "but I don't think that's the *prime directive* here. If you follow my meaning."

McCoy blanched. He'd momentarily forgotten that

45

Rimillia wasn't a Federation planet. It was a mere technicality in their case, since they could join whenever they chose to, but they weren't a member yet, and technology transfer was thus forbidden. Scotty could help with their impulse engines because they already knew the secrets of those, but McCoy knew nothing about their genetic-engineering capabilities. He might have revealed more than he should just by bringing it up.

But Haidar defused the situation, saying, "We have scientists trying just that. Unfortunately, when Joray's party won the last election, they diverted most of their funding to the rotation project."

"Because genetics was a dead end!" Joray said. She turned to McCoy. "They've been trying to mutate the cyclone trees for years, but the best they could do was extend their range another kilometer. In the meantime, things just got worse and worse. 'Be patient,' they kept telling us, but finally we ran out of patience. Their solution might work in another century, but we have no assurance that it would *ever* succeed. Besides, we need relief now."

"Spinning the planet won't solve things immediately," Haidar reminded her.

"No, but it will begin the process. Waiting for your geneticists to come up with a miracle is like waiting for the storm to hit before you shutter the windows."

"Speaking of which," the pilot said, turning his head toward them, "we only have a few minutes left. Should I take us back to the capital?"

Joray glanced to the dark half of the sky. McCoy peered past her, trying to make out detail in the gloom. Was the sky darker than before? It was hard to tell. But the few clouds that projected up into the sunlight were billowy and moving fast; on any other world they would presage a storm.

"Yes, I think we've seen enough anyway," Joray said.

The car banked around and flew back the way they had come.

Haidar asked McCoy, "Would the Federation help us with our genetic-engineering project, the way you are helping Joray with her little folly?"

He glanced at Kirk, who gave him a warning look. "Well," McCoy said, "I guess that would depend on the kind of help you need. If you've already got your own project going, then I'm sure we could provide some assistance. . . ."

"What Dr. McCoy means," said Kirk, "is that we will offer whatever help we can that doesn't violate our noninterference rules. We'll have to see what you've done so far, and what you're capable of doing, and base our decision on that. But we will at least check into it." He looked out the window at the approaching storm. "In the meantime, of course, we'll continue our work on the impulse engines."

"Of course," Haidar said, but she was smiling when she said it.

Her smile didn't last long, however. A sudden gust of wind slammed into the hovercar, pitching everyone against the left side. Another gust tossed them the other direction; if they hadn't been strapped in, they would have all wound up in each others' laps. Even so, McCoy realized now why the interior of the car was so heavily padded.

The car steadied out for a moment, but then

another gust, even stronger than the first, shook it, and the pilot aimed for the ground. "Sorry, Coordinator," he said. "We'll have to seek shelter."

"Very well."

The car plummeted toward the city below. McCoy wondered if it was out of control, but just as he was about to reach for his communicator to call for an emergency beam-up, the pilot hit the repulsors and brought it to a halt just a few feet above one of the narrow streets. He could easily have crushed a pedestrian with a maneuver like that, but what few people McCoy could see were already running for the doorways of the surrounding buildings. Metal shutters were rising out of slots in the walls to cover the windows. In what seemed only a few seconds, the city transformed itself from a peaceful, pleasant center of activity to a besieged, heavily defended fortress.

Wind whistled past, slewing the car from side to side and shoving it to the ground a time or two, but the pilot kept it moving toward a flat wall in one of the low, rounded buildings. Just before they got there, a door slid aside, and the car nosed into a small enclosure just barely big enough to hold it. It was just a bare garage, big enough for an aircar and not much else. Evidently it existed for just this purpose, to shelter anyone caught in a storm. There must have been thousands of them scattered around the strip city.

The door closed behind them, and the roar of wind diminished. Joray and Haidar opened the doors and stepped out of the car, and the others followed them to stand on the flat stone floor of the garage. The heavy door rattled and boomed with the force of the wind. McCoy noticed a small window set in a normal-sized door beside the big one, and he walked over to it and looked out. It looked thicker than the windows on the *Enterprise,* and McCoy wondered if it was just because of weaker materials or if this window really needed to be that thick. Outside, litter and dust and other unidentifiable debris blew past at an astonishing pace. McCoy thought he saw a loose stone actually tumbling down the street, but he couldn't be sure because in the next instant it disappeared in a torrential downpour. The window streaked with water, then a moment later filmed over with wet, heavy snowflakes.

McCoy turned away from it, amazed at how fast and furiously the storm had hit.

Haidar was grinning at him. "Welcome to Rimillia," she said. "If you think this is bad, wait until the rotation starts. Weather patterns will change catastrophically. When the cold face sees the Torch, megatons of ice will vaporize into worldwide storms. Imagine this—" she waved at the shuddering building around them, and by implication the storm beyond "—magnified a thousandfold. That's what awaits us if we go through with Joray's insane plan."

Chapter Five

Sulu WAS STILL on the bridge when the landing party returned. Dr. McCoy was obviously unhappy with the way the visit to the planet had gone; Sulu could hear him haranguing the captain before the turbolift had even come to a stop. When the doors opened, Kirk stepped out first, with McCoy right on his heels.

"Look, Jim," he was saying, "All I meant was that they could bring in some geneticists from one of the research stations. They could do a gene scan, run a few computer simulations, and tell them whether or not there's any merit to the idea of redesigning the cyclone trees. With some of the new modeling software they've got they could tell in a week if it's going to work, without having to actually grow anything at all. And if it *will* work, then there's no need to go through with this ridiculous scheme to rotate the whole damned planet."

Kirk sat in his command chair and took a deep breath. "If I didn't know better, Doctor, I'd think the lovely Miss Haidar had gotten to you. Despite what she says, this 'ridiculous scheme' is the only real hope they've got at the moment. By the time we could get a qualified geneticist here from Starfleet, the window of opportunity would be past. And if it turned out that the cyclone trees couldn't be reengineered for more extreme climates, then they'd really be stuck, wouldn't they?"

Spock had been watching the weather patterns on the planet; now he looked up and asked, "Redesigning the cyclone trees?"

"McCoy thinks they can solve their oxygen problem by planting more trees," Kirk explained. "Trouble is, there's no room for them unless they can somehow be hardened to grow farther out into the hot and cold faces of the planet."

Spock considered the idea for a moment, then said, "That would be a stopgap measure at best. The Rimillians have already overtaxed their planet's resources and cut down one perfectly functional forest in the process. The current generation might be persuaded to leave the new plantings alone, but it is illogical to assume that later generations would treat a new forest any more delicately than the previous generations did the last one. People seldom learn from their ancestors' mistakes."

McCoy looked over at him with narrowed eyes. "That's a fine thing for you to say, Mr. All-logic-because-his-forefathers-were-too-emotional. Vulcans learned from their ancestors, didn't they?"

"Vulcans had little other choice," Spock said stiffly.

51

"Well, as far as I'm concerned, neither do these people."

"Fortunately, Doctor, they feel otherwise."

McCoy turned away and looked at the planet on the main viewer. "Trust you to prefer the mechanical solution over the biological one. You'd rather risk everything on a—a technological tour de force than try something that might require a little ingenuity."

Sulu looked to Chekov, who gave him an almost imperceptible shake of the head that said clear as words, *There they go again,* before he busied himself with the navigation controls.

Sulu couldn't help looking back at the doctor and the captain. Was McCoy serious about redesigning the local flora?

The captain said, "I'm sorry, Bones, but it's really out of our hands. Unless you think you can run the necessary genetic scans and simulations yourself. You're more than welcome to give it a try if you want. If you really think the cyclone trees can be reengineered successfully, you have four days to prove it."

McCoy whirled around angrily. "Me? Dammit, Jim, I'm a doctor, not a botanist."

Sulu felt a shiver of excitement run down his spine as he cleared his throat and said, "No, but I am."

Everyone on the bridge turned to stare at him.

"It's one of my hobbies, actually," he went on.

"Is it really?" McCoy asked dryly.

"Yes, sir." Sulu swallowed, wondering why he had stepped into an argument between his captain and the chief medical officer.

McCoy looked from Sulu to Kirk, then back again.

52

"Well, I'll be damned," he said. "Have you ever resequenced a plant's genetic code before?"

"Yes, sir," Sulu said nervously.

McCoy turned back to the captain. "Well, Jim, I guess it's time to fish or cut bait. Request permission to steal your helmsman for a few days."

"Granted," Kirk said. "Mr. Sulu, you're reassigned to Dr. McCoy."

"Yes, sir," Sulu said for the third time. He stood up and approached McCoy, wiping his suddenly sweaty hands on his pants. What had he gotten himself into?

"Relax," McCoy said. "It's not like we have to save the whole planet or anything. Just a ninety-kilometer-wide strip of it."

"Oh, good," Sulu said as he followed him into the turbolift. "I was afraid this was going to be difficult."

Spock would have liked to beam down with the landing party, but he knew it was illogical to have all the ship's senior officers leave during a yellow alert. So while he waited for the captain's return, or for someone to shoot at the ship again, he had busied himself with a sensor study of the planet below.

He had learned a great deal about it during the hour and a half that the captain had been gone. The sunlit side reached temperatures of nearly four hundred degrees Celsius, while the cold face fell to under two hundred below. The difference would have been even more extreme except for the atmosphere, which served as a convection mechanism to pump heat from the hot side to the cold. The air was thin, less than two-thirds of a standard atmosphere, but it still carried plenty of heat and moisture. That in turn drove powerful storm systems, the likes of which Spock had never seen before.

They did not follow the usual global patterns, for there was no Coriolis force to steer them into cyclonic rotation. Instead, they developed linearly, driven by air currents that began when warm air rose from the hot face, then flowed at high altitude to the cold face, where it cooled, fell, and flowed back across the surface to the hot face. Consequently, the storms nearly always approached from the cold side of the planet, which meant that temperatures in the habitable zone plunged to the freezing point or below within minutes of their arrival. The more desirable property was thus not exactly in the middle of the twilight band, but a few kilometers to sunward of it, where solar heating could counteract the effect of the storms. Of course, during periods of low storm activity it would become uncomfortably hot there. . . .

He had also learned a great deal about the Rimillians themselves, from their style of architecture (heavy, to withstand the storms) to their patterns of settlement (from the center of the habitable zone outward). There was also a vast interconnected system of underground shelters, recently constructed, in which the world's population would wait out the early stages of rotation.

He also found isolated outposts hundreds of kilometers into either face, all heavily insulated and sealed tight as space stations, where research was presumably being conducted. From the *Enterprise*'s present orbit he couldn't see either the hot or the cold pole, but he was willing to bet there would be outposts there as well.

A few of the outposts, and a few sites within the

inhabited zone—fifteen in all—were shielded with energy screens, through which the *Enterprise*'s sensors would not reach.

The impulse engines had been easy to spot, scattered evenly all over the planet. Heightened activity around thirty-seven of them indicated the ones that had been sabotaged. Most of these were near the populated area, where guerrilla teams could strike at them and withdraw quickly. Their contribution to the total power output would be nearly negligible, but the stresses on the planet's crust from their absence would not be so insignificant. Uneven thrust would cause ground quakes, at the very least. Depending on the thickness of the planet's crust it could cause deeper rifts, which would spawn volcanoes that could render vast sections of the planet uninhabitable even after the rotation was complete.

With that thought, Spock had done a deeper scan, and he had discovered something truly interesting: The planet had once had a normal day/night cycle. There could be no other explanation. The surface evidence had been worn away by the constant winds on the dayside, and by glaciation on the nightside, but in the undisturbed strata underneath lay clear indication of continents. Continents that had once borne life. Ancient riverbeds still wound down from the highlands to equally ancient seas, and fossil-bearing shale and coal deposits spoke of a once-thriving ecosystem. Spock had followed the strata upward, watching how the organic content slowly dropped as the planet's rotation slowed and living conditions became more harsh. Eventually, over a billion-year span, it had all died out, save for the narrow band where the Rimillians now lived.

Now, as Dr. McCoy and Mr. Sulu left the bridge, Spock said to the captain, "I do not hold out great hope for the doctor's project. My studies of the planet and its geological history indicate that the current situation has persisted for over a hundred million years. If it were possible for the native vegetation to exist farther from the temperate zone, it would have evolved to do so long ago."

Kirk looked up at him. "So you think rotating the planet is the right answer to the Rimillians' problem?"

"It is the only permanent one," said Spock. "The current biosphere—or perhaps I should say 'biostrip' —is far too small to remain stable under the stress their current population has placed on it. We are seeing only one possible failure mode; I have identified at least seven others that could occur even if this current one were mitigated, all equally disastrous."

The captain laughed softly. "They call it the Edge, Mr. Spock. Sounds like it might be an appropriate name in more ways than one."

"Indeed." Spock swiveled completely around in his chair to face Kirk. "They could use that term to describe more than just their current situation, as I understand it. From the accidental destruction of their homeworld, to the risky interstellar exodus at sublight velocity, to their final choice of colony site and now this decision to revive it at great risk, all of Dumadan history seems to be a balancing act on the knife edge of fate. Their perseverance in the face of adversity is truly astonishing. A lesser race would have given up long ago."

Kirk shook his head. "Some of the Rimillians are in favor of that now, by the looks of things. There was a protest demonstration going on outside the meeting hall while we were there. They wanted us to bow out of their business. One person even shouted, 'Let us die in peace.'"

Uhura spoke up from her communications center. "I've been monitoring their radio transmissions, and I've found three different programs advocating that very thing. The speeches I've heard all claim that their troubles are some sort of divine retribution for the way they've treated the planet."

Spock said dryly, "There is no need to invoke a deity to explain their imminent demise, but they do seem to have cause and effect correct in its essentials."

"They know they've caused their own problems," Uhura went on, "but these people say that's evidence they aren't fit to survive."

"Do they call themselves Denialists?" Kirk asked.

"No, sir. Why?"

"That's the group that Coordinator Joray accused of kidnapping their chief scientist. She didn't mention this death cult. I wonder how many others are opposed to the spin project?"

"I will endeavor to find out," Spock said, turning to the computer with the intention of setting it to scan the local news media for mention of any more.

"While you're at it, Mr. Spock, see if you can find any evidence of Professor Kostas, or any likely places where the Denialists could be holding him. Now that Scotty's on the job down below, rescuing him should be our first priority."

Spock felt one of his previously unexplained observations slide smoothly into place. "I believe I have already discovered fifteen such sites."

"Oh?"

"Yes, sir. There are fifteen structures on the planet's

surface that have been shielded from our sensors. Those shields do not seem to offer protection from the elements, or from attack. They are energy-field disruptors only, and apparently exist solely for the purpose of blocking sensor scans, or transporters. It would therefore seem likely that the missing scientist is being held in one of those sites."

Kirk considered that for a moment, then shook his head. "It doesn't make sense. We wouldn't be able to find him even out in the open unless we already had his ID trace in the transporter files. They could hide him anywhere. Keeping him under a shield would just call attention to him."

"True, Captain, but they do not know that. There has been no technology transfer from the Federation to this planet, therefore they are largely unaware of our capabilities. Lacking precise knowledge, they would tend to err in the direction of caution, which would mean keeping him under shields."

"Hmm." Kirk pondered the idea for a moment. "What about transporters? Do they have those? Maybe they're just shielding valuables from theft."

"I do not think so. They do have the technology, but theirs is still in the early stages of development, and is very expensive to use. Anyone who could afford access to a Rimillian transporter would not need to steal."

Kirk had heard of plenty of rich thieves, but he had to admit that even they seldom spent more on a heist than they got out of it. Besides, fifteen sites was way too few if it was really people protecting their valuables. To hear Joray talk, the entire centerline of the Edge would be shielded if that were the case.

"I think you're probably right, Mr. Spock, but just on the off chance that they're legitimate installations, we'd better check first. It wouldn't do to go barging in on some classified government project. Besides, maybe we can narrow down the possibilities. I don't like the idea of making fifteen simultaneous raids." He turned to Uhura and said, "Open a channel to Joray." She moved to comply, but he suddenly said, "Belay that."

"What's the matter, Captain?" she asked, pausing in midmotion.

"Security's the matter," he replied. "Our signal can be shielded from interception, but we don't know if Joray's equipment is secure. I'd be willing to bet that Haidar has it tapped, and if she's really behind all this then we don't want to tip her off to what we're doing."

"A wise precaution," Spock said.

Kirk nodded. "Give me the coordinates for those sites, and I'll go ask Joray in person if she knows what they are."

Spock recorded the information and handed Kirk the isolinear chip, then thought better of it and downloaded the coordinates into a tricorder, keying it to a global map with the sites marked and labeled. The lack of knowledge worked both ways; the Denialists didn't know the *Enterprise*'s capabilities, but he had no idea whether or not the Rimillian computers could read isolinear chips.

Kirk took the tricorder, said to Uhura, "Inform the coordinator that I'm beaming back down," and headed for the turbolift.

Chapter Six

SCOTTY WAS much less happy than the captain about returning to the surface. He'd gone back to the ship just long enough to pick up his tricorder and circuit analyzer; then he'd beamed back down to begin the long task of repairing the planetwide system of impulse engines.

The new chief of the project, a much younger man than Professor Kostas, met him at the first installation he visited, only a few dozen kilometers from the Edge, and near where the equator would be on a normal planet. "I'm Dobry Neron," he said, offering his left hand in greeting. "And I'm very glad to see you." Despite his youth he had worry lines in his forehead, and by the look of his bloodshot eyes he probably hadn't slept in a week.

Scotty transferred his tricorder to his right hand and shook, saying, "Don't you worry, lad, we'll have all this up and running again in no time. Now, show me what the saboteurs did to her and we'll get to work."

Neron looked skeptical, but he said, "Of course. This way, please."

Scotty had beamed down in the entry airlock; Neron led him through the inner doorway into the vast hangar that housed the engine. They paused to take it all in: an imposing hulk of machinery on an even more massive concrete pedestal. It was mounted horizontally so its thrust would be tangential to the surface, but to keep it from ripping free the engineers had set its forward thrust plate against a concrete wall nearly twenty meters thick, from which braces ran forward at an angle deep into the ground.

"Anchored to bedrock, I assume?" Scotty asked.

"Oh, yes," replied Neron. "And though it's not visually apparent, we've angled it downward three degrees, so the stress won't be completely shear. There's enough of a compression component to the thrust vector that the support will actually become dynamically locked to the planet when the engine fires."

"Very good," Scotty said, impressed despite himself. After what he'd seen in Joray's briefing room he had expected to find boards nailed in Xs, and maybe even a coal chute, but perhaps these people understood engineering after all. Unconventional design didn't necessarily mean bad design, he reminded himself.

He stepped closer and looked up at the engine itself. At first glance it seemed more like a warp drive than an impulse engine, because of the tall, cylindrical matter-antimatter reaction chamber that towered over everything. Scotty knew what the warp core was for, though: for a project this big, normal hydrogen-fusion reactors wouldn't provide enough energy. Only antimatter carried enough kick to influence an entire planet's spin. In these engines the power generated in the warp core went into normal impulse-style subspace field coils, and finally vented through a typical matter-infusion reaction drive that passed the superheated exhaust plasma through a vectored nozzle to wring the last few ergs of thrust out of it.

That last stage would be loud as hell in an atmosphere, Scotty realized. Noise-cancellation earphones would definitely be a good idea when they fired this beast.

"How many hours of test time has this design undergone?" he asked. He climbed up a metal-grating staircase to the first level of the catwalk system that encircled the entire engine, and began to make a close-up circuit.

"We've run one test engine out in the hotlands for over forty days without failure," said Neron. His ears—pointed and edged with light gray fur like the other Rimillians'—twitched a couple of times. He seemed a bit nervous at having a Starfleet engineer asking him questions, but Scotty supposed he would get over it.

"At what load?" Scotty asked.

"Fifty percent. We've run it up to one hundred on five separate occasions with no significant problems."

"Good." A sudden thought hit Scotty. "How long are your days here?"

Neron laughed, a quick bark, quickly stifled. "Since we have no natural cycle of our own, we use the day length of our homeworld. Just a little over twenty-one of your standard hours."

"Hmm," Scotty said. A bit shorter than Terran days, but long enough for forty of them to be a real test. He jacked up his mental score another notch. Maybe these people knew what they were doing after all.

Then he came to the Schofield convertors. Forty superconducting magnets arranged in an evenly spaced ring, they interacted with the ionized warp plasma to power the subspace coils. Except there were more than forty of them in this engine, and they were anything but evenly spaced.

"What have you done here?" asked Scotty, pointing to the gaps in their spacing.

"Those are the Bischoff taps," Neron said nervously.

Scotty rolled his eyes skyward. "I know what they are, laddie, though we've got another name for 'em. What I'd like to know is how you expect the plasma flow to stay stable when they're unevenly spaced like that."

"We had to leave room for the pressure sensors," Neron said, pointing to a cable leading into the gap Scotty had pointed out. "We compensate for the imbalance by drawing off unequal power loads from the coils. The net effect is the same as if they were spaced evenly and identically loaded."

Scotty nodded slowly. "Aye, I suppose it could work. Seems needlessly complex t'me, but it's too late to change the design now. But next time you build an impulse engine, try taking your pressure readings in the Backlund junction, here, where there aren't any coils in the way." He pointed to the narrow flowpipe between the antimatter reaction vessel and the Schofield converters.

"We call that the Silva coupling," Neron said apologetically.

Scotty took a deep breath, and let it out slowly. "Silva coupling," he said. "Right." He didn't really care what they called it; it was whether or not the Rube Goldberg contraption would work that worried him.

But they had already done days of test firing, he reminded himself. Whether or not the engines would work wasn't the issue. Whether they would work *together* was the big unknown.

He turned away from the power-conversion section. "So let's see what the saboteurs did to it," he said.

Neron led him up another four flights of catwalk. Scotty was puffing hard by the time they got to the top; if he had to climb up and down these catwalks much, he would need an oxygen mask to counter the thin air.

When they reached the upper level, the damage was instantly apparent: the engine's entire control section had been melted to slag.

"Well, they knew what they were goin' for, an' there's no doubt," Scotty said when he saw it. Instead of attempting to damage hardware that was meant to stand up to antimatter reactions and hundreds of g's of thrust, the saboteurs had gone for the most fragile yet most necessary item of all. What had once been a fairly sophisticated, if unusually designed, computer was now a useless heap of plastic and silicon.

Some of the interior parts hadn't been melted as badly, but the whole unit was still toast. From the way those parts had been spared from damage, however, Scotty guessed that this had been done with a beam weapon rather than a bomb, and from the angle of the shadows made by the catwalk railings, it looked like the saboteur had stood down below, probably just inside the door.

"Is it the same way with the others?" he asked.

"Yes," said Neron. "Then of course there's the central control station at the north pole. They crashed an armored hovercar into that." He gestured over his shoulder.

"Ah, that's inventive," Scotty said. Then he realized where Neron had pointed. "Wait a minute," he said. "North is that way?"

"Yes," Neron said, narrowing his eyebrows. "Why?"

Scotty looked at the massive engine, its plasma exhaust nozzle pointing to his left. He felt his mental compass shift around and lock into a new orientation. If north was behind him, then . . .

He began to laugh, for it truly didn't matter, but he found it somehow appropriate that Rimillia would be different from ninety-nine percent of the rest of the planets in the galaxy.

"What's funny?" Neron asked.

Scotty shook his head. "Do you realize," he said, wiping a tear from his eye, "that when we start up these engines—assumin' you've got 'em all pointin' in the same direction, that is—then you'll have the only planet in this whole sector that spins backwards?"

This time Coordinator Joray met Kirk in a much less formal setting. She had invited him to beam directly to her living quarters on the third floor of the executive mansion, where she had retired for a nap after their meeting.

"I'm sorry to have disturbed your rest, Coordinator," Kirk said as she greeted him in the anteroom where he'd beamed in.

She was wearing different clothing now, a floor-length turquoise green robe with a black sash tied loosely in front. Kirk wondered if it was what she slept in, or if she had put it on just before he'd arrived. If it wasn't her sleeping attire, then she slept in the nude, because from the amount of leg and chest it revealed when she moved, he was certain she wasn't wearing much, if anything, beneath it.

He smelled a faint aroma of spice, like cinnamon, perhaps, but he couldn't tell if it came from her or from something else in the room.

"Don't apologize, Captain," she said warmly. "When you call on someone here, you're just as likely to catch them sleeping as awake. We don't have any official day or night on Rimillia; people here just sleep when they are tired, and get up when they want." She led him into a sitting room and waved him toward one of two high-backed couches facing one another beside a stone fireplace, which crackled with open flame. "And believe me, I certainly don't mind getting up for you. Make yourself comfortable. Would you care for something to drink?"

Despite the pleasant company, Kirk was eager to get the information he needed and go. He had a scientist to rescue. But diplomacy was part of his job as well, so he said, "Yes, thank you," and settled onto the couch. "Whatever you're having."

She disappeared through an arched doorway, and

Kirk heard clinking and pouring sounds from beyond. He took the opportunity to scan the room with his tricorder, looking for bugs, but he found none.

Unlike the meeting halls he had been in before, this place seemed more warm and homey, a living room rather than a showcase. The windows were shuttered against the storm that still raged outside, but the inner faces of the shutters glowed with bright yellow-white light, illuminating the room almost as well as daylight. Most of Joray's personal belongings had apparently been packed away already in anticipation of the rotation, but a few paintings remained on otherwise smooth white walls, and a few items of blown-glass sculpture—apparently by the same hand or at least of the same style—rested on shelves and pedestals beneath them. Some holographs and other knickknacks of personal interest decorated the mantel, and the furniture, which consisted of the two couches, four single padded chairs, and end tables near each of them, remained as well. The table nearest the fireplace, on the end of the couch opposite Kirk, was piled with books. That would be Joray's favorite spot, Kirk thought, and sure enough, when she returned with two crystal glasses of purplish liquid, she handed one to him and then sat beside the books.

He took an unobtrusive sniff, then a sip. Not bad. Juice of some sort, unfermented, slightly chilled. It had a little bite on the tongue, and a tangy aftertaste.

"Berggren berry," she said. "I keep it for special occasions."

"It's very good."

She nodded. "They grow in the wetlands where the glaciers melt when they reach the Edge. One berry per plant, and the plants have poisonous thorns. Very hard to harvest. A gallon of it would sell for enough to keep a whole family fed and clothed for a year."

Kirk shifted his mental gears into "2158 Ridley Cabernet" mode. "Then I promise to savor it," he said.

Joray laughed. "Gulp it down, Captain. I'm the world coordinator." She took another sip, then said, "I couldn't have afforded even a taste before I was elected, and to tell you the truth I don't even like it much, but I drink it now mostly so there will be less for Haidar and her kind."

Kirk laughed despite himself. "It seems there's no love lost between the two of you."

"None at all," said Joray. "I know she's behind the sabotage."

The building shuddered in a heavy gust of wind. Kirk was glad it was made out of stone, and that they weren't any higher than they were. "Are you sure of that?" he asked. "It seems like there are plenty of people who oppose the rotation project."

Dismissively, Joray said, "Oh, yes, there are three distinct groups, but two of them aren't militant enough to have done it. The Sealers—they're the ones who advocate putting domes over the Edge and sealing it up like a space colony—aren't violently opposed. They just think it's a waste of effort. The Nihilists think we deserve to die because of what we've done to the planet."

"My communications officer says they have quite a presence on the radio spectrum."

"Oh, yes, don't get me wrong. They're politically strong, and will probably cost us the election next term if we don't succeed, but they're pacifists. Only the Denialists, whom Haidar leads, are capable of sabotage and kidnapping for their cause."

Kirk sipped his Berggren berry juice. "I see. Well then, now that we're alone, do you know where she's keeping Professor Kostas?"

"No. Probably in one of her rich friends' mansions. She's had three days to hide him; he could be anywhere on the Edge by now."

"Or maybe beyond it," Kirk said, holding out the tricorder with its display set to the shielded locations Spock had found. Some of them were deep into uninhabitable territory. "Do you know offhand what's at those sites?"

She looked at the map. Kirk showed her how to expand the scale for greater and greater detail, and at last she nodded. "Yes, of course. These five—" she zoomed the display back out to planetary scale and leaned forward to show him the sites she meant, inadvertently exposing the tops of her breasts as her robe fell open "—are government information vaults. These eight—" she pointed again "—are known Denialist strongholds, but we've been watching them since before the kidnapping, so it's not likely they could have slipped him in without us knowing it." She gathered her robe up more closely and cinched the belt, then said, "But the other two are not familiar to me. What drew your attention to these areas?"

"They're shielded," Kirk replied, trying to keep his mind on business. "My science officer thinks whoever captured the professor might be trying to hide him from our sensors under an energy barrier."

"That makes sense."

"Mr. Spock usually does," Kirk said. He grinned,

and added, "With your permission, then, I will organize landing parties to check out these two unknown sites and search for your missing scientist."

"Please do," Joray said. She pointed at one of the locations that sat square in the middle of the Edge. "And pay special attention to this one," she said. "Unless I'm very much mistaken, that's near where Haidar lived before she was elected to the council."

"I'll see to that one personally." Kirk swallowed half the remaining juice in his glass and set it down on the end table. "Thank you for your help. I'll let you get back to your nap now."

But before he could get up, Joray laughed and said, "Thank you, Captain, but I'm wide awake again now, and I enjoy the company. Please stay at least until you're done with your drink."

Kirk settled back onto the couch. He itched to get back to the ship and check out these sites, but it would be rude to leave now, and also rude to just bolt what remained in his glass and go. And besides, the world coordinator was easy on the eyes, and her lightly furred ears and starburst pupils added just enough exotic flavor to stir his sense of adventure. So he said, "Just for a few minutes. Then I really must go."

She nodded. "You're a busy man, I know. Being a starship captain must be an exciting life."

"Yes, it is that," Kirk admitted. "Maybe even too exciting at times. But I've never complained."

Joray curled her legs up beneath her. "Oh, no, I can't imagine you doing that. So tell me, where's the most exciting place you've ever been?"

Her question brought a hundred images to mind, from the planetwide amusement park at Omicron Delta, to the war-torn Eminiar VII, to very edge of the galaxy itself. But Kirk had been around enough to know what she was really asking, so he gave her the answer she wanted. "Actually, I find Rimillia quite fascinating."

She smiled. "You're being diplomatic. I'm afraid I never learned that skill."

"On the contrary," Kirk protested. "I've met with quite a few heads of government, and you're by far the most . . . pleasant to deal with."

He didn't expect her to laugh, but that's what she did. It took her a moment to bring it under control, and by the time she did Kirk found that he'd lost his momentary annoyance and was laughing with her.

"What did I say that was so funny?" he asked when they'd both recovered.

Joray wiped her eyes with a sleeve. "Captain, I must be the galaxy's least experienced planetary leader. I inherited this job when the previous coordinator was assassinated two years ago. I won her seat merely because I was the most vocal organizer for the rotation project, and her supporters knew I would make it my highest priority. But until the day I was elected to this office, I lived in a thousand-unit apartment complex forty kilometers into the cold face."

Kirk nodded. "I suspected something like that. You're too open and direct for a professional politician. You know what you want and you go straight for it. I find that refreshing."

"Do you really?" she asked mischievously. She uncoiled from her couch and crossed the two steps that separated them, and sat down beside Kirk. "Then you won't mind if I sit a little closer, will you?"

The cinnamon aroma that he had noticed earlier grew stronger now. It was definitely coming from

Joray, but whether it was a perfume or her natural fragrance, he couldn't tell. Whichever it was, Kirk liked it.

He wished he had the time to appreciate all she was offering him, but he really couldn't just now. "Of course I don't mind," he said, making room for her on the couch. "But I really did mean it when I said I could only stay a few minutes. I have to rescue your scientist and get your rotation project back on-line before I can, ah, take the time to enjoy your company properly."

Joray laughed. "That was very diplomatic as well. All right, Captain, I'll let you go. But only if you promise you'll come back as soon as your work is done." She leaned forward and kissed him, her lips soft and warm and tasting of cinnamon. It was no perfume; it was her. Kirk's pulse rate began to rise.

"That's a promise I'll be glad to keep," he told her. He wondered what had become of his intentions not to get personally involved with the Rimillian leaders, but then she kissed him again and he knew exactly what had happened to them.

Chapter Seven

SULU'S FIRST DUTY under McCoy's command was to beam down to the planet and retrieve some samples of the local flora to study. It was a logical starting point, and a job he'd gladly taken, since it allowed him to set foot on another alien world, but he hadn't realized until now just how difficult it would be to find a suitable beam-down site.

He and Ensign Vagle, the transporter operator, had been staring into the sensor display with growing frustration for the last twenty minutes. After the reception the *Enterprise* had gotten on arrival, Sulu wanted to avoid people as much as possible, and he also wanted to avoid the Rimillian storms. Unfortunately the only places in the entire habitable zone that were both storm- and people-free were also free of vegetation. When the weather allowed going outside, it seemed the Rimillians headed for the parks.

There were a few little pockets within the parks that didn't have anyone in them at the moment, but they were small and Sulu had no way of knowing whether they would have any useful specimens. The best way to find out was probably to go see in person, so he finally just picked one at random and said, "Okay, send me here."

"No problem," Vagle said as he keyed in the coordinates.

Sulu stepped up on the transporter platform, his tricorder in one hand and his sample bags in the other, and a moment later the park took shape around him. He was on the side of a steep hill, which explained why there were no people around. There were a few trees, at least. He stepped toward a low, bushy one with bright orange leaves, but just as he reached out to snip a branch from it he heard a growl and a spiny, reptilian creature about knee-high leaped out at him.

He quickly jumped back, but the creature was faster. It clamped onto his left thigh with its toothy mouth and shook its head as if trying to rip his leg completely off.

Pain shot all the way up his left side. "Yow!" Sulu yelled, whacking at the creature with his tricorder, but it hung on stubbornly, even when he hit it squarely on top of its head. He dropped the tricorder, grabbed his phaser from his belt, and stunned the thing—and his leg in the process—but even then it didn't let go. He had to tug its jaws open by hand. At least the stunned leg didn't hurt anymore.

He flung the creature back into the bush, wiped its saliva on his pants, and took his communicator from his belt. His leg was beginning to bleed. He paused to retrieve his tricorder and sample bags, then said, "Sulu to *Enterprise*. Beam me back up."

A moment later he stood in the transporter room. "What happened?" Vagle asked him when he hobbled down off the platform.

"We only scanned for humanoid traces," Sulu said sheepishly. "Evidently they haven't hunted everything to extinction yet down there, because I found one wild animal, at least."

Fortunately sickbay was only a few steps away. Sulu endured McCoy's less-than-gentle chiding while the doctor force-healed the puncture wounds, and a half hour later, much chagrined and still stinging from the bite, he beamed back down to the same park, which was now nearly deserted. He gave the creature's lair a wide berth, since now he had nearly the whole park to choose from. A cold wind blew in from the dark side of the sky, rattling the bushes and making Sulu shiver, but he figured he could snip off a couple of samples from the various species he encountered nearby and beam back to the ship before the storm hit.

There was vegetation everywhere, all the way from grass and flowers to bushes and trees. Judging by what he saw in this one small park, it came in as many shapes and colors and aromas as on Earth. Rimillia evidently didn't suffer for diversity, despite its small habitation zone. Sulu started with the bushes, since they were readily available, but he had come primarily to get genetic material from a cyclone tree, so he kept his eye out for one of those. They might have been common once, but now they were indeed rare; by the time he discovered a gnarled old specimen, its multiple trunks twisted round and round in a tight spiral, cold rain was already falling.

Cyclone trees, it turned out, were incredibly tough. It took Sulu nearly a minute to cut loose a piece of bark with a sample knife, but that wasn't really the best specimen. He needed a branch tip, where cells were actively growing. That would make the genetic investigation much easier. But the branch tips were all out of reach.

He didn't have time to find a smaller specimen, so he clipped his sampling equipment to his belt and pulled himself up onto the lowest branch. The bark was slippery as well as tough, especially when wet, and the exertion of climbing in Rimillia's oxygen-poor air made stars swirl in his eyes, but he climbed up until he could reach a small branch and snipped it off. A gust of wind rattled the tree and drove the first few wet flakes of snow at him, but he hung on and stuck the sample in the bag before heading back down.

The branches were even slipperier now, and Sulu was shivering with the cold. He missed a step and grabbed the trunk for support, but just then another gust of wind came through and blew him right out of the tree. He had one exhilarating moment of free fall before he landed on his back with enough force to knock the wind out of him. He gasped for air, but what he got was too low in oxygen to do him much good, and he felt himself losing consciousness. He scrabbled with numb fingers for his communicator, but the world grew dimmer and dimmer and his motions grew slower and slower. He forced himself to calm down and store up his strength before he fainted.

The storm hit with all its fury, though, and by the time he could get enough breath to call for beam-up—perhaps a minute—he had an inch of snow on him.

The warmth of the *Enterprise*'s transporter room and the higher oxygen content of its air were a welcome relief. Vagle stared in openmouthed wonder as Sulu shook the snow off of himself, leaving puddles on the smooth floor.

"Don't say a word," Sulu told him as he squelched his way off the transporter platform and into sickbay.

He told McCoy the same thing as he handed over the sample packets, but the doctor ignored him and said, "My God, you're going to catch your death of cold. Get out of those wet clothes and get something warm to drink."

"Gladly," Sulu said. He stumbled off toward the turbolift to go to his quarters, but he turned back around at the door and said, "I'll be right back and we can get started on the gene sequencing."

"Take your time," McCoy told him. "I've got to set up for more patients. The captain and Spock are leading a rescue mission to the surface, and there could be trouble."

"Rescue mission?" Sulu asked. He'd evidently missed something while he was gone.

"That's right," McCoy said. "He and Spock think they've found where the hostage is being kept, and they're going after him."

Sulu's first thought was *Without me?* But he'd been reassigned to do botanical research with Dr. McCoy, and besides, right now he was in no shape to go anywhere but to his quarters. Still, it felt odd to be missing out on all the action.

McCoy recognized the glint in Sulu's eyes. Damned fool kid! What was it about people under thirty that made them think they were invincible? Sulu had already been laid low in less than an hour today by a feral house pet and a chill, yet there he was, disappointed because he couldn't go out and let people shoot at him in the name of duty.

And Jim—he didn't even have youth as an excuse. Not that he was an old man, but he was at least old enough to know he wasn't invincible. Besides, the captain of a starship had no business risking his own neck on landing parties time after time the way he did. Especially not ones like this. This was a job for the local police if McCoy had ever heard of one, but he bet Jim had never even asked them to do it. He was such a dominating personality that nobody else would have suggested it either, until well after Jim had already made his own plans, and by then it was too late.

Why did he do it? McCoy wondered. *Got to keep myself in shape somehow,* he would say when McCoy confronted him about it, despite the fact that the gymnasium records showed him to be the top user by far. The truth was he was addicted to excitement. He got a rush out of charging into danger, and of charging right back out again with the pot of gold or the brass ring or whatever the token of success for the day happened to be. The actual result never seemed to matter to him as much as the fight to get it.

What he never seemed to see, in all his brushes with danger, was how close he came to not *coming* back. He'd always made it so far, so he assumed he always would, while McCoy, when he wasn't dragged along for the ride himself, waited in sickbay to see how badly damaged his friend's corpse would be when the survivors dragged him home.

The waiting was worse than actually going along.

With a start, McCoy realized he'd just answered

why Jim always went on these missions himself. He couldn't bear to sit on the bridge and wait for the landing party to report.

Well, at least McCoy could do something useful while the shooting was going on down below. As Sulu squelched his way home for dry clothing, he made another walk-through of sickbay to make sure everything was ready for casualties. The exam tables were vacant, their diagnostic computers waiting for patients. The surgical instruments were lined up and ready. The handheld sensors had all been calibrated and their power supplies checked, and the hyposprays were filled with the most likely needed painkilling and tissue-regeneration drugs. The entire sickbay blinked and beeped and whirred happily, waiting for patients that the doctor hoped would never arrive.

But by the looks of the situation on Rimillia, McCoy suspected he'd be using his shiny collection of tools all too soon.

Chapter Eight

Spock was just as concerned about the captain as McCoy. Unfortunately, he would not have the chance to look out for Kirk's welfare even as much as the doctor might, for the captain was leading the second landing party. Kirk had decided to make a simultaneous raid on both suspected strongholds, so the Denialists could not move their captive once they realized their cover was blown.

There would be only two people per team. Spock would take Lieutenant Hughes, a three-year veteran of the ship's security force, while the captain would take Ensign Turner, who had served two. Both men had been on the planet once already, and though their exposure to it had been minimal, they were still the most experienced security personnel available. All the same, Spock was uneasy about Turner. His performance on the job had always been exemplary, but he brewed alcoholic beverages in one of the science labs during his off-duty hours, and Spock was not sure how much faith he could place in someone who created mind-altering substances as a hobby, even if his use of them was moderate.

"Captain, I believe we should take larger parties," he said when they assembled in the transporter room and began to check their gear.

"I'd like to, Mr. Spock," Kirk replied, "but remember, we don't know for certain that these sites are rebel strongholds. They're suspect, that's all, so we're going in to investigate, and take appropriate action once we find out what's there. I don't want to beam down an army and find out we're trespassing on a legitimately shielded private residence."

"Your target could possibly be such," Spock said, "but the probability that the site I am to investigate is a residence is vanishingly small, considering that it lies four thousand kilometers into the cold face of the planet."

"Maybe it's a ski chalet," Kirk said. He was struggling to get his boots into the pant legs of a white insulation suit, one of four he had borrowed from the airlock in the government meeting hall. The bulky clothing would help keep them from being identified, and in Spock's and Hughes's case it would provide an extra layer of insulation over their own environment suits, which were designed to retain heat against the vacuum of space rather than the supercooled atmosphere they would encounter at their destination.

Spock checked that his own suit was sealed tightly, and that his phaser and tricorder were easy to reach with his gloved hands. "I find that equally unlikely, Captain," he said as he worked. "At the temperatures we are likely to encounter, snow, if it even exists, would be no more slippery than rock. Hardly conducive to skiing."

Kirk finally got his legs through, and finished suiting up. "Well, then, Mr. Spock, look at the bright side. You won't have to watch your footing."

"That is true."

Kirk did a final check of his suit, phaser, and communicator. "Ready?" he asked.

Spock hadn't yet put on his environment-suit helmet. He did so now, pulled the insulation suit's hood over it, and said, "Ready." A tiny speaker just above the neck ring transmitted his voice for the others to hear.

"Ready," said Lieutenant Hughes, doing the same. Spock heard him over the radio link as well as the external speaker.

"Just a minute," said Turner, who was still adjusting his suit. He tucked his uniform tunic into his pants—Spock noted with disapproval that it was stained on the side—then fastened his insulating oversuit. "Okay, now I am."

"Good, then let's do it," said Kirk, stepping up onto the transporter platform. Turner stepped up beside him while Ensign Vagle keyed in the coordinates for their beam-down point. "Energize," Kirk said. Vagle slid the activation controls forward, and Kirk and Turner disappeared in twin columns of light.

Spock and Hughes stepped onto the platform as soon as they were gone, and a moment later they, too, were on their way.

They arrived in the dark. They were prepared for it; Spock unclipped his infrared flashlight and switched it on. The visor in his helmet was already tuned to its wavelength, so he could see clearly whatever the beam touched. He swept it around in a circle, turning his head to follow it, while beside him Hughes did the same with his own light.

They had arrived on one of the few level stretches of ground in a vast terrain of jumbled rock and ice. House-sized boulders lay strewn about like gravel, washed there by the immense floods that occurred every sixteen years, when the Spark heated this side of the planet and melted the oxygen and nitrogen caps. Atmospheric circulation provided some local melting even now; a small stream gurgled and splashed along the bottom of a washout gully only a few meters away. It looked deceptively like a stream on any terrestrial planet, but Spock knew that this one would freeze him solid in an instant if he were to touch it with unprotected skin.

He and the lieutenant would have to be very careful here, even more careful than if they were in space. Here the familiar-looking surroundings could lull them into underestimating the danger, but they had to remember that nothing was what it seemed. He held his flashlight on an expanse of ice and watched it sublime beneath the infrared beam. Not water ice, then. Probably carbon dioxide.

From where they had beamed down, the terrain all around them looked untouched by any hand. That was by design; Spock preferred having a moment to get his bearings before he advanced upon the Rimillian installation. If his targeting had been accurate, then it should be just beyond the large slab of ice directly before him.

He took a step toward it, noting that his footing did indeed seem secure in the environment suit's cleated boots. When he peered around the edge of the ice, he saw the installation about fifty meters away, glowing brightly in the infrared with its own heat radiation. It was a squat metal cylinder, like a storage tank, about twenty meters across and half that high. A small rectangle set in the side looked about the right height to be a door. There were no windows.

Lieutenant Hughes stepped up beside him and had a look. "Doesn't look much like a ski chalet, does it?" he asked.

"Indeed not," Spock replied. "It looks industrial, or perhaps scientific. Or military. We will separate and approach it from different sides. Rendezvous at the point opposite the door, and we will make a close inspection for other entrances on our way back around to this side. Keep your phaser ready, and remain in radio contact at all times."

"Understood," Hughes said. He drew his phaser and moved off to the right, his feet crunching the hard snow with every step.

Spock moved to the left until he judged he was ninety degrees away from their beam-down point, then began advancing on the structure. He had only taken a few steps, however, when he noticed a narrow line of bare rock in front of him. He paused before it, wondering what had caused it. It was too straight to be natural, but Spock could see no obvious purpose for it. Something had melted the path, though.

He followed it with his flashlight and saw that it

extended to a glittery block of ice, where its path was bent about sixty degrees.

"Lieutenant," Spock said. "Do you see a straight line melted in the ice before you?"

"No, sir," Hughes said.

"Watch for one. I believe there is an electronic defense perimeter here." Spock bent down to look at the rock. It had an unnaturally smooth surface on the side facing the installation: obviously a mirror. Spock sighted down the line. Sure enough, he could see a rosy glow from another rock at the far end of the straight path. "Yes," he said, "I detect a low-intensity infrared beam, ankle-high." It wouldn't produce much heat, but here it wouldn't take much to melt a pathway. Taking out his tricorder, Spock scanned for other, less-obvious radiation, but found none.

"I see it now," Hughes said.

"Step over it and proceed," Spock said. He did so himself, keeping his tricorder on scan.

They found two more perimeter lines, one waist-high and another at chest level. Spock also found a mechanical trip wire that was not energized, and therefore didn't register on his tricorder. Whatever this facility was, its owners seemed quite concerned about intruders. What that indicated about their intentions did not bode well, but on the other hand he suspected that their paranoia might work to his advantage. They would place their trust in their detection devices, and thus might be less prepared than usual if he and Lieutenant Hughes were to successfully penetrate their defenses without triggering them.

Scanning every step of the way with his tricorder, he reached the smooth wall of the cylindrical structure on the side opposite where they had arrived. Hughes met him there, and they split up again to circumnavigate it, walking around tall drifts of snow.

Spock continued scanning, but he found only a smooth iron-alloy wall of undetermined thickness. His tricorder would not penetrate it; evidently the sensor-blocking shield conformed to the surface. That would work both ways; no internal sensors could detect *them* either, and Spock had seen no evidence of optical cameras. On the nightside of the planet like this, that was not surprising.

He met Hughes again at the door, which was blocked by another snowdrift. "I saw no other openings but this one," he said.

"Me either," Hughes replied. "Looks like this is it."

The lack of other entrances did indeed cut down the number of decisions to make, but it didn't improve Spock's assessment of the odds. A single entrance would would undoubtedly be rigged with an alarm, and whatever security forces lay in wait beyond would all be focused on the doorway. He scanned with the tricorder, but the shield blocked him from reading anything.

There was no lock in evidence; just an L-shaped handle. Spock was about to grasp it and see what happened when he had a sudden thought.

"Footprints," he said aloud.

"Sir?"

"There are no footprints here. I see no evidence of recent storm activity, yet I see no evidence that anyone else has come or gone by this door, either. I believe no one has."

"They've got to get in and out somehow," Hughes said.

"Assuming that this facility is staffed at all," Spock countered. "In any case, there is one surface we have not examined: the roof."

"I didn't see any way up," Hughes pointed out.

"They would not need a way up," Spock said. "The preferred form of transportation on this planet is the hovercar. They would merely land on the roof to begin with."

Hughes leaned back and looked up the flank of the cylindrical tower. Spock followed his gaze. Only ten meters, but that was still out of reach. But he had learned one thing in his investigation that they had not known before; the shield did not extend beyond the surface of the structure.

Spock flipped on his environment suit's communicator. "Spock to *Enterprise.*"

"Enterprise," came Uhura's voice.

"Beam us aboard again, then back to the top of the installation."

"Yes, sir."

A moment later they stood on its flat metal surface. Spock had hoped to find a hatch there; he had not expected to find two dozen of them. Their circular outlines dotted the entire top of the facility in an even hexagonal array. Fortunately, one hatch defied the pattern; it stood alone near the edge of the roof, and it had a small pillar beside it.

Cautiously, checking for more trip wires or infrared beams along the way, Spock and Hughes walked over to the odd hatch. Spock scanned the pillar with his tricorder, and this time he got some information. It stuck up out of the shield, no doubt acting as an antenna so people inside could communicate with the rest of the world. Or vice-versa.

There was a keypad atop the pillar. The tricorder detected a lock circuit inside, set for a five-digit access code. The designers had been smart enough to store the code in encrypted form, so Spock couldn't simply read it from his tricorder screen and key it in, but every lock has its weakness and Spock soon found this one's: once the code had been entered, the lock mechanism merely sent an electronic pulse to an electric motor, which then opened the hatch.

It took only a moment to set the tricorder to send that same pulse. The hatch squealed as stress patterns changed in the supercold metal; then it slowly tilted upward, revealing a stairway leading down. Bright lights blinked on in succession down the stairway.

Spock waited for any sign of alarm from inside, but nothing else happened. He stuck his tricorder down as far as he could reach, pushing it below the energy shield, and scanned for human presence, but it came up negative. That didn't necessarily mean there wasn't anyone there, but if there was, they were behind another shield inside the first one.

There was a limit to how much caution they could exercise. Spock knew the captain's methods well; he and Ensign Turner were probably already inside their target, perhaps even making contact with its inhabitants by now. If the two separate investigations were to be anything like simultaneous, it was time for Spock and Lieutenant Hughes to make their move as well.

"Let us see what awaits," Spock said, and he started down the stairs.

The interior of the structure was all catwalks and girders and pipe. It was obviously not a living facility. What it *was* was less obvious, until Spock realized that the long tubes leading up from floor to ceiling were arranged in the same pattern as the hatches on top.

"Those are launch tubes," he said. He felt his body react to the realization; adrenaline heightened his senses and shifted his metabolism to a higher pace. Nothing was without price, however; it also heightened his human side, disturbing his Vulcan calm and distorting his perception of events. Spock never knew whether or not it was a fair trade-off, but he had learned to live with it.

"Planetary defense?" Hughes asked hopefully, but by the tone of his voice he suspected the answer already.

"The government denied knowledge of this facility," Spock told him. "Therefore, it almost certainly belongs to the rebels." He spotted a control console on the ground level, and started on down the stairway. "If we can disable them without sending an alarm, that might win us a strategic advantage in a future conflict."

When he got a good look at the computer, he realized that would be more difficult than he had hoped. A display screen showed an active link to each photon torpedo, constantly reporting its status and allowing instant reprogramming of its target from a remote command center. The moment he and Hughes interfered with the system, whoever was monitoring the torpedoes would know of it.

They would have to disable the torpedoes completely, then, and do it all at once. Perhaps they could set one to detonate in the launch tube—after they had a chance to get clear, of course.

Yes, they should give some thought to their escape. The site wasn't manned, but it could still be dangerous. "Lieutenant," Spock said to Hughes, "locate the shield generator and see if it can be disabled without triggering an alarm."

"Yes, sir." Hughes moved off through the machinery.

Spock turned back to the computer, looking for clues for how to bypass the command signal, but he was still puzzling it out when the activity lights flickered and the status display for missile number one changed from STANDBY to READY.

"Lieutenant, did you disturb anything?" Spock asked.

"No, sir," Hughes's voice came over the radio link. "At least I don't think I did."

The rest of the missiles were receiving instructions as well. Spock checked the status monitor and saw that those instructions were indeed coming from outside.

Spock didn't believe in coincidence. If Hughes hadn't triggered anything, and Spock was fairly sure he hadn't either, then that left only one other person who might have set something like this in motion at this particular moment: the captain. Kirk had evidently encountered resistance.

Then there was no need for secrecy here anymore, either, especially if the missiles were about ready to be launched. Spock drew his phaser and fired it into the control computer, blowing it into a spark-spitting jumble of wreckage.

"Forget the generator," he said. "It will be faster to simply get free of the building and call for beam-up." Then, remembering what had happened to the ground site after the *Enterprise* had been attacked earlier, he said, "I believe we should do that *now.*"

He rushed toward the ground-level doorway, not caring about triggering any more alarms. If this facility was like the last one—and he saw no reason why it would not be—then it contained a self-destruct mechanism. He might have disabled that along with the control computer, but he might not have, and he didn't want to stick around to find out the hard way.

The door was stuck from disuse, but Spock kicked it beside the latch and it sprang open. Hughes was right behind him, and they both ran out into the rock and ice. Spock had never turned off his environment suit's communicator, so now he simply called, "Spock to *Enterprise,* two to beam up."

Before Uhura could answer, however, he heard a loud whoosh from behind him, and a bright ball of coruscating light shot into the sky. The torpedoes apparently had local intelligence as well, and after losing their command signal at least one of them had launched for its programmed target.

A second one flashed upward, then a third. They were apparently all operational, and firing one at a time after separate retry cycles.

There was no answer from the *Enterprise.* Nor would there be until after the attack was over; they would have to go to maximum shields to repel this many photon torpedoes.

"We are on our own!" Spock said sharply. "Follow me."

The environment suits hampered fast motion, but Spock's Vulcan physique and the extra energy from his suddenly heightened metabolism nearly made up for it. Hughes was keeping up nearly as well, though; apparently the human panic reaction had its uses, too. He was running for the cover of a boulder, but Spock realized a big enough explosion could roll it over on him and shouted, "The stream! Get into the streambed!" That would put them below the level of the explosion, and possibly give them more protection from the blast wave.

"Right!" Hughes said, veering to the side. Spock was behind him now, but he quickly closed the gap. The steady stream of photon torpedoes launching behind them lit their way with brilliant white light. The gully was only ten meters away, then five, then—

Too late. The self-destruct charge went off just as Spock was about to leap. The force of the explosion blew him clear past the gully, tumbling him head over heels across the ice field beyond to finally smash into a boulder, cracking his faceplate and at least a few ribs, by the feel of it. And his right leg hurt as well.

Debris rained down around him. Spock pulled himself to the far side of the boulder and waited it out. "Hughes," he called. "Lieutenant Hughes."

"Here," came a faint voice.

"Are you all right?"

"Yeaaaa . . . no. I've got a . . . suit breach."

A ragged sheet of steel spun down out of the sky and clanged against the rocks only a few meters away from Spock. The destruct charge had obviously not been a photon torpedo, or the metal would have been vaporized. As would Spock and Hughes, but by the sound of things, they hadn't escaped yet even so.

"Spock to *Enterprise,*" Spock called again, but he once again got no response.

"How bad is your suit breach?" he asked.

No answer.

"Lieutenant Hughes?"

"It's . . . not good," Hughes responded. "I don't . . . damn that's cold."

Spock tried to stand and go to Hughes's aid, but when he moved his right leg he felt a sharp stab of pain. He had broken a bone.

"Spock to *Enterprise*," he called again. "Come in, *Enterprise*. This is a medical emergency."

"Too . . . late," Hughes whispered.

"Lieutenant!" Spock called, but he got no response.

And now he realized that the pain in his leg was not all from the fracture. His own suit had been breached as well. It *was* cold.

"Spock to *Enterprise*," he called again. And again, and again and again.

Where were they? A sudden thought sent an entirely different chill racing down Spock's back. Could the photon torpedoes have penetrated the shields? He aimed his tricorder into the sky and set it for maximum sensitivity. The range was far too great for detailed analysis, but it should at least be able to detect the *Enterprise* against the background of empty space.

It should, but all he read on the display was the expanding cloud of a matter-antimatter explosion. The *Enterprise* was no longer there.

Chapter Nine

KIRK AND ENSIGN TURNER appeared inside a small storage building. Kirk had chosen it as a good spot to arrive without being noticed, and from the lack of any cries of alarm it had apparently succeeded at that; but private also meant dark. They could have materialized at the bottom of a well for all he could see.

He was just reaching for his light when Turner turned on his own, illuminating the tool-filled interior of the shed. It was barely big enough for two men to stand side by side; certainly not big enough to swing a cat in, as Chekov would say.

Turner took a step toward the door, but the moment he moved, something flew out of the dark and struck his left hand. His light spun out of his grasp, and both he and the captain whirled, drew their phasers, and fired. The blue energy beams fanned out and struck the walls, but in their light and the light from the fallen flash they could see no sign of an assailant. Nor was the attack repeated.

"Rake," Turner said at last. "I stepped on a rake."

Kirk stifled a laugh. "Well," he said, "I think we stunned it."

Turner picked up his light again, and he and Kirk stepped carefully over shovels and more rakes and around wheelbarrows to the door. Kirk had expected it to be locked, and it was, but no one ever worries about locking a storage shed from *inside.* He found a pry bar among the tools on the wall and bent the latch tang outward until it no longer held anything, then cautiously eased the door open a crack. Gray twilight seeped in through the gap, and Kirk motioned Turner to switch off his light so they could see out without giving themselves away.

They were about twenty meters away and off to the side of the main building, a wide, low mansion with many windows along the front. The grounds looked well kept, with trimmed bushes lining the walks and trees carefully planted so they wouldn't shade the windows. They cast barely a hint of shadow now; it had been storming recently. Snow lay ankle-deep on the ground. None was falling now, though, and from the look of the sky the storm might actually be breaking up. Time to move, then, before people came outside and started shoveling off the walks.

A brilliant plan came to Kirk all at once. He looked to the wall just inside the door, and sure enough, there were half a dozen wide-bladed shovels stacked there. He picked up two of them and handed one to Turner.

"Here's our ticket to go wherever we please. Come on."

"You mean we've got to *work?*" Turner asked jokingly. "That wasn't in the contract."

Kirk liked this ensign. Cool under pressure. Or at least he hid his nervousness well. "Always check the fine print," he told him.

He eased the door open and stepped out into the snow, glad for his tall service boots. The walks were obvious beneath their white covering; Kirk cut across the yard to the main path from the front gate of the estate, and began shoveling his way toward the ornate double doors in the middle of the mansion. The shovel grated on the stone walk, and the wet snow thumped heavily when he tossed it aside.

"What do we do when we get to the door?" Turner asked, shoveling along behind Kirk.

"Ring the bell and ask for money," Kirk said. He was starting to sweat beneath his insulating suit. Shoveling wet snow was hard work, and in this oxygen-poor air he began panting immediately. They should have started closer to the door. Too late now.

Too late, in fact, to ring the bell. They'd been spotted. Two more snowsuited men came around the side of the house, heading for the shed, but they stopped when they saw Kirk and Turner.

"Hey," one of them said, walking closer. "Who are you? How'd you get in here?"

Kirk stood up and rested against his shovel in the least-threatening pose he could manage. "We're new here," he said, trying to mimic the Rimillian accent with its stressed vowels. "Got caught in the storm before we could check in. In fact—" Kirk leaned closer and lowered his voice. "—we haven't even had a chance to go to the bathroom yet. Could you tell me where—"

The man rolled his eyes. "Inside, through the kitchen and to the right."

"Thanks." Kirk set off toward the house, Turner following right behind.

"Around back, you idiots!" the man shouted.

Kirk obligingly turned to the side and followed the two sets of tracks to the back door.

"I'd hate to have *him* for a boss," Turner whispered when they'd rounded the corner.

"I'll take that as a compliment," Kirk replied. He looked up into the sky. There was no sign of a shield there, but he really didn't expect any. Only the most powerful energy fields caused visual distortion. But he knew it was there, and they had probably already come within its influence. From here on in, there would be no communication with the ship, and no emergency beam-out if things went wrong.

The back door was much less impressive than the front. Kirk and Turner walked right in as if they belonged, and found themselves in a small entryway. Arched doorways opened in three directions, to the kitchen on the left, some sort of utility room on the right, and ahead into the house proper. Kirk went straight in, figuring that would give him the most options. Besides, if he were holding someone captive in the house, neither the kitchen or the utility rooms would be his first choice of prison.

There were three chefs at work in the kitchen, and Kirk could hear someone scooting something heavy along the floor to the right. None of the staff paid any attention to the two snowsuited men as they walked down the hallway, peeking into the open rooms as they passed. They found the dining room, the library, two sitting rooms, and an office, but no bedrooms and no sign of the scientist. Kirk turned to the left through one of the sitting rooms and emerged in a long hallway with doors opening off on either side. This looked more promising.

Most of the doors were closed. Kirk tried the latch on the first one and opened it to find a room with a wide slab of padded plastic hovering in midair about knee-high in the middle of it. Small shelves hovered beside it on either side, and after a moment Kirk realized he was looking at a bed and two nightstands. There was a doorway beyond the bed that led into a bathroom, but he didn't go see if the toilet was similarly designed. From the lack of personal items on the nightstands it didn't look like anyone stayed here regularly; so this must be the guest wing. That might be good; it depended on how well the kidnappers were treating their hostage.

But they made it all the way to the end of the hallway and found nothing but empty rooms. It seemed like the house was practically deserted.

Then why was it shielded? And why were there three chefs for a place where nobody lived? Something wasn't right here.

Kirk had just looked into the last bedroom when he heard someone approaching from behind. He turned around and saw a woman carrying an electronic device of some sort in one hand—and an equally unfamiliar weapon in the other. Kirk didn't know if it was a phaser, laser, or projectile launcher, but the dark hole in its center pointed directly at him.

He didn't reach for his own weapon. Even though a Starfleet phaser was probably unfamiliar to her, that would be too obvious a move. So before the woman could speak, he said, "Hi. We're here with a message from Haidar concerning the professor."

"Haidar?" the woman said. "What are you talking about? She doesn't know he's here."

But now we do, Kirk thought. He nodded knowingly. "Of course not," he said. "And of course the message isn't officially from her. But we have instructions to turn it over to you. Mr. Turner, the isolinear chip, please." And Kirk reached toward *Turner's* phaser.

Turner obediently handed it over. Kirk checked to make sure it was set on heavy stun, taking his time, then held it out toward the woman. "Here you go," he said, then he fired.

She folded without a sound, but her weapon and the electronic device she'd been holding hit the floor with a loud thump. The floors here were obviously not stone; though they were covered with carpet, that hollow bonk sounded more like wood underneath, and if that was the case then it would transmit sound all through the house. Kirk and Turner sprang into action, pulling the woman into one of the vacant bedrooms and dropping her on the floating bed. It dipped down, then rose back up to normal height as its suspensor field compensated for her weight.

Turner had just closed the door when they heard footsteps in the hallway, and a male voice said, "It sounded like it came from down here." Another voice said, "Check the rooms." The sound of doors opening and closing came down the hallway.

They were moving too fast to be making a thorough check. Kirk pointed at the bathroom, and together he and Turner grabbed the unconscious woman and carried her inside, where they laid her on the floor at the foot of an upright coffin-sized cabinet that must have been an ultrasonic cleaning tank. Whatever it was, it wasn't plumbed for water. Nor was the toilet, which Kirk was relieved to see was at least enclosed below the seat.

Turner sat on it, once again panting for more air, but Kirk forced himself to go back for the electronic gadget and the hand weapon. He ducked back inside the bathroom just as the outer door opened, and he and Turner held their breath, waiting for a cry of alarm or a phaser blast through the wall. But after a second the door closed again and the footsteps went on.

Kirk looked at the electronic device. It was too small to be a shield generator, but it wasn't anything else he was familiar with either. It had a row of six green lights across the face, with a gray button below each of them, and a single large yellow button below those. Kirk was tempted to push it, but he didn't want to find out the hard way if it was a self-destruct.

He would keep it, though. Once they got it back to the ship they could figure out what it was. He wished he could just beam it back now, and beam down a whole security team, but that wasn't an option. Even if they could get out of the building without anyone else spotting them, the woman they had stunned would wake up in half an hour or less, and the men in the hallway would probably miss her before that. The moment they thought their cover had been blown, they would either move the professor or kill him, depending on how desperate they were. No, it was just him and Turner, but if they played their cards right they could do the job.

Holding the gadget, he stepped out into the room again and went to the door. He heard the two men conferring in low voices partway back down the hall, then their footsteps receded again.

"Come on," Kirk said, easing open the outer door. "They're suspicious of something; I bet now they'll lead us right where we want to go."

"I'm not sure if 'want to' is the right term," Turner whispered, "but it's probably where the action is, all right."

They slipped out into the hallway and followed the sound of footsteps through the center of the house and into the other wing. Kirk was growing uncomfortably hot in the insulating suit, but he was reluctant to remove it; the anonymity it provided had already helped them twice.

Third time's a charm, he thought as he peered around a corner and saw the men he was following just starting down a set of stairs. They were wearing the same white oversuits; Kirk bet they were the same men he had seen outside. Two more men in regular indoor clothing stood guard at the top of the stairs. Kirk felt pretty sure he knew what was down below.

He waited for the ones from outside to disappear down the stairs, then whispered, "Cover me, Mr. Turner," and stepped out into the hallway. He held up the gadget and walked toward the guards, saying, "They forgot this."

Their response was not what he expected. One of the guards said, "What? That's Marina's!" and drew his weapon. Kirk dropped him with his phaser before he could take aim, and Turner took out the other guard, his phaser beam passing uncomfortably close to Kirk in the process. Both guards slumped to the floor, and Kirk and Turner rushed up to them and pulled them away from the stairs so they couldn't be seen from below.

"In there," Kirk said, pointing to a closed door beside the stairway. He pulled it open and saw another woman just rising from a desk, but he stunned her before she was even out of her chair and she sat back down heavily and fell forward onto the desk. Kirk and Turner dragged the unconscious guards into her office and left them on the floor.

Fifteen minutes, Kirk thought. That's all they could count on before one of the four people they'd stunned woke up and spread the alarm. Of course the people down below were already alerted that somebody unauthorized *might* be in the building, but they didn't know for sure yet. Kirk tried to think of a good way to exploit that situation, because he didn't like the odds of success if they were to just charge down the stairs with phasers blazing. Three chefs, he kept thinking. That was enough to feed a couple of dozen people.

He wished there was a back way into the basement. Everyone would be guarding the main stairs; if there was another way down, Kirk and Turner might be able to sneak in and rescue Kostas right behind their backs. There might actually be one, too, but they didn't have the time to search it out.

But they could make one. This wasn't a starship, with nearly indestructible duranium composite deck plating. The floors here were made of wood.

"Okay, here's the plan," he said to Turner. "Give me a minute to get back over to the other side of the house. I'll signal you when I'm ready, and when you get the word I want you to fire down the stairs with one of these weapons." He picked up one of the guards' pistols and held it out to Turner. It was massive, and the barrel was hollow and finned for cooling; he was willing to bet it was a heavy-duty disruptor. "That way maybe they'll think it's their own police, and it should also make enough noise to cover what I'm doing."

"And what will you be doing?" Turner asked.

"Cutting a hole in the floor with my phaser. As soon as you get their attention over here, follow me. I'll be in the room we hid in before, or below it."

"Got it," said Turner, hefting the gun experimentally.

Kirk slipped out into the hallway again and hurried silently back through the house. When he was in the far bedroom again, he flipped open his communicator and said softly, "Kirk to Turner. Go."

Almost immediately, a loud zipping sound and a bang echoed through the house, followed by seven more at closely spaced intervals. Kirk immediately fired at the floor, turning his phaser up to Disrupt and sweeping the beam around in a wide circle. The carpet burned and stank, but Kirk didn't care about that; he finished the circle and stood aside as the flaming disk fell away.

No one fired up through the opening, so he cautiously peered down. He'd cut his way into a recreation room, by the looks of things. The piece of floor had damaged a gaming table of some sort. Nobody had witnessed its fall; Turner's diversion had worked wonderfully. Kirk stamped out an arc of the burning carpet, then swung down through the hole and lowered himself to the table, and from there to the floor.

He heard loud voices through the doorway in the far end of the room. There was no other door, so he crept up to have a look, and sure enough there at the end of a long room full of electronic equipment were at least ten men, all armed with the same kind of pistols the upstairs guards had, all aimed up the stairway. A couple of them fired, and Kirk hoped that Turner had gotten clear before they did.

The distraction wouldn't last much longer. Kirk took his chance and stuck his head out the door, and the moment he did he saw two more guards who hadn't joined the party at the stairs. They were standing to his right on either side of another door, a heavy one that had been bolted with a solid metal bar all the way across it.

Perfect. The room they guarded was next to the rec room. Kirk pulled his head back in before they could spot him, went all the way to the back of the room, and started another hole in the wall. Turner dropped through the one in the ceiling while he was cutting.

"Are you all right?" Kirk asked him.

"Fine, except for my wrist," Turner said. "I slipped on the floor and fell on it."

Kirk laughed. "If that's the worst you get out of this, you'll be lucky. Look sharp, it's falling through."

He'd cut a tall oblong; when he closed the gap at the bottom of it the loose slab toppled into the next room. Kirk waited a moment for disruptor fire, but there was none, so he stepped through.

There was quite a bit of smoke, and only a single dim light panel overhead, but Kirk could see well enough to recognize Professor Kostas standing in the far corner, as far away from both the main door and the one Kirk had cut as he could get. His cell was practically empty; besides the professor it contained only a small rectangular table and a single wooden chair.

"It's okay," Kirk told Kostas. "We're here to rescue you."

Kostas blinked disbelievingly, and opened his mouth as if to speak, but no words came out.

"I'm James Kirk, of the Federation *Starship Enterprise*," Kirk told him, realizing that the professor had no idea who this was bursting in on him with such strange weapons. "Do you know where the shield generator is?"

Kostas found his voice. "Out there," he said, pointing toward the locked door.

Kirk remembered the banks of electronics he had seen, and all the men who guarded them. He and Turner would never be able to find and disable the shields before they were overpowered.

"No good, then. We'll have to go out the way we came in." He held out his hand to help the professor toward the hole in the wall, but just then there was another loud *zip-bang* and Turner dived in through it instead.

"They've seen us!" Turner shouted, rolling to his knees and snapping off a phaser burst back into the rec room.

More bangs as violet energy bolts flew through the hole in the wall and blew scores of smaller holes in the wall across from it. Turner fired again, his phaser beam scintillating in the smoky air, and they heard someone fall in the other room. The firing stopped momentarily, then another fusillade poured through the hole.

Kirk added his phaser to Turner's, but the angle was

wrong to hit anyone. That worked both ways, but Kirk knew the stalemate would only last for a few seconds at most. They had to make a break, and they had to do it now.

Just in case the easy route was open, he pulled his communicator from his belt and flipped it open. "Kirk to *Enterprise*. Come in, *Enterprise*."

No response. The house was still shielded. They were still on their own.

He looked upward, thinking he could cut another exit through the ceiling, but what he saw there stopped him cold. The entire ceiling was studded with the hexagonal plates of a wide-area cargo transporter grid. The floor was carpeted as in the rest of the house, but he was willing to bet there was a grid below that as well. Suddenly he knew what the big yellow button on the device in the briefcase was for, and he bet there was another button like it on one of the control consoles in the next room. A panic button, in case security was breached. It would drop the shields and activate the transporter all at once, and beam their captive to another location.

Well, Kirk would just see about that. He raised his phaser to fire at the ceiling, but before he could depress the stud he felt the confinement beam lock his body rigidly into place for the scan. He and Ensign Turner and Professor Kostas were about to go for a ride.

Chapter Ten

CHEKOV, along with Sulu's replacement, Ensign Brady, had been holding the *Enterprise* in position halfway between the two beam-down sites. Those were over a quarter of the way around the planet from each other, but it was possible to keep them both within range if the ship stayed put. That required breaking orbit and using constant impulse power instead of centripetal acceleration to counter the planet's gravity, but the starship had power to spare. They could hover on impulse engines for weeks if they had to.

It was a tougher job than a simple orbit, though, and it took Chekov's complete attention to keep the ship from drifting. He had hardly looked up from the navigation console since the two landing parties had beamed down. He had set his monitors to display the planet, with color-coding to mark the shields and any changes of energy level at either of the two sites the

107

captain and Spock were investigating. So he saw the shields go down at the captain's beam-down site, and he immediately hit the intercom.

"Transporter room, can you get a lock on the capta—" he began, but a string of brilliant white starbursts rising from the surface, one after another, stopped him cold.

"Positive lock on both the captain and Ensign Turner, sir," Ensign Vagle, the transporter operator, said. "Do you want me to beam them aboard?"

How fast were those torpedoes moving? Sublight velocity, but would the *Enterprise* have time for a transporter cycle before they hit? Chekov didn't think so. The away team would just have to wait a moment. Chekov hated making that decision, but he, saw no other choice. If he had the time, he could check with McCoy, who was technically in command, but the doctor was in sickbay, and Chekov had the conn.

"No," he said, noticing even as he said it that the energy signature of a transporter trace was beginning to grow at the site. "Cancel transporter! Shields up!" he shouted, stabbing at the buttons himself. The shields had been down to permit using the transporter, but with the ship on yellow alert they had been on standby and now quickly came up to full power. "Incoming photon torpedoes. I track five, no, six, no—holy *chort*"—he switched momentarily to Russian in his excitement—"they're firing their whole arsenal at us!"

The torpedoes were coming from Spock's beam-down point. Chekov knew the science officer was probably in trouble, and the captain as well, but there was no way the *Enterprise* could beam either of them back on board until the attack was over.

Even shielded, Chekov didn't want to see what twenty—no, twenty-one—photon torpedoes would do to the ship. "Evasive action," he said. "Full impulse."

The engines were already running; the moment Brady hit maximum thrust, the starship streaked away at full acceleration. They were already aimed away from the planet; now it began to dwindle in the screens like a deflating balloon. But the torpedoes kept coming. They were lighter and faster than the ship, and the first one caught up only seconds later. The *Enterprise* shuddered as the aft shields took the hit, then again as the next torpedo struck.

Chekov deflected their course by sixty degrees, and the next two torpedoes missed, but the ones farther away veered to follow the ship. A steady stream of them drew a dotted line all the way back to the planet. There was no way Chekov could outmaneuver them all.

"Warp power!" he shouted. "Get us out of here!"

Brady pressed the warp engine engaging control, and the *Enterprise* shook as another torpedo hit the shields, but that was the last one to reach them. The field generators in the engines' twin nacelles wrapped the ship in a bubble of subspace, and planet, torpedoes, and everything disappeared in a streak of light.

"That's enough, Mr. Brady," Chekov said. "Return to impulse." When the ship dropped back into normal space, Chekov searched for Rimillia in the vastness behind them. The engines had been set for warp six, normal cruising speed, and even a second at that speed had taken them far across the star system. The sensors were designed for greater distances than that, however. They quickly located the planet, and Chekov plotted a return course.

When they got back, hovering at a much greater height to give them more time in case of another attack, they scanned the two drop sites for the away teams. Uhura immediately reported, "I'm getting a transmission from Mr. Spock. He needs immediate beam-up."

"Transporter room," Chekov said, "lock on to Mr. Spock and Lieutenant Hughes and beam them aboard."

"Beaming now," Vagle said. "Got them. They're both—my god, sickbay, I'm beaming two patients straight over."

Intraship transport was dangerous; if Vagle thought it was worth the risk to beam the injured men to sickbay, then they had to be badly hurt. Chekov wanted to ask what had happened to them, but he had a more pressing problem at the moment. He could find no sign of the captain.

"Transporter room, did you beam the captain on board before our shields went up?" he asked.

"No, sir. I couldn't get a lock on them."

"Uhura, can you locate the second away team?"

"Negative," she reported. "Neither communicator is responding."

"But the site is no longer shielded."

"We did see a transporter trace right after the shields went down," she reminded him. "He could be anywhere now."

Chekov groaned. She was right. "Transporter room,

scan the planet for the captain's and Ensign Turner's ID traces."

"Yes, sir." Vagle's voice sounded tight; whatever he'd seen had shaken him badly. But he did his job. Moments later he said, "I don't find their traces anywhere, Mr. Chekov. But there are seventy new shielded sites that could be blocking my scan."

Seventy? Chekov looked to his own board, and sure enough, there were the new shielded sites, scattered all over the planet. And that was just on the side they could see from here. All but one of them were decoys, no doubt, but the Denialists were rich; they could afford that kind of expenditure to help hide their captives.

That didn't mean Chekov would quit looking. Even the rich could screw up.

"I'm plotting a high-speed, power-assisted orbit," he said, keying in the coordinates as he spoke. "Continue your scan. Mr. Brady, ahead half impulse."

The starship swooped around the planet, its engines forcing it into a curved path much tighter and faster than gravity alone would have allowed. In three minutes they had made an entire circuit, but Vagle confirmed what Chekov's own instruments told him.

"He's just not there," Vagle said. "And now there are over a hundred places where they could be hiding him."

Vagle was good at his job. His emergency beam-in procedure automatically split the two patients' signals and reoriented them so they were already lying on the tables when they were reassembled.

McCoy and Nurse Chapel were still cleaning surgical instruments up off the floor when the patients arrived. Fortunately, sterility was not a problem with energy beams; McCoy merely flipped on a handheld scanner and turned to the closest exam table, but what he saw there made him recoil in shock.

Two frozen corpses lay on the tables, frost already shrouding their outersuits. McCoy, in his short-sleeved medical tunic, felt the intense cold coming from them almost as if he had just stepped into a freezer. Their faceplates were completely frosted over, and it took a moment for him to realize who they were; he had subconsciously been expecting Kirk and Turner, but the tall one was obviously Spock, which meant the other one was Hughes.

Hughes had a long gash in both his oversuit and the environment suit beneath it, running from his right shoulder across the chest and abdomen all the way to his left leg. A quick pass with the scanner and a glance at the overhead monitor confirmed what McCoy already knew: he was dead. Besides the freezing damage, he had massive internal trauma from whatever impact had torn open his suit.

But Spock's monitor showed signs of life. His body temperature was far too low for even a Vulcan to survive for long, but he hadn't been exposed nearly as badly as Hughes to the intense cold of the planet's dark side. There was no helping Hughes, but Spock could be saved if they got him warmed up again fast enough.

"Quick," McCoy said to Chapel, "help me get this suit off him." Heedless of the intense cold, they tore the oversuit off and tossed it to the floor, then unfastened the environment suit beneath that. Its heating system had failed from prolonged contact with the supercold ground, but the two layers of insulation had offered some protection. When McCoy pulled off the helmet he saw that Spock's hair and the tips of his ears were rimed with white frost from his own breath, but at least the Vulcan was still breathing.

"Spock, can you hear me?" McCoy asked.

Spock struggled to speak. "Yes," he said at last. "I . . . am . . . cold."

"You're damned right you are, but we'll take care of that." McCoy looked up at the monitor again. "And your broken leg. Do you hurt anywhere else?"

"Everywhere," Spock murmured; then, gathering his strength, he said, "But I believe . . . my ribs are the only other injury."

Nurse Chapel, standing beside him on the other side of the exam table, took his hand in hers. She looked as if *she* had been wounded as well. McCoy knew how she felt about the science officer; it had to be hard for her to see him lying there like this. It was hard enough for McCoy, and Spock generally irritated the hell out of him.

The monitors confirmed Spock's assessment, though McCoy never trusted them completely when dealing with Vulcan physiology. He would do a more thorough check later; the first thing he needed to do was raise Spock's body temperature before he went into hypothermic shock.

The fastest way to do that was with a Wasner biophaser, essentially the same device as the phaser weapons carried by the ship's crew, but tuned to heat rather than stun or disintegrate the tissue of its target. McCoy grabbed the rectangular handheld unit from the pile of instruments he'd rescued from the floor, flipped it on, and passed the whirring device back and forth over the science officer's body. He had to be careful not to overdo it; Spock's own metabolism would kick in soon and the combined effect could easily overshoot the mark.

He settled for two degrees below normal, then switched over to an anabolic protoplaser to start the healing process in the ribs and the leg bone. The built-in anesthetic function also helped cut down the pain that Spock had to be feeling from the tissue damage.

"I think you're going to make it," McCoy told him.

"That is comforting knowledge, Doctor," Spock replied evenly, his Vulcan reserve already back in working condition.

"Course, I can't guarantee your extremities," McCoy went on, unable to resist a little dig now that he was sure Spock was going to live. "Frostbite's pretty tough to reverse. I think I can save the fingers and toes, but I'm afraid you might lose those pointy ears."

"I am not amused," Spock said.

"Good," said McCoy. "That means you're back to normal."

He finished setting the bones and did another scan for injuries he might have missed, but aside from bruises and scrapes, Spock was back in good health. Or at least as good a health as could be expected for someone who had been nearly blown up and frozen at the same time.

"Okay," he said to Nurse Chapel, "we can transfer him to recovery now."

"Yes, Doctor," she said, her relief evident in her voice. She took a long, lingering look at the science officer, then went off to get an antigrav gurney.

Spock tried to sit up. "Recovery? I am needed on the bridge. We must have taken damage from the attack, and the captain—"

"Hold it right there," McCoy told him, pushing him back down to the exam table. "You were just about killed down there. I've got you patched together again, but your body needs time to heal completely. I'm holding on to you for at least a day."

"You cannot."

McCoy shook his head. "I can and I will. I'm the doctor here. Now prepare to be moved; I might need this exam table soon. The captain still hasn't checked in."

Both of Spock's eyebrows shot up. "What news *do* you have of him?"

"Not much," McCoy said, his voice softening. "The shield went down where he was just before all hell broke loose for you. That's the last I heard before I got busy. Here, let me check again." He walked over to the comm panel. "McCoy to bridge," he said. "Is there any word yet from the captain?"

"No, sir," Uhura replied. "We're still searching for him."

"Great," McCoy said sarcastically. He turned back to Spock. "One dead, one wounded, and two missing in action. I don't know what you guys did down there, but you sure stirred things up."

Chapter Eleven

THERE WAS MORE LIGHT in the room where Kirk and Turner and Professor Kostas arrived. A lot more light. All three winced under the sudden glare, but Kirk immediately shielded his eyes from the two skylights —he'd arrived looking straight into them—and checked out the room for more guards or for anything that might offer an escape route. The first few seconds after a capture, before the situation was brought under control, were often the most crucial in breaking free.

Unfortunately, this one had been planned ahead of time, and it was already under control. There were no open doors, no guards who hadn't yet brought their weapons to bear, nothing but shelves of boxes lining three walls and a rack of cylindrical metal canisters on the fourth. They were apparently in a storeroom. Not a large one, either; Kirk estimated it at about four meters by six.

That and the lack of a transporter grid overhead told Kirk that they had at least forced the Denialists into plan B. They hadn't expected to need this, so they hadn't prepared for it as completely as they had Kostas's first prison.

The sparse furnishings from that room had beamed across with them; the table and chair filled a quarter of the available floor space. Not everything had come along for the ride; Kirk's and Turner's phasers had been edited out of the transporter signal, as had their tricorders and communicators. Kirk lowered his hand and turned to the professor. "Do you have any idea where we are?" he asked.

Kostas looked up at the skylights. "Well," he said slowly, "considering that the sun appears directly overhead, I would guess we're at the hot pole."

"The hot pole." Kirk shuddered. That was a descriptive enough phrase. "I assume you mean the point facing straight at the sun."

The room's single door opened, and a woman stood there, holding one of the Rimillian beam weapons aimed right at Kirk's chest. "Correct," she said. "The outside temperature is hot enough to melt lead, so I would not advise any heroic attempts to escape. We may just let you."

"Who are you?" Kirk demanded, trying to decide whether or not he could jump her before she could fire. He reluctantly decided not. He might be able to take just her, but behind her, in a much smaller version of the control room he'd seen in the mansion, he could see four more people, all armed, standing ready to back her up.

All the same, she retreated a step, interposing the

partially open door between them. "I'm your host for the next four days. You can call me Marybeth."

That was such an obviously Terran name that it had to be an alias, but Kirk supposed it would do as well as any other. He asked her, "Do you realize that by illegally imprisoning a Starfleet officer you have committed an act of war against the Federation?"

Marybeth laughed. "The Federation will never declare war on a backwater planet like this. You've got Klingons and Romulans and who knows what else to worry about."

"Ah, but the *Enterprise* is already here," Kirk said. "When they realize you've taken their captain prisoner, they'll tear this planet apart looking for me."

She shook her head. "An apt metaphor, considering what you and Mr. Kostas propose to do, but I'm afraid I have some bad news for you, Captain. The *Enterprise* had a rather unfortunate encounter with some photon torpedoes, and is no longer with us."

Kirk felt as if he'd been physically struck in the stomach. "The *Enterprise* . . . is destroyed?"

"Yes. We're sorry, really we are. We'd only intended to force them to raise their shields so they couldn't beam you away before we did, but evidently the torpedoes were too much for them. The ship exploded before even half the salvo reached it."

"You're lying," Kirk said coldly. She had to be lying. The *Enterprise* couldn't be destroyed, not by photon torpedoes from some technologically benighted planet like this. Not without *him* on board. A captain should go down with his ship.

She shrugged. "It no longer shows on our sensors, and there's a big plasma cloud where the torpedoes hit. But that's not the issue, Captain. The destruction of our entire race is the issue, or rather saving us from it, and we intend to hold you here until your window of opportunity for killing us all is passed."

At that, Kostas spoke up. "You'll doom yourselves to slow asphyxiation," he said. "Do you prefer that?"

"We prefer uncertain life to certain death," she replied. "I do not intend to argue with you. You will be held here until the danger is over."

"I want to talk to Haidar," Kirk said.

"Haidar is not involved," Marybeth answered quickly.

"Sure she isn't. I can see her pulling your strings from halfway around the planet."

She gave him an angry look, then said, "Don't bet on it," and shut the door.

"Looks like I pushed a button, at least," Kirk said. He was growing uncomfortably hot in his insulated suit, so he stripped it off and tossed it into a corner.

Ensign Turner did the same with his; then he began to circumnavigate the room, looking for weaknesses. Kirk looked around from where he stood, taking it all in. The walls on three sides, behind the shelves of boxes, looked like some kind of foamed ceramic, probably to insulate against the intense heat outside. The other wall, the one with the rack of metal canisters and the door in it, was lighter weight, some kind of plastic by the looks of it. It actually shook when Turner shoved against it with his hands.

He rattled the door, which seemed equally light. "We could probably go right through this if we wanted to," he said.

Kirk's first impulse was to do it, to act *now,* but he knew what awaited them in the room beyond. And their kidnappers undoubtedly knew the door was flimsy; they would be ready for an escape attempt. Nor could Kirk count on the *Enterprise* to help them out even if they did escape. He buried that thought, unable to consider the magnitude of what it meant, except that they must wait. "Not yet," he said. "Unless we can figure out a way to incapacitate at least five armed people, busting down the door isn't going to do us any good. We may only get one chance at it, so let's save it for a better moment."

Turner nodded and continued his survey of the room.

"Well, at least we won't starve," Kirk said, pulling a box off the shelf and looking inside it. It held clear plastic packages of what looked like cookie-sized rounds of shortbread. He held a package out to Kostas and asked, "What are these?"

"Budz bits," the professor answered. "A rather expensive cracker." He sat in the single chair by the table and sighed. "Whatever else I may say about our captors, I must admit they lay a fine table. Apparently even way out here."

Turner tipped one of the metal canisters and it sloshed. "Thought so," he said. He turned it so he could reach its spigot and dribbled a few cc's of its contents into his cupped palm. "Some kind of juice," he said. "Sweet."

"Not Berggren berry, then," Kirk said. "That's fairly tart."

Kostas laughed. "Ha! Even Haidar herself wouldn't leave a cache of Berggren berry juice for prisoners to drink. That is probably just Kenan root extract. The most common drink on the planet."

"Root beer?" Kirk asked disdainfully. "Doesn't anyone here believe in alcohol?"

"What's alcohol?" Kostas asked.

Turner looked at him in wonder. "Don't you have beer here?" he asked. Then he answered himself before Kostas could. "Of course you don't. Not if you're storing highly sugared wort at room temperature. One yeast cell and you'd have a keg of ale in no time. That means you must not have yeast around here, do you?"

Kostas shrugged. "What's yeast? What's ale?"

Turner tasted the extract again. "I could probably show you," he said, "but it wouldn't be a very good introduction. This stuff's got way too strong a flavor, and besides, the brewing conditions here are terrible. Too hot, for one."

Kirk set the box of crackers back on the shelf. "You mean you can brew beer out of that stuff without any special equipment?" he asked.

Turner nodded. "Well, it may not be beer, since beer is mostly hops and malted barley, but I do have the yeast." He laughed. "No brewer goes anywhere without his yeast. It'd be practically impossible. It's in the air wherever you brew. It gets into your hair, on your skin—and into your clothes." He untucked his tunic and pointed to a stain along the left side. "Sometimes it gets there in more concentrated form than others. I was experimenting with a Romulan ale yeast earlier today, trying to see what kind of porter it would make. But I spilled a little of the culture on my shirt while I was making the starter, and then you called me to duty on the away team before I could change, and here it is. Romulan ale yeast."

"Romulan ale," Kirk said, wheels turning in his head. "That's the most potent nondistilled liquor in the whole quadrant."

"That's right," Turner said. "It'll reach thirty percent alcohol, at least, before the yeast stops working. And smooth . . . you can hardly tell there's any kick to it until it's too late."

"Oh, yes," Kirk said, smiling. "I've had plenty of experience with Romulan ale. But it sounds like you haven't." He nodded to Kostas.

"No, I'm afraid not."

"Good," said Kirk. "Mr. Turner, how long would it take for that yeast to make Romulan ale out of this extract?"

"It'll never make Romulan ale out of this," Turner said. "The ingredients are all wrong. But I can probably make a pretty alcoholic root beer out of it."

"How long?" Kirk asked again.

Turner blushed; he'd let his fascination with the hobby carry him away from the question. He said, "It usually takes a week or so, but in this heat it could go a lot faster. I'd guess a couple of days."

"And how many of these canisters can you inoculate with that little patch of yeast?"

Turner looked at the rack of them. "Well, the more yeast you use the better your odds of a smooth brew, but in a pinch all it takes is one cell per container. Why?"

"Then inoculate all you can," Kirk told him, "because I think that's our ticket out of here."

Scotty looked around at the tall concrete wall he and the Rimillian engineer, Neron, had beamed in next to. They were now at the north pole, but no visual cues would have given that away; the sun was low on the horizon as always, the temperature was mild, and the place was as crowded with people as anywhere else in the Edge.

But most of those people held weapons, Scotty noted, and atop the wall were heavy phaser cannons. And he and Neron had arrived outside the wall, not inside it, which meant the computer center it enclosed was almost certainly shielded.

"Why here?" Scotty asked as Neron led the way toward the gateway and the tunnel beneath the wall.

"Why the north pole, you mean?" Neron replied.

"Yes. You know it's going to get cold here once you start her spinning. Unless you keep the axis perpendicular to the orbital plane, but then you won't have any seasons."

"Oh, no, we're giving it a twenty-degree tilt to match our homeworld," said Neron. "Even after all this time, our biorhythms are still tuned to Duma."

Scotty tried to visualize it in his mind. "Are we at the current pole, or where the new one is going to be?"

"We're at the new pole. For convenience, we put it on the Edge as well." They approached the gate and Neron put his palm on an ID plate set into the wall beside it. A moment later the gate slid aside, but he didn't enter yet. "Here, put your hand on the scanner," he said, and when Scotty did so, Neron tapped in a code number on the keypad beneath it. "There, now you're authorized to come and go as you like," he said.

"Thank you," Scotty said, trying not to show his annoyance at having to endure all this security. It wasn't Neron's fault that his people were divided over the project.

They walked on into the compound. When they

emerged from under the wall, Scotty saw a cluster of typically Rimillian buildings, all squat and massive and interconnected by enclosed causeways. The roof had caved in on one of the buildings. That was undoubtedly where the aircar had crashed. Evidently the phaser cannons on the walls had been a late addition, or else their operators had been bad shots.

"So why here?" Scotty asked again.

"Well, to start off with," Neron replied, setting off down the main avenue toward the damaged building, "it's safest. Most of the engines are near the equator, where their thrust will do the most good. But that means most of the quakes will be there as well. Up here at the pole, we should be relatively safe from that. Also, even though it's eventually going to wind up being pretty inhospitable here, this and the south pole are actually going to have the mildest climates while the planet is spinning up to speed."

"Ah, I see your point," Scotty replied, getting the correct mental image now. The rest of the planet would have to make a few very slow passes through day and night before the planet picked up any appreciable rotation, but the poles would remain in twilight. By the time it got cold here, they wouldn't need the facility anymore. Provided everything worked the way it was supposed to, of course.

Construction workers were hard at work repairing the computer building. Scotty and Neron stepped around piles of roofing material and ducked to avoid scaffolding as they went in through the front doors and down a long hallway into the building's central chamber.

It was an even bigger mess inside. The aircar had been winched out through the hole it had made in the roof, but it was obvious where it had hit. The entire circular room had been lined with racks of electronics, bank after bank of them in concentric rows, but now a pie-shaped wedge of them were ripped apart by the impact and scattered across the floor. Above the computers, occupying about ninety degrees of arc along the wall, a big situation map of the planet had mostly escaped destruction, but dozens of smaller panels below it had been smashed by flying debris. People were already at work repairing the damage, but they had a long way to go. Too long, in Scotty's opinion.

"Aye, an' that's a sorry sight," he muttered when he saw how little had been done, and how much there was yet to do. "I sure hope your backup controls fared better than this."

Neron looked at him with a surprised expression. "Backup?" he asked.

Chapter Twelve

SULU SNEEZED. He wiped off the gene scanner's monitor with a tissue from the box Nurse Chapel had thoughtfully provided him, and continued the scan. He had most of the cyclone tree's DNA sequence recorded now; he was just scanning the cells' cytoplasm for loose fragments in case any might express themselves in the adult organism. Another few minutes and—

—and nothing. The monitor flickered, and the sampling instrument itself beeped a warning. Good grief, had he shorted something out with his sneeze? No, the condition lights on the computer interface were blinking red, indicating that the problem was over there. Sulu stared blearily at the monitor, trying to clear his head. He'd been at it for over twelve hours, and he was beginning to see double. No, it was the damned gene sequencer again. It had been acting up all day, dumping data and locking up without warning. Sulu resisted the urge to slap it alongside its CPU housing, and instead pressed Reset for the hundredth time that afternoon. While the computer restarted itself, he leaned back and rubbed his eyes.

A moment later McCoy stepped into the lab. "Problems?"

Sulu nodded. "This genetic scanner has definitely seen better days."

"Hah," said McCoy. "Tell me about it. If we'd met with the *Hoffman* when we were supposed to, I'd have a new top-of-the-line instrument sitting there now instead of that tired piece of junk."

Sulu sneezed again, then said, "I did actually make some progress before it went down again. Here, let me show you."

He called up the cyclone-tree genome that he had finally managed to assemble from three different scans, and fed it into the gene sequencer's growth-simulator program. Slowly, as the computer crunched through the billions of calculations for the interactions between genes, a picture began to build on the monitor. It didn't look much like a cyclone tree—in fact, it looked more like a sea urchin—but it was better than the gray goo that Sulu had gotten out of his first few runs.

"I'm still having trouble identifying the activation triggers," he explained. "Cyclone trees are apparently like most other life in that most of its genetic material is inert in any given organism, but of course the triggers that switch the genes on and off aren't the same as ours. I'm experimenting with the various proteins I've found in the cells, but so far I haven't found them all. This is just something that *could* come out of this genetic code if we turned on the right genes."

"Well," McCoy said dubiously, "somehow I don't think that particular combination is going to do us much good. But keep trying. We haven't got much time to prove our point." He shook his head. "But without Jim here to run things, I don't know if the rotation would proceed on schedule anyway."

From just behind McCoy, Spock said, "I assure you, the captain's absence will not prevent us from accomplishing our mission."

McCoy whirled around angrily. "What are you doing out of bed? Get back in the recovery room!"

Spock didn't move. "I cannot assume the captain's duties from a convalescent bed," he said.

"Well then you'll just have to let someone else do it," McCoy said, "because you're staying put until I say you're healed. Is that clear?"

"Perfectly, Doctor." Spock folded his arms over his chest. "With the chief engineer also off the ship, and the first officer confined to sickbay, you are technically in command. Do you intend to pursue the captain's agenda, or your own?"

Sulu held his breath. He hated it when McCoy and Spock got after each other, and this time looked to be a bad one. McCoy was turning red in the face, and his Southern accent grew more prominent as he said, "Ah, so that's why you're so hot to get back upstairs, isn't it? You want to make sure that this harebrained scheme to cook every living creature on the planet goes through before we can prove there's a better way, don't you? You like the brute force, mechanical approach so much that you won't even give us a chance."

"That is illogical, Doctor." Spock's voice never

revealed emotion, but Sulu had been around him long enough to know when he was angry. For a Vulcan to say someone's statement was illogical was tantamount to calling them a fool. Spock looked directly into McCoy's eyes as he said, "If you were actually to prove that biological methods are superior in this case, then of course I would support their use. However, at this point you have nothing but simulations, and not very promising ones at that." He nodded to the screen with the urchin-like ball of spines on it.

"We're just getting started," McCoy protested.

"That is obvious," Spock said. "What is much less clear is whether or not you can decode the genetic map of the native life and alter it—even in simulation —into something that will survive in a harsher environment, and do that in the three days remaining to us. We must, therefore, proceed with the repairs to the impulse-engine system, and we must use it if your efforts here are unsuccessful."

"That's illogical, Spock." McCoy stabbed a finger at his chest. "The damned rotation project is the only thing that's got a deadline on it; we've got months to come up with better cyclone trees before the atmosphere gets so bad they can't breathe it."

"You have three days," said Spock with finality. "We cannot let the only other alternative pass by without proof that your plan will succeed."

"Damn your computerized logic, Spock," McCoy said. "You have no more proof that *your* plan will succeed."

"No," Spock said. "I do not. But it is the option the inhabitants of this planet have chosen, and unless and until they choose otherwise, it is our duty to help them carry it out."

"Oh, so now it's *their* fault. That's just wonderful, Spock. I love how you weaseled out of that." McCoy reached out and took the science officer's arm. "Now, get moving. I wasn't kidding when I ordered you back to bed."

Spock took a few grudging steps back down the corridor. "I protest this treatment, Doctor. I could do my duties from an antigrav chair without further—"

"And I could follow you around the ship with a hypospray waiting for you to keel over again," said McCoy. "But frankly I've got better things to do with my time. Like save a planet from your pointy-eared logic."

Sulu shook his head as the two officers quarreled their way down the corridor. He looked back to the screen. Maybe if he tried activating *this* sequence here . . .

The place smelled like a brewery. Ensign Turner liked it that way, though he was a little worried about how fast it was happening. It was too hot to brew a proper ale. The yeast was acting too quickly—flash-fermenting—converting all the sugar in the wort to alcohol in one vast orgy of replication. It would stop just as suddenly, and unless Turner caught it at precisely the right moment and sealed the canisters while there was still a little activity, he would have flat beer.

Of course that would probably be for the best, he supposed. It would give their captors one less clue that their beverage supply had been contaminated.

Turner wondered how quickly they would notice it anyway. Romulan ale had a nasty habit of sneaking up on a person, but usually that person was at least expecting *some* alcohol. On the other hand, that Kenan root stuff had a pretty overpowering natural flavor; it might mask the alcohol long enough to do the trick.

And if not, well, he and the captain and Professor Kostas would have plenty of brew to drown their sorrows in.

He was sitting on the floor with his back against the metal rack. The cool air current from the room's single ventilation duct blew down this wall, and helped evaporate the sweat that poured off his body. At this rate he was going to need a couple gallons of fluid a day to replenish what he lost to the heat. He was glad he'd left half the canisters untouched; a couple gallons of Romulan ale per day—even the ersatz root beer this wort would produce—would be enough to kill anyone but a Romulan.

Professor Kostas sat at the table in the only chair. Captain Kirk had pulled a crate of canned goods up across from him and was sitting on that, showing Kostas how to play checkers with some Budz bits.

Turner shifted position to stretch a kink in his leg, and Kostas looked up from the table at him. Smiling, he asked the captain, "Are all your crew members as resourceful as Mr. Turner here?"

Turner looked over at Kirk. The captain seemed to be waiting for him to speak, so he said, "Of course they are. We're the best crew in the galaxy." Then he remembered that the rest of them were probably a thin cloud in space now, and he took a deep breath and looked away.

"They're alive," Kirk said firmly. "No question."

"I certainly hope so," Turner replied.

Kostas nodded. "What about this engineer of yours

—Mr. Scotty, I believe you called him? Is he equally inventive?"

Kirk laughed suddenly. "Mr. Scott is a veritable genius when it comes to inventiveness."

"Does he know computers?" Kostas asked.

"Like the back of his hand," Kirk said proudly. "Don't you worry, he'll have your control system up and running again with plenty of time to spare. And no slur on your own abilities, but I'd be willing to bet he'll find a way to improve on the design while he's at it."

"Oh, I hope not," said Kostas. His face wrinkled into a mask of deep concern. "I spent the last two years tuning that computer to exactly the right configuration for the job. You can't just go altering things willy-nilly with a neural net; you have to proceed gently, a little bit at a time, and give the system a chance to respond gradually. A heavy-handed touch will throw it into complete disarray."

Turner could tell that the captain was irritated by the mere implication that his chief engineer could possibly screw up, but Kirk kept an even tone when he said, "His touch could hardly be as heavy as the saboteurs' was. But I'm sure he understands the danger. If gentleness is required, then I'm sure Scotty will be gentle."

The squeal of metal against metal rose to a momentarily unbearable pitch before the bolts holding the ruined computer console gave way with a loud clang. Scotty backed away as the crane swung the wreckage overhead and the clawed hand released it to fall into the pile of crushed equipment near the door. The console tumbled down the pile with all the grace of a cargo pod falling off an a-grav plate, and skidded to a stop beside the front-end loader that was scooping up the ruined electronic parts and carrying them out of the building. The clatter and boom echoed in the immense computer hall.

"Very good," Scotty shouted to Neron over the din. "Once we get this cleared away, we can start on the *real* work."

Neron smiled halfheartedly. Watching a sixth of the control system's intelligence being wrenched loose and carried away obviously hadn't put him in the best of spirits, but for the first time in the day and a half since he'd arrived here Scotty couldn't be happier. They were actually *doing* something now. It was more triage than repair work at the moment, but once they got the hopeless stuff out of the way they could bend to the task of hooking together what was left.

"I never thought I'd live to see the day when I'd appreciate a neural network," Scotty said, "but I thank my lucky stars that's what you built here. If you'd used a regular digital processor, what you'd have now wouldn't even make a good adding machine, but a neural net, now that's another kettle o' fish entirely. It might be a wee bit confused at first, what with all the missing connections, but at least it should remember most of its programming."

"I suppose we'll find out soon enough," Neron said. His fur-rimmed ears quivered like a nervous horse's.

"Aye, that we will." Scotty slapped him on the back. "Cheer up, laddie. This is your big moment t'shine. If we pull this off, people will be singin' songs about you for thousands of years to come."

The prospect didn't seem to cheer the Rimillian much, but Scotty supposed he had a right to feel glum once in a while. Truth was, being a hero had never appealed much to Scotty, either. He preferred engineering over entertaining, puzzles over parades. And this was going to be the greatest puzzle he'd ever been asked to assemble.

A neural net was a special kind of computer, so named because its millions of processors were linked together with billions of interconnections, much like the cells of a brain, rather than in a single chain of command like a more conventional computer. In theory the net could process information faster and work on much bigger problems, and experimentation had proved that theory at least partially correct.

The problem was, they did their work by trial and error. Those billions of pathways couldn't be controlled by any external means; the interactions between processors had to be left to the processors themselves. There were general rules, of course, which the programmer could alter at will, but those were more like traffic signs than physical laws. They influenced the patterns of motion, but individual vehicles could still use the roads however they wished. That meant that after you switched on the computer, what actually went on inside it was largely a mystery. You fed in a problem on one end, and it spit out an answer on the other, but the methods it used could vary from moment to moment.

The machines learned, of course. In time, certain pathways became favored over others and overall performance improved dramatically—until the input changed enough to force a paradigm shift and the machines had to learn from scratch what to do with the new data.

That unpredictability had made them popular for artificial-intelligence research, but they had fallen out of favor over a century ago for general use. Parallel processors and subspace information buses that bypassed speed-of-light limitations had solved the speed problem in conventional computers, and were far more reliable as well.

But neural nets still excelled at one function: They could adapt. Given a situation with constantly varying input from thousands of separate sources—say, seismometers and angular-momentum sensors—and control signals going out to thousands of separate devices—say, impulse engines—a neural net could churn through the problem in real time while a normal computer would simply overload and crash.

And there was one added advantage that Scotty was most glad for now: If you removed part of a neural net, you could reconnect what was left into a functional, although somewhat less intelligent, version of the original. It would take all the time they had left, but Scotty was willing to bet he and Neron could make those reconnections and get the control system back on line before the window of opportunity for the rotation passed.

The only question was whether the lobotomized computer would still be able to handle the job. Having Professor Kostas back would help immeasurably in making sure it would, but Scotty didn't know if that was going to happen or not. The captain's rescue attempt had gone badly, and both of them were now captured. Scotty wanted to go after them himself, but he knew that would be foolish. If he was captured as well, then the project would really be doomed.

No, he had to stay and help Neron make repairs, and hope what they could do on their own would get the job done. And as Neron had said, they would find that out soon enough.

Chapter Thirteen

Two days. If he hadn't made marks on the wall each time he slept, Kirk would have lost track even this soon. With the constant sun overhead, his and Turner's sleep cycles were the only markers of time's passage. Kostas was no help; his concept of a day was completely variable. When he was interested in something he would stay awake until he was finished or grew exhausted, and when he wasn't—as had been the case since he'd been kidnapped—he took short catnaps every few hours.

The long delay in breaking out chafed at Kirk, but he knew he had to make his plans carefully. As the woman, Marybeth, had said, even if they broke out of their prison there was only the hellish landscape outside to escape into. Kirk needed to learn more about the situation, figure out what he was going to do when he gained the upper hand before he made his move. Like the prisoners of war in centuries past, he needed to observe his captors' movements until he could predict their every action, and thus exploit their moment of greatest weakness.

The trouble was, they had no regular schedule that Kirk could discern. They were evidently as bored with their job as Kostas was with being a prisoner; they came into the storeroom cell for food and drink about as often as the professor slept. They didn't prepare meals for the prisoners, but with all the prepackaged food that wasn't a problem, save that it cut down on the number of opportunities to overpower someone and make an escape. The real problem was that it didn't seem like everyone ate at the same time, so it would be hard to get them all drunk at the same time by simply letting them take one of the fermented beverage canisters.

Marybeth complained about the smell and made bad jokes about their personal hygiene, but without any experience with fermentation she didn't connect it to the bubbling root beer, which Turner kept on the bottom of the rack so she wouldn't discover it until Kirk decided it was time.

They did get more frequent bathroom breaks out of the situation, which allowed Kirk to scout out the rest of the building in which they were being held. His first impression when they'd beamed in had been right: the entire facility was small, and had probably been a scientific outpost before it was converted to a jail. Besides the storeroom where they were being held there was only the communications room with its banks of electronic equipment along the walls, the bathroom, a tiny galley (which explained why nobody brought prepared meals to the prisoners), and a single bunkroom for the staff.

Like the other buildings Kirk had seen on Rimillia, this one had an airlock, and two full-blown environment suits hung stiffly from pegs just inside the inner door. Kirk wondered how long they would allow a person to survive in the intense heat outside, but he didn't particularly want to find out the hard way. Maybe he could get Marybeth to tell him.

He stopped on his way to the bathroom one time and asked her directly: "So do you ever go outside, or are those just for decoration?"

She had backed off to the middle of the comm room, her pistol held ready, after opening the storeroom door for him. She might have been bored, but she was still alert; even though two of her four companions were also there with her, she kept her eyes on Kirk when he nodded toward the suits.

"We don't need to go out," she said. "We're in constant contact with headquarters. We can beam in anything we need."

They didn't have a transporter of their own, Kirk noted, so they would have to be in contact with somebody. That might be a weakness he could exploit.

"What about repair work? Storm damage, things like that. You must have to go out occasionally."

"Our job is to guard you," she replied. "If we have any problems, we call for help and someone else fixes them."

"I see." Kirk took a couple more steps toward the bathroom, then turned back around. "If you're in

139

constant contact, have you transmitted my request to speak with Haidar?"

Marybeth reddened. "I told you before, she is not involved."

"Of course not," Kirk said. "But a message could nevertheless be sent to her, couldn't it? You could arrange a meeting on neutral ground somewhere."

"What makes you think she'd listen to us? Or to you, for that matter?"

Kirk waved a hand at the tiny outpost. "Even if she doesn't approve of your methods, she sympathizes with your cause. She wouldn't have any reason to fear being taken hostage as well. And I suspect she would like to hear what I have to tell her."

Marybeth shifted her weapon slightly, but not enough for Kirk to make a move to take it from her. "What do you want to tell her?"

"You're not her," Kirk replied, shaking his head. "But you can tell her I may have information she can use in her campaign to change the government's mind."

"Why would you do that?"

"Because she can help me find out what happened to my ship, and my crew. It's possible some of them beamed down before the torpedoes hit, or escaped in life pods. It may not yet be too late to rescue them. Haidar can put the resources of the government to work on finding them."

He thought he saw a flicker of emotion come over her when he mentioned the *Enterprise*. Remorse? Whatever it was, she closed down on it immediately. "I will send a message to my cell leader," she said. "She can decide whether or not to risk speaking with Haidar."

Kirk suspected it wasn't much of a risk, but of course they would have to keep up the pretense that the councilor had no part in his capture. "Thank you," he said simply; then he went on into the bathroom.

It was a tiny cubicle, with a coffin-sized ultrasonic cleaner instead of a shower, and a chemical toilet. Water was at a premium here, so he hadn't been surprised to see that, but he had never seen a toilet designed quite like this one. It didn't use any water at all; instead a frictionless surface let all the waste slide into a collection chamber where it was burned to ash. Kirk had assumed there was a phaser or a molecular disruptor of some sort inside to do the job, but when he had asked Kostas if it could be removed and used for a weapon, Kostas had told him it didn't work like that. Toilets were old technology, and disruptors used too much energy anyway; the Rimillian system sprayed a powerful oxidizing agent into the collection chamber and burned the waste that way.

Kirk could see possibilities in that. The ale was coming along fine, according to Turner, and the three prisoners had just sampled some before Kirk left to use the bathroom and found it surprisingly smooth, but it never hurt to have a backup plan. As soon as Kirk was alone in the bathroom he bent down to examine the toilet's injection system, looking for a way to remove some of the oxidizer. The stuff was easy enough to find: inside an access hatch at the base of the stool was a clear plastic bottle, about half-liter-sized, a quarter full of greenish liquid. There hadn't been anything like that in the storeroom, so Kirk couldn't just take a bottle from there. He wondered how he could take some of this bottle's contents back with him now. He couldn't very well pour it into his boot.

He searched the rest of the bathroom, hoping to find where they stored the full bottles, but there was no cabinet. Just the ultrasonic shower, the stool, a regular water sink, and a wastebasket beneath that.

And an empty oxidizer bottle in the wastebasket.

Kirk quickly unscrewed the quarter-full one and swapped the empty one into its place. With luck, Marybeth and the other guards would just think the extra people were using it up faster than usual.

The bottle sealed itself automatically, like a gas canister, which was a good thing because there was only one place Kirk could hide it. He sucked in his stomach and tucked the bottle into the front of his pants, leaving his uniform tunic untucked to hide at least some of the bulge it left there.

Marybeth was still in the central room when he opened the bathroom door. If she noticed anything unusual, then she thought just what he wanted her to think: she blushed slightly as he walked past her to the storeroom.

The Romulan root beer had worked every bit as well as they had hoped. Perhaps better. The prisoners had only drunk a few ounces each, but Turner was asleep when Kirk returned, and Kostas was humming happily to himself as he stacked canned goods in an improbable arch over the table. It looked like it should collapse in a hail of cans at the slightest disturbance, but Kostas calmly set one after another in place without even jiggling it.

"Doing some recreational engineering?" Kirk asked him.

Kostas nodded. "It came to me in a vision, and I had to test it out."

"I'll bet it did," said Kirk. Oh, yes, this just might work. He wondered if now would be a good time to have the professor playing with dangerous chemicals, but they didn't have forever to wait for him to sober up. Kirk pulled the oxidizer bottle from his pants and held it out to him. "Can you do anything with this?"

"What sort of thing do you mean?" Kostas asked, taking the bottle.

"I was thinking about a bomb. An oxidizing agent this powerful should make quite an explosion if you mix it with the right stuff, shouldn't it?"

Kostas looked at the bottle dubiously. "Well, yes, I suppose it might, but we don't have any of the proper equipment to test it with, or—"

"We've got a whole storeroom full of stuff," Kirk said. "That'll have to do." He reached for the nearest box, looking inside to see if it might contain anything volatile. Canned goods. He reached for another box.

He and the professor were still at it a few hours later, without much more success than a few charred Budz bits, when they heard footsteps approaching the door. They hastily hid the oxidizer bottle and pretended to be adding more cans to the arch when Marybeth opened the door and said to Kirk, "She has consented to an audience. Come in here."

Kirk had been so absorbed in his latest project he had nearly forgotten that he had other irons in the fire. He switched his mental gears and followed Marybeth into the communications room. She waved her beam weapon at a circle drawn in the middle of the floor, and he stood in the center of it. They were doing a blind transport, then. No ID trace, and therefore untraceable; the remote transporter would simply beam whatever was in its target area to wherever it was programmed to send it. Even if the *Enterprise* were still around and searching for him, without an ID trace they couldn't tell what was included in the beam. A good trick.

Marybeth nodded to one of her compatriots at the controls. He flipped a switch, and Kirk noted its position. It was almost certainly the control for the energy shield.

A moment later he felt the confinement beam lock on to him, and in the next instant he was standing in a much larger, much more comfortable room, like those in the first government building he had visited. It was furnished with two well-padded armchairs, and food and drink waited on a low table between them. Four men stood well back from both Kirk and the chairs, and all held weapons trained on him.

"Sit down," one of the guards said.

"I'm pleased to meet you, too," Kirk told them, choosing the chair on the left. He looked around at the room, noting that its contents had not been packed away yet as Joray's had. Of course not; these people didn't expect the rotation to happen.

The guard spoke into a communicator, and a moment later Haidar shimmered into existence where Kirk had. She looked at the guards, then at him. Nobody told her to sit, Kirk noted.

She did anyway. "I am taking an incredible risk for you," she said. "I hope you appreciate it."

"That remains to be seen," said Kirk. "I might, if you give me reason to."

"And what would you consider sufficient reason?"

"News of my ship and crew. Your jailor told me it had been destroyed with all hands on board. Is that true?"

Haidar looked genuinely shocked. She was either a good actress or she honestly didn't know that part of the story. "She is not 'my' anything," she said indignantly, "and obviously whoever she does work for is misinformed. Your ship is fine, and is orbiting overhead as we speak. I talked to your first officer less than three hours ago."

Kirk leaned back in the chair and closed his eyes, relief flooding through him. Yes. He'd known it couldn't be true.

"Captain?"

He looked over at Haidar again. She actually seemed concerned. Were she and Marybeth playing the good cop/bad cop routine on him, or had he grossly miscalculated her involvement in the conspiracy? There were, after all, other councilors who might have done it.

"Thank you," Kirk told her with absolute sincerity. "You have definitely earned my appreciation. Now let me earn yours."

"How do you propose to do that?"

"By giving you good news as well. Unless of course Mr. Spock has already filled you in."

She shook her head. "We spoke only of your disappearance."

That would be like Spock, Kirk supposed. Strictly business, and *his* business at that. Kirk picked up one of the snifters of purple juice from the table and took a sip. "Ah," he said. "Berggren berry. Better have some; I've heard it's rare."

Haidar gave him a hard look, obviously wondering where he had encountered Berggren berry before, and obviously not liking the answer she came up with.

He smiled at her and said, "What I said at our last meeting wasn't all talk. When we got back to the ship, I set Dr. McCoy and Mr. Sulu—our, uh, resident botanist—on the task of genetically tailoring your cyclone trees to survive farther from the Edge. When they succeed in finding a viable mutation, I stand ready to give you evidence of it, which you can then use to force a recall vote in your council."

"Evidence of it?" Haidar asked. "Not the mutation itself?"

"Not unless Starfleet approves. But if you know it's possible, you can either find it yourselves or petition the Federation for membership and then ask for it as a full member. Either way, your problem with the rotation project will be postponed, perhaps indefinitely."

Haidar took a snifter of juice and sipped at it. "A generous offer, Captain," she said, "but ultimately empty, I suspect. How can your doctor do in two days what our own scientists have been unable to do in years?"

Kirk grinned. It felt wonderful to know that McCoy was still alive, and that the *Enterprise* still awaited its captain. He said, "He's the Federation's finest medical officer, and he's got some of the Federation's finest equipment to back him up. If it's at all possible, he'll find out."

Kirk winced at the memory of McCoy complaining about his gene scanner and simulator, but the statement was true enough. It was the Federation's finest when it was installed only a few years ago, and it would still be sufficient for the job. Whether or not the cyclone trees were up to it was a different question, but Kirk knew that McCoy and Sulu—and even the gene scanner—would perform.

"Why the sudden change of heart, Captain? Or is this just a ploy to escape your captivity?"

Kirk laughed. "No, I've already got that taken care of," he said. "Though if you want to save everyone some trouble you could tell Mr. Spock that we're being held in a scientific research station at the hot pole."

Haidar smiled at him. "I will pass that information along, but I don't know how much good it will do him. Or you. There are hundreds of science stations at the hot pole, many of them legitimately shielded against solar radiation. Unless you think he's prepared to search every one of them personally, I suspect that knowledge will do him little good."

Kirk knew Spock well enough to know that he would search every building on the planet if he thought it would help. And if he knew where to concentrate his search, he would keep a constant watch for any sign of Kirk in that area. Which meant that Kirk would only have to lower the shield— or escape beyond its reach—for a few seconds before Spock locked on to him and beamed him to safety.

"Of course I will do everything in my power as well to negotiate your release," said Haidar.

"Of course," Kirk said, allowing just the slightest bit of sarcasm to creep into his voice.

Haidar flushed red. "Captain, I resent this insinuation that I would condone such a thing as your being held hostage. I oppose the rotation project, but I act within the law in my opposition to it. I would work for your release in any case, whether you had agreed to help me or not."

"Good," Kirk said. "I'm glad we understand one another, because I work within the law, too. Yours as well as my own, as long as I am here, which means that I will support the official government-sponsored program for rehabilitating your planet. I will give your people anything Dr. McCoy comes up with, but it will be up to you to decide what to do with it. Is that clear?"

"Perfectly." Haidar stood up. "We will talk again, Captain. Hopefully under more comfortable circumstances." She turned to the guards, who had waited patiently throughout their conversation. "Beam me back to my office." She stepped back to the spot she had beamed into.

The guard spoke into his communicator, and a moment later she dissolved in a column of sparkling light.

Kirk had stood up as well, but the guard said, "Please remain seated, Captain," so he sat back down. Perhaps someone else wanted to talk with him as well. But he was just reaching for a snack when the transporter containment field locked him into position, and a moment later he was back in the storeroom with Turner and Kostas. Evidently they had just refocused the beam on his chair in case he made an escape attempt.

Both his cellmates looked up in surprise; they obviously hadn't been warned he was returning.

"How did it go, Captain?" Turner asked.

Kirk shrugged. "It's hard to say. She might help us, or she might not." He leaned back and sighed. "Well, we at least got a couch out of the deal."

Chapter Fourteen

SPOCK HAD BEEN accessing the computer for visual scan data of the surface when Councilor Haidar called. He was on the bridge again, after finally winning his freedom from Dr. McCoy. Why that man persisted so in his relentless assault on the Vulcan way of life, Spock would never know. It seemed to fill a completely emotional need on the doctor's part, and was therefore unknowable. Whatever else it was, Spock found it distracting, especially when he needed to locate the captain.

He was glad to have the bridge largely to himself. It was ship's night, and the only other people at the controls were the helmsman, Benjamin, and the combined engineer/navigator, Goodloe. They were busy with their own jobs, which gave Spock the rare opportunity to work uninterrupted at his science station.

150

Sickbay's patient terminals had allowed him only limited access to his normal resources. He had been unable to perform more than the most rudimentary of searches, nor had he been able to do the high-speed correlations that the incoming data he did receive required. Now he was trying to make up for lost time, but the incoming call provided yet another delay.

Uhura was not at her station to receive it, so Spock cleared a monitor for it and said, "*Enterprise,* Spock here." When Haidar's image appeared he added, "What can I do for you, Councilor?"

She shook her head. "It's what I can do for you that matters at the moment. I just spoke with your captain. He is being held in a research station at the hot pole."

"Indeed?" Spock said. He reached out with the intention of redirecting his sensor scans to that area, then stopped with the motion only half done. Logically, he had no reason to trust such a statement from a person who benefited from the captain's absence.

"Yes," said Haidar. "The Denialists beamed him to the meeting location and back again just a few minutes ago. If you were scanning for transporter use at the time, you might have some evidence of which station he's at."

Yes, Spock thought, they might—if they'd been scanning for that. The *Enterprise's* sensors were powerful but not limitless; Spock had reasoned that their best chance of locating the captain would be through penetrating the shielded defenses rather than attempting to intercept and filter through every transporter trace on the planet for sign of him, but he had evidently been mistaken. He would not make that same error again. As soon as he finished talking with Haidar, he would reset the computer to make continuous scans, and send out probes in polar orbits to cover the areas the *Enterprise* couldn't reach from its present position. In the meantime, Haidar herself could be his best source of information.

"What is the captain's condition?" he asked.

"He seemed fine. Restless, but anyone would be in his situation."

Spock nodded. She was no doubt correct, but Jim was restless in any situation. "What did the kidnappers demand for his return?" he asked.

Haidar shook her head. "They don't intend to release him until after the danger of rotation is over."

"I assure you, madam, that the resources of the *Enterprise* will be more than sufficient to repair the sabotage even without Captain Kirk at the helm. Therefore, holding him hostage serves no useful purpose."

"I'll remember to tell them that if they contact me again," Haidar said. "In the meantime, Captain Kirk told me that Dr. McCoy is actually working on adapting the cyclone trees for harsher climates. If he were to succeed, the Denialists would have even less reason to hold him."

Spock resisted the urge to remind her that no reason, less another reason, was still no reason. As little as they valued logic, humans nonetheless reacted badly to having theirs corrected, he had learned. Haidar was not technically human, but she was closer to it than to Vulcan so he merely said, "The doctor is indeed attempting to redesign your forests. So far he has had little success, but he clings to his hope with characteristic determination. If you wish, I will pass along your assessment of the situation and see if it spurs him into heroic action."

Haidar blinked her eyelashes repeatedly, as if something had just become lodged in both eyes simultaneously. "Why Mr. Spock, I believe you are mocking me, and possibly your doctor as well."

"I would never mock you, madam," Spock said. "It would serve no useful purpose."

McCoy was finally beginning to see some progress. He and Sulu were still a long way from designing a heat- and cold-tolerant cyclone tree, but at least now when they ran the genome map they had made through the simulator they could come up with the original plant again. That was actually a big step forward, because it meant they had finally figured out the activation triggers that controlled the genes. Now they merely needed to figure out what the individual genes coded for, and they could assemble the features they wanted into a new species.

Right. Sulu's last simulation, after duplicating just one amino acid sequence that he'd thought might code for thicker sap, had looked more like a toadstool than a tree. A thirty-meter-high toadstool, to be sure, but still not quite what they were looking for, especially with the winds it would be expected to withstand.

That had been just one gene, and their parent tree's chromosomes contained millions of them.

It was late. McCoy and Sulu had both been at it all day. Sulu's cold was getting worse, and it sapped a lot of his energy, despite all McCoy's efforts to minimize the symptoms. It galled him to realize that chicken soup would probably do his patient just as much good as anything else he could give him.

They sat side by side in the lab, hoping that two minds and two sets of eyes would improve their odds of figuring out the problem. The new scanner that waited for them in the hold of the *Hoffman* had multiple user terminals, but this model had just the one, so they had to share. It allowed for closer brainstorming, but as McCoy was beginning to realize, you had to have two functioning brains to create more than fog.

"Why don't we call it a night," he said when the toadstool appeared on the screen. "Get some sleep, and hit it again in the morning when we're fresh."

"Okay," said Sulu, not making any move to get up. "You first." He brought the genome map back onto the screen and highlighted another sequence for activation, then set the simulator to running again. It would take five minutes or so for it to assemble everything and present the phenotype on the screen.

"Listen here," McCoy said, "I'm the doctor here, and—"

The intercom interrupted him. He tapped it on and said, "Sickbay."

"Spock here. Councilor Haidar called with news of the captain. I assume you would be interested in a summary of our conversation."

"Of course! Is Jim all right?"

Sulu leaned closer to the communicator, too.

"She reports that he is physically healthy, though restless from captivity. He seems to have attempted to bargain with her, using your tree-mutation project as an inducement. I have attempted to dissuade her from false hope, but she—"

"You *what?*"

Sulu jumped backward from the force of McCoy's outburst.

"I told her that you were having little success, and that—"

"You damned idiot! If it'll get Jim back, you should have told her we were on the edge of a breakthrough."

"But you are not," Spock said, "unless you have achieved it within the last hour."

Vulcans! Spock apparently wouldn't tell a lie even to break Jim out of jail. Not that McCoy liked the idea, but there were principles and then there were principles.

"Well, as a matter of fact," he said, winking at Sulu, "we have."

Spock wasn't fooled for a second. "You are aware that if you claim to have succeeded, you will be required to produce at least the simulated genome, if not a force-grown specimen of the actual plant."

"Don't tell your grandma how to suck eggs, Spock," McCoy drawled. "You just call that councilor back and tell her we're hot on the trail."

"Doctor, I cannot in clear conscience—"

"Tell her I *told* you we were close to a breakthrough," insisted McCoy.

Spock was silent for a moment, then finally he said, "Very well, Doctor. Let us hope you can actually produce something to back up your claim."

"Don't sweat it," McCoy told him. "We're closer than you might think."

"I have no doubt of that. Spock out."

McCoy switched off the intercom. "Damned pointy-eared boy scout," he muttered.

Sulu laughed. "We all have our crosses to bear," he said.

McCoy looked back to the screen, now showing a palm tree with tentacles dangling from the tips of each frond. "Don't we just," he said, pulling his chair closer and settling in for a long night.

Chapter Fifteen

KIRK PACED THE ROOM like a caged tiger. It had been twenty minutes since one of the guards had come into the storeroom and gathered up supplies for dinner, including a fresh canister of Kenan root extract. This was one of the doctored ones; Kirk had grown tired of waiting for Haidar to release him, and he had decided it was time to make his move.

Trouble was, he couldn't tell if anyone had drunk enough of the stuff to make any difference. Or if more than one of the guards had partaken; it might have been just the one having a snack. No sound came through the door, not even snoring, to indicate what might wait on the other side. Kirk was tempted to just kick down the door and go see, either overpower the guards or die in the attempt, but he knew that would be foolish. If there *weren't* drunk, die would be just what he would do, because those weren't phasers they carried. They were molecular disruptors, and there was no stun setting that he had seen.

On the other hand, if anyone had drunk the ersatz ale now was the time to take advantage of it, because Kirk doubted they would give him a second chance.

He also had a crude bomb that Kostas had made, by the simple expedient of filling a plastic bag with alcohol distilled from the Romulan root beer and inserting it into the oxidizer bottle. A sufficient shock would burst the bag, and the oxidizer and the alcohol would mix explosively. It wouldn't have much blast strength, since the bottle didn't offer much containment, but then again Kirk didn't want to blow up the building, either. That would be fatal to everyone, prisoners included. He just wanted to cause enough confusion with it to overpower his captors—but that would be a great deal easier if they were already drunk.

Turner and Kostas sat at the table, contemplating the arch that Kostas had built. It was an imposing structure, reaching up nearly head-high, and as thick as a tree trunk at its base. It tapered as it curved upward until at its peak a single can hung suspended by the pressure from either side. The guards had left it alone, probably unwilling to touch it, and after he'd sobered up Kostas hadn't wanted to fool with it any more, either. Now Kirk looked at it, and he felt a smile begin to grow. Maybe they could test the waters without exposing themselves to unnecessary gunfire.

"How's your throwing arm?" he asked Turner.

Turner looked up. "Sir?"

"Ever play baseball?"

Turner frowned. "Ever play what?" he asked.

"Never mind," Kirk told him. "What I want to

know is whether or not you can hit a head-sized target at close range with a can of sliced peaches. Or whatever this stuff is." He nodded to the arch.

"I can probably do that," Turner said, rising from the box he was sitting on.

"How about you, Professor? You're pretty good with an arch; how are you with applied ballistics?"

Kostas shrugged. "It has been many years since I played varago, but I used to be quite good at it."

"Good," said Kirk. He had no idea what varago was, but he took Kostas's statement as an affirmative. "Gentlemen, arm yourselves. I think it's time we laid in a new course."

Turner lifted the box he'd been sitting on up to the tabletop and pulled out two fist-sized cans from it. He hefted them experimentally and smiled. "Yeah, these will do."

Kirk picked up the bomb in his left hand and held out his right for a can. Turner tossed him one, then dug into the box for a replacement. The professor took two as well, but Kirk shook his head and said, "I'm sorry to break the news to you, but we'll be needing a distraction. If you would like to do the honors . . ." He nodded toward the arch.

Kostas laughed. "I would be glad to. To tell you the truth, I was wondering if I would be able take it apart gracefully anyway." He reached for the single can at the top. "Whenever you're ready, Captain."

Kirk stood back to where he had plenty of room for his throwing arm and had a good angle on the door. Turner took up position on the other side. "Ready any time you are, Captain," he said.

Kirk nodded to Kostas. "Go," he said.

Kostas snatched the can away with a quick upward

Jerry Oltion

snap of his wrist. There was a soft *snick* of metal on
metal, then silence. The sides of the arch held their
positions for over a second, then began to creep closer
together. It looked like they might simply meet and
buttress one another again, but just before they
touched, one of the cans near the bottom of the
rightmost pillar shifted position and that entire side
crumpled. Cans hit and bounced on the floor and off
each other, clattering like meteors on an unshielded
hull.

Then the second arch fell like a toppling tree on top
of them, and the roar of their impact was like a wave
smashing into rocky headlands. Cans rolled every
which way across the floor.

Kirk heard a muffled thump from the other side of
the door, then a curse and more thumps coming
closer. The door popped open and the guard who had
come in earlier stepped in, shouting, "All right, what
are you—yow!" He stepped right on a rolling can and
his foot shot out from under him just as Kirk and
Turner both threw cans at him. Their missiles missed
completely, but it didn't matter. He went down with a
thump that shook the building, his head hitting hard
against the doorsill and his pistol flying out of his
grasp.

Kirk snatched the pistol out of the air. He peered
around the edge of the door into the control room,
then pulled his head back fast. Two more of the guards
were waiting with their weapons drawn, and though
they seemed be having trouble just standing up, one of
them fired the moment he saw Kirk. Fortunately his
aim was off, and his energy bolt merely burned a long
streak in the wall.

He kept firing, though, shot after shot striking the

door, the walls, the table, cans on the floor, anything. Kostas had been nearly in his line of sight; he dived for cover behind the couch that Kirk had brought back from his meeting with Haidar. Kirk and Turner dragged the unconscious guard out of the way so he wouldn't get killed by his own man.

"Looks like he's an angry drunk," Kirk said to Turner over the *zzzzip-bang!* of energy bolts and vaporizing targets. He fired a couple of shots through the doorway to make the guy take cover, then transferred the bomb to his right hand. It was now or never. The guards were as drunk as they were going to get.

Kirk threw the bomb straight for the center of the control console, then ducked back into the storeroom, putting a wall between him and the explosion. He heard a *whump* and felt the building shudder; then the crackle of flames filled the air.

He risked another look. The control console hadn't taken much damage, but it was covered in flame, and short circuits were shooting sparks every which way. That would probably be good enough. The controls for the shield were in that console, and as soon as it went down, the *Enterprise* could get a lock on the captives and beam them away.

One of the guards had grabbed a flame suppressor, but Kirk fired his disruptor and shot the whirring device right out of his hands. The other guard fired back at him, and Kirk jumped behind the door, but the disruptor beam came right through and seared a line across his chest. He'd been lucky; a direct hit would have gone right through *him*. He didn't feel lucky, though. His chest felt like it was on fire.

Turner had maneuvered around behind Kirk; now he threw a can through the open doorway, and it hit one of the guards square in the head with a solid *thunk*. He dropped like a switched-off robot. That left just one guard, but only for a second; Marybeth and her fourth man had evidently been asleep in the bunkroom, but now they charged out, disruptors blazing—and stopped when they saw their control panel ablaze.

"You idiots!" she yelled. "We'll all fry to death!"

"As soon as the shield goes down, the *Enterprise* will beam us out," Kirk shouted back.

"They don't know where to look!" Marybeth screamed. The crackle of flames nearly drowned her out, but he heard her add, "And we can't call for our own pickup, because you've burned out the radio."

Kirk smiled. Let her panic. If Haidar had kept her promise—and she couldn't afford not to, for everyone would know for certain that she was involved if she didn't—then Spock already had a pretty close fix on them and was just waiting for the shield to go down to get a final look.

Another shot zinged out of the control room. Kirk fired back to force Marybeth and the others to keep their heads down, expecting beam-up at any moment. The shield generator couldn't last much longer. But when a few more seconds went by and he was still in the station, he began to wonder.

And instead of dying out as he'd expected them to do when the alcohol had all been consumed, the flames rose higher. Evidently the insulation on the wiring had caught fire, and probably the padding on the chairs and anything else combustible, too. The stench of it was awful, and sooty black smoke billowed everywhere.

They had to get out of here, and they had to do it

fast, before they all died of smoke inhalation. "Cover me!" Kirk told Turner. He fired two more shots into the control room, tossed the pistol to Turner, and leaped through the doorway. He made a running dive into the airlock, disruptor bolts passing over his head the whole way, and slammed the door behind him. Two energy bolts punched holes through it and through both of the environment suits that hung on the wall behind it. Half a dozen more shots that didn't come through the door had to be Turner firing back.

Kirk tugged one of the environment suits off the rack and checked for damage. The energy bolt had gone through the power pack on its back, rendering it little more useful than an insulated coverall. He pulled down the other one and saw that the holes merely passed through its sides. The cooling wires on the left had been severed, but that was better than nothing at all. Fortunately it didn't have to hold air against vacuum; it only had to keep him from frying in the intense heat outside.

He pulled it open and tugged it on over his uniform. All he had to do was make it past the shield and as long as the *Enterprise* was still searching for him he would appear on their sensors.

He heard more weapons firing, and another energy beam shot through the door just over his head. Turner and Kostas couldn't keep their captors at bay forever; even if the smoke didn't get them, eventually Turner's pistol would run out of charge or the guards they had knocked out would revive and join the fight again.

The environment suit was designed differently from those of Starfleet issue. Kirk had to pull off his boots to get his feet in the legs, and instead of a separate helmet this one was permanently attached to the shoulders. He had to stick his head up through it after he slid his arms in the sleeves; then after that it was a simple matter of sealing up the flaps over the chest and switching on the power. He immediately felt the superconductant cooling web on his right side draw away the heat from his recent exertion, but the left side remained warm.

"Beggars can't be choosers," he muttered, his voice echoing in his helmet. He crawled to the other side of the airlock—keeping low to avoid more stray energy bolts—and tugged open the door.

He felt the heat like a physical wave washing over him. Light even brighter than inside made him squint, and he held his hand up to shade his eyes so he could see. The ground outside the door was rocky and parched, and streaked with yellow and orange minerals that sparkled in the sunlight. No pools of molten lead, but Kirk didn't doubt that they could exist here. His left side was already growing uncomfortably hot. Kirk couldn't see any other buildings in his field of view, but he supposed they could be scattered fairly loosely and still all be effectively at the hot pole.

He crab-walked out the door, then stood up once he was out of the line of fire from inside. He didn't pause to look around, but just ran straight out into the desert. The shield for a single building wouldn't extend very far; he could run beyond it in no time.

Or maybe not. For one thing, he was already gasping for air, but even so, after he'd run for half a minute and he was still on the planet he slowed down to pant and turned once around. Maybe the whole complex was under one great big shield.

Then again . . . The station he'd been held captive

in was already just a small rectangle in the distance. Beyond it lay no others, only more sun-scorched desolation leading off all the way to the horizon. Kirk's left side felt like a roast on a spit, but the sun hung like a yellow spotlight about forty-five degrees high, pouring still more of its relentless heat on him. He turned around to put the side that still had cooling capacity toward the light, but that didn't help a whole lot. The air itself was like fire.

Then he realized what he was seeing. The sun was at forty-five degrees elevation? But they were at the hot pole! Kirk looked overhead, but he saw only the deep violet sky and a few wispy high-altitude clouds.

He couldn't have been beamed back to a different station after his meeting with Haidar, could he? Impossible. Turner and Kostas had stayed here, and so had the guards and Kostas's improbable arch and the cans of Romulan root beer.

Squinting into the glare, Kirk saw the answer: Mirrors above the skylights, aimed to reflect the sun straight down into the storeroom where the prisoners had been held. Put there to fool them—and their captors—into thinking they were at the hot pole, and to keep them from revealing the true location to anyone after they were freed.

And also to make the *Enterprise* search the wrong area for them even if Haidar did tell Spock where they thought they were.

Kirk almost turned back to join the fight again. If he could find his communicator, maybe he could raise the ship that way.

Wait a minute. Shouldn't these environment suits have some kind of radio link? It would be bad design to let someone go out in such a harsh environment without a way to contact their base. It wouldn't broadcast on the same frequency as his communicator, but he bet Uhura was scanning for any signal with his voice pattern in it.

Kirk examined the chest-mounted controls. They weren't labeled, but there were only four buttons, and he knew the biggest one was the power switch. He poked at the others and found the temperature controls, up and down on separate buttons, which left the topmost button to be the radio. He pushed it.

"Kirk to *Enterprise*," he said. "Come in, *Enterprise*."

Nothing. He tried it again, this time holding the button down. Still nothing. As unlikely as it seemed, maybe he wasn't yet out from under the shield. He took a step—

—and walked off the transporter platform.

Ensign Vagle was grinning from ear to ear. "Welcome aboard, Captain!" he said. "Sorry for the delay; you weren't where we were looking at first."

Kirk ripped open the front of the suit and ducked his head down through it, letting the helmet hang over his back. "Get a full security team down to that station," he said. "Complete environment-suit protection if you can't beam them directly in. Ensign Turner and Professor Kostas are still down there."

"Right away, sir," Vagle said. He made a move to the intercom, but something on his control board drew his attention again. "Shield is down now," he said. "Positive ID on Turner, and two other people right beside him. I don't know which one is Kostas. Should I beam them all aboard?"

"Let me see your phaser first," Kirk said. Vagle

handed it over, and Kirk made sure it was set to stun, then took aim at the platform. "Energize," he said.

Vagle shoved the slides forward, and three figures materialized on the platform: Turner, wounded in the leg and side, with his pistol aimed at Marybeth, who in turn held hers against Kostas's head. Clearly things hadn't gone well after Kirk had left.

But now the situation was reversed. "Drop your weapon," Kirk said to Marybeth, and she reluctantly —and ungracefully—did so. It clattered to the floor, and Kirk winced, but it didn't go off. Marybeth released Kostas without waiting to be told to, and he bent down and picked up the pistol before he stepped away from her.

"Beam the others up, too," Kirk said to Vagle. "You, straight to sickbay," he said to Turner, and while Turner limped out of the room, Kirk stepped to the intercom and said, "Get me security to transporter room one. We have a prisoner who needs an escort to the brig." Her companions appeared on the transporter pad, but they were in no shape to fight. Smoke inhalation or the heat had brought them to their knees, gasping for air. Kirk kept them covered anyway, but he looked to Marybeth and said, "You've kidnapped a Starfleet officer and committed an act of treason against your government. Whose law would you prefer to be prosecuted under first?"

She held her head up proudly, and her starburst eyes glittered as she said, "My own people will judge me a hero, if I've delayed you long enough to keep you from destroying our planet. You and your—"

"Save the speech," Kirk told her. "You'll need it for the trial. On your own world, if that's what you want."

Four security officers arrived and led her and the others away for holding until they could arrange to turn them over to the Rimillians. When they had gone, Kirk turned to Kostas and said, "Now let's just hope she isn't right. Come on, I'll introduce you to Scotty."

Chapter Sixteen

WHEN SULU RETURNED to sickbay in the morning, after taking nearly three hours of sleep to recharge his brain, he was sure McCoy had solved the genome problem. The doctor was grinning like the Cheshire cat, and even whistling a little tune as he tapped merrily at the scanner/simulator's keyboard. But when Sulu looked over his shoulder to see what he'd come up with, he saw a round orange blob with prominent ribs down the side and needle-sharp spikes sticking out from the ribs.

"A pumpkin cactus?" he asked dubiously as he sat down beside McCoy.

"Good morning to you too," McCoy said. "And no, if you'd check the scale you'd see it's microscopic. I think I must have switched out a growth hormone somewhere, or else this variant only exists as pollen."

"Then why are you so happy?" Sulu asked.

"Because the captain is back, without a scratch. Well, okay, he got a first-degree burn on his chest," he amended, "but he's a lot better off than he could be."

A voice from the recovery room said, "That's better than some of us can say."

"Pipe down in there!" McCoy called out. "That's Turner. He took a couple of direct hits. He keeps asking for Romulan ale to kill the pain."

"That's just my first choice," said Turner. "A good bitter would do."

McCoy shook his head. "I knew it was a mistake to put the convalescent ward this close to the lab."

Sulu laughed. The doctor's mood was contagious. With the captain back on board, all seemed right with the ship again, even if the cyclone trees were still being stubborn. He shuffled back through the images the computer had saved of the runs McCoy had made while he was gone. The genome certainly held some interesting variations: he saw fruits on some, massive root systems on others, even flowers the size of Jeffries-tube hatch covers on others. Some didn't even look like the same genus, like the ones that grew in thick mats of entwined bushes or the pollen grain that had just been on the screen.

Sulu stopped at one that looked promising. Tall, triangular, with lots of greenery for oxygen production. It looked like a Christmas tree, one of those too-good-to-be-true ones that came off the tree farms on Leslie's World or Bayless IV. Then he looked at the scale bar along the side and whistled softly. "Two hundred meters! That's incredible!"

"It's also incredibly finicky," McCoy said, pointing at the growth-zone indicator next to the scale bar. "It'd grow fine in the middle of the Edge, except the tops would stick up too far into the light. It doesn't like too much sun. Besides which a forest of 'em would shade the whole damned rest of the Edge. The side that's too shady already. People'd love that."

"Oh," said Sulu. "I guess that might present a problem." He flipped to the next screen, a flagpole with a line of wind socks all along its length, apparently for filtering food out of the wind.

"That one—" McCoy began, but the intercom interrupted them.

"Bridge to sickbay." It was Uhura.

"Sickbay. McCoy here."

"There's been some kind of disturbance on the planet," Uhura said. "Two people killed, one badly injured. They can't stabilize her, and they're asking us to beam the survivor up here for treatment."

"Of course!" McCoy said, already rising out of his chair. "What kind of injuries?"

"Phaser wounds," Uhura said.

McCoy did a double take. "Phaser wounds? Not disruptors?"

"That's what they said. That's why they want us to try saving her. They hoped we would have more experience with that type of injury."

"Well," said McCoy, "they're probably right about that. Beam her straight to sickbay."

"Can I help?" Sulu asked the doctor's departing back.

"Hard to say," McCoy replied. "Come on in if you want, but keep out of the way unless I ask for something. Nurse Chapel!" he called down the corridor. "Trauma, phaser burns, table one."

Sulu followed him around the curved hallway to the emergency room. Chapel was already there, and the patient arrived just as McCoy did. She was slender and had silver hair, but she was lying on her side with her back toward Sulu, so he couldn't see her face. Her back was where the action was anyway; she was burned in a diagonal stripe from shoulders to hips, as though she had twisted and fallen when she'd first been hit. That motion might have saved her life; it had spread the effect of the beam over a wider area.

McCoy rushed to the table and immediately checked the life signs on the overhead monitor, then gave her something from a hypospray. He and Chapel exchanged terse instructions as they worked furiously to stabilize their patient, who even Sulu could see was in critical condition. Her body was limp as a rag, her heartbeat on the monitor was fast and irregular, and her blood pressure was almost nonexistent. Two of the other indicators on the monitor were also bottomed out, but Sulu didn't know if that was good or bad.

McCoy moved around to the other side of the table and lifted the patient's head to look into her eyes. "My god," he said, looking up to Nurse Chapel, "it's Coordinator Joray."

Chapel was passing some kind of whirring instrument back and forth over the burned area. She didn't look up as she said, "They didn't mention that little detail when they asked for our help?"

"No," said McCoy, obviously annoyed. "Not that it would affect our treatment, but it's kind of nice to know when you're working on the head of the planetary government."

Sulu cleared his throat and said, "They probably didn't want to mention who it was over a clear channel, for fear someone would take advantage of the situation while she was gone."

"Good point," said McCoy. He looked up at Sulu. "That means Jim probably doesn't know yet, either. That's something you could do for me."

Oh, great, thought Sulu. He would almost rather have McCoy's job than be the one to tell the captain that the world coordinator was dying in sickbay. He went to the intercom and made the call anyway.

It seemed only moments later when Kirk rushed into the emergency room. "How is she, Bones?" he asked, bending over Joray.

"Not good," McCoy said. "She's been hit bad, and the beam went deep. She's got internal injuries from the heat and radiation, including neural damage in her spine. Somebody was definitely shooting to kill, and they damn near succeeded."

"And they did it with *my* phaser," Kirk said, visibly restraining his anger. "Either mine or Turner's. That's the only way they could have gotten one."

"You think it was Haidar?" McCoy asked.

Kirk shook his head. "I would have said so without hesitation yesterday, but now I'm not so sure. She's just one of who knows how many suspects at this point." He balled his hands into fists. "But of course the Denialists will claim somebody from the *Enterprise* did it. We'll have to be ready for that."

Sulu suddenly realized another implication they probably hadn't thought of yet. "There were two other people killed," he said. "I wouldn't be surprised if they were council members too. Probably on Joray's side."

Kirk turned away from the exam table, either unable to look anymore or needing to concentrate on the new information. "If that's so," he said, "then the balance of power would shift to the Denialists." He

173

looked up at Sulu. "How are you coming on the mutation project?"

"Uh . . . well, I just got here this morning," Sulu began, "and I haven't yet seen what Dr. McCoy did after I went to bed, but—"

"We haven't solved it yet, Jim," McCoy said, still not looking up from his patient. "We've got the genetic map done, and we're simulating new organisms, but we haven't found the right combination yet. We will, though."

"You're sure?" Kirk asked him.

"No, I'm not sure," McCoy said, exasperated. "If I had the equipment I was supposed to have by now, I could tell you in twenty minutes whether it was possible, and have the code for it in an hour, but with what we've got to work with it's going to have to be trial and error until we hit the right combination. Or find proof that it can't exist. Success could happen on our next run, but it could be six months or longer before we know if we *can't* do it."

Kirk said, "Well, you'd better hope you can, because I'll bet you anything the new council votes to postpone the rotation. And if they do that, then your project is the only thing that will save this planet." He looked back at Joray. McCoy and Chapel continued working on their patient, frantically trying to stabilize her condition. The fate of an entire world rested in their hands, and apparently in Sulu's as well.

"No pressure," said Sulu as he headed back into the lab.

In the last few hours, Scotty had watched Professor Kostas's expression shift from horror to grim determination to grudging acceptance as he came up to speed on what Scotty and Neron had done so far to repair the sabotage. He had finally accepted the necessity of their computer surgery, and had even suggested a few more modifications they could make to compensate for the decreased processing ability, but this latest news had shifted him around full-circle to despair again.

He sat in a swivel chair before one of the input/output terminals, elbows on the desktop, resting his head in his hands. Neron and Scotty and Spock, the bearer of bad tidings, stood in a huddle around him.

"Dead?" he asked again.

"Only Councilor Telinga," Spock replied stoically. "And Coordinator Joray's personal assistant, Lexi. Thanks to Lexi's heroic intervention, Joray herself is still alive, though in critical condition, aboard the *Enterprise*."

"Leaving the council deadlocked," Kostas said. He looked up, his star-shaped pupils wide with anger. "I'll bet Haidar is pleased."

Spock shook his head. "When I informed her, she professed surprise and dismay, and has sworn to find and punish those responsible. Whether she is sincere, I could not tell without physical contact."

Scotty, still holding on to the logic probe that he had been using to trace the computer's new pathways, said, "But what does she intend to do with the council, man? Does she plan to let us finish our job here, or is all this work going to come to nothing?"

"It is too soon to tell, Mr. Scott. She is not the leader of the council, nor will she be unless Joray dies. She is still only the minority advocate. But as I understand the political system here, now that there is a balance of power in the council, Haidar could still force a vote if she can demonstrate sufficient public support. Unfortunately, that is a distinct possibility."

"They didn't have the support before," Kostas said. "What makes you think she might now?"

Spock said simply, "Fear. As the deadline for rotation approaches, many of your people are having second thoughts."

"That's no surprise," Neron said disgustedly. "The political climate has changed more often than our software in the decade since we started this project." He looked away, and Scotty followed his gaze from Spock to the computer consoles they had been working on for the last three days. Thick bundles of optical cable snaked across the gap where the hovercar had crashed, reestablishing the links between the remaining processors. Scotty had lost count of how many thousands of circuits he had connected and tested, or how many thousands more remained to be done, but for the first time since he had begun this job, he had actually thought they might have a chance to succeed. Now he wondered if they would get the chance to try.

Surprisingly, it was Kostas who said, "Actually, I don't blame them for being afraid. I have had nightmares ever since we started, and that was when I thought we would have an intact computer to control the subspace interactions. Now—" He shuddered. "I just don't know. Perhaps it is folly to proceed."

Spock said, "I assure you, Professor, that to do nothing would be the greater folly. Your atmosphere *is* becoming unbreathable, and your present living space can no longer support your population. Those problems will not solve themselves."

"Ripping apart the planet won't solve it either," Kostas said. He pressed his hand to his forehead, as if he could force his doubts away. "I wish we could know, really *know* that this would work the way it's supposed to. We put our faith in physics and engineering, we make our calculations and build our machines, but it's faith nonetheless. We don't know until we try it if a new device will really work. Sometimes they blow up."

Scotty had heard that argument before. He waved his logic probe at the scientist. "Now, laddie," he said softly, "you don't think we Earthlings got all the way out here by being timid, do you? Sure things blow up sometimes, but that doesn't mean you shouldn't try 'em. It just means you should take precautions, and learn from your mistakes."

Neron said, "The professor has a point. A mistake here will kill us all."

"So we make sure we don't make any," said Scotty. "That's what all this control computer is about, isn't it? What waitin' for all the planets to line up on the opposite side of the sun is about? We're takin' precautions."

"But have we taken enough?" asked Kostas.

Spock said, "You have addressed all the failure modes you can identify, have you not?"

"Yes, but what about the ones we can't identify?"

"As Mr. Scott has said, Earthlings did not make it this far by being timid. Nor did Vulcans, nor your own ancestors for that matter. When you have done all you can in preparation, it is time to throw the switch."

Kostas waved his hand in dismissal. "Oh, yes, I know that. And I understand it, intellectually. I even feel it on occasion, when things are going well."

Spock raised an eyebrow, but when he didn't speak the professor went on.

"We Dumada have already destroyed one planet, and we stand on the brink of destroying our second. I understand those people who would rather not throw that switch this time."

Neron looked at him with wide, astonished eyes, but he said nothing.

"Even if it dooms them to slow death through resource depletion," said Spock.

"Even so." Kostas took a deep breath and sat up straight in his chair. "Look, I understand them," he said. "I even sympathize with them. But I don't necessarily agree with them. Until now I was sure I didn't, but now I simply don't know."

Scotty hefted his logic probe. "Well," he said, "I certainly hope it doesn't affect your work, because even though we've hooked this beast back together while you've been gone, you're still the only person who knows how to retrain it to do the job, and we've only got a day left to do it in."

"Point seven two," Spock said. "And counting."

Chapter Seventeen

McCoy checked Joray's vital signs for perhaps the hundredth time that day. They changed constantly; now her electrolytes were out of balance. Last time it had been kidney failure, and before that her blood pressure had dropped again. Her body was just not stabilizing, and McCoy was having to do it all himself.

It was like juggling eggs, and it had been like this for hours now as system after system became overtaxed and shut down. Turner had been healed and sent back to his quarters to sleep it off already, but Joray's wounds had been too extensive to repair all at once; she didn't have the strength for it, so McCoy had been forced to heal only the most vital organs first. He had hoped to continue her treatment as she recovered, but she wasn't improving enough to justify putting any more stress on her system. In fact, by the way more

179

and more problems kept cropping up, it was obvious she was just circling the drain.

Jim, on the other hand, seemed to be circling sickbay. He showed up every few hours to see how she was doing, and to bug McCoy and Sulu about their genetics project. McCoy kept telling him he would be the first to know if there was any change in either one, but Jim needed to look in on things himself. The constant waiting was driving him crazy. He was worried about Joray, and he was worried about Rimillia. The clock was ticking down to zero without a clear indication of what he should do when the alarm went off.

So when the doors swished open about an hour and a half after his last visit, McCoy didn't even bother to look up from the hypospray he was setting for sodium and potassium. He merely said, "No, Jim, she's no better."

"I'm sorry to hear that, Doctor," said a woman's voice, and McCoy looked up, startled, to see Jim all right, but with Councilor Haidar at his side.

"What are you doing here?" he asked, almost instinctively protecting his patient from the person he was certain had tried to kill her.

If she noticed, she didn't let on. "I am here to see our coordinator," she said. "The council needs to know her condition. And I am concerned as a friend."

McCoy bit his tongue and turned to Joray with the hypospray. He'd been sympathetic toward Haidar until now, but if she was behind this attack on Joray—and it sure looked like she was—then he didn't want her in his sickbay.

Joray didn't react when he injected the electrolytes, but the monitor overhead showed their slow dissemi-

nation throughout her bloodstream. Turning back to
Haidar, McCoy said, "You can see for yourself she's in
pretty rough shape. Phasers set on 'kill' do that to
people. But with luck, and a little time, I think she'll
recover."

Haidar stepped closer. Kirk held back, and he gave
McCoy a warning look, but McCoy reflected it right
back at him, Haidar be damned. She seemed oblivious
to that exchange as well. "Just as you think you will
create a new cyclone tree for us any time now?" she
asked sweetly.

"We're working on it," McCoy told her.

"I'm sure you are. It's a curious position for you to
be in, don't you think, Doctor? On one hand, you are
attempting to save the coordinator's life, while on the
other you attempt to destroy her life's work."

McCoy felt the sting in her words, but he said, "I'm
trying to save lives all the way around. There's no
ethical dilemma in that."

"And so am I, Doctor," Haidar said. "We are all
working for the same thing. Only our methods differ."

McCoy slapped his hypospray into his palm.
"Somebody's method included a phaser in the back,
and now I've got a patient in critical condition and
you've got a deadlocked council. I don't call the
person who did that an ally."

Kirk spoke up. "I'm sure the councilor doesn't
either, Bones. She was the one who sent Joray here for
help."

McCoy looked at her again, surprised. "You did?"

"I was there when she was attacked," said Haidar.
"The council had just recessed; we were all there."

"Then who do you think was behind it? Did you see
who fired the shots?"

Haidar shook her head. "I don't know. All I saw was someone wearing an oversuit, and they beamed away as soon as they fired at us. It could have been anyone. There are so many factions. Denialists, Sealers, Nihilists. All growing more militant in their opposition as the final hour approaches. We thought your presence here would keep them in hand, but now that the council is deadlocked, we're afraid they may go to war after all."

"And so you came up here to see how likely it was that Joray would die and give you a majority," said McCoy.

Haidar nodded. "That is true, as far as it goes. Her death—or even her resignation—would break the tie and allow the new majority to stop this insanity before it destroys us."

McCoy put down his hypospray. "Well," he said, "I'm sorry to disappoint you, but she's in no shape to tell us whether she wants to resign or not. And despite *someone's* best effort to do her in, I'm not going to let her die, either. So you're just going to have to solve your problem some other way." He took a deep breath and said, "I've been trying to develop one possibility for you, and I'll keep at it, but frankly we're not having the sort of success I'd hoped for. You may have to come up with something else."

She said, "Thank you, Doctor, for your assessment of the situation. I will report to the council what you have told me."

She turned to go, but Kirk took her by the elbow and drew her toward the lab. "Before you leave," he said, "perhaps we can get Mr. Sulu to show you what progress they *have* made on the cyclone trees."

"I'd like to see that, Captain," she said, allowing him to lead her that way.

McCoy watched them go. He wondered what Kirk was up to, bringing her on board the ship like this. Kirk had been sure she was behind the kidnappings, and it made sense that she had arranged the assassinations as well. Even if she had been there, that didn't prove anything. In fact, it was just the sort of alibi you'd expect from someone who'd arranged it in the first place.

But then why had she called the *Enterprise* for emergency care, rather than letting Joray die? Maybe she'd had no other choice. Joray's own allies had been there as well; if one of them had suggested it then it would have been done anyway, so maybe Haidar had decided to take the credit for the inevitable.

Or maybe she wasn't the one behind it all. Haidar wasn't the only Denialist on the council.

The idea of working for their benefit rankled McCoy. But letting Joray's people actually make living conditions *worse* with their risky solution to the problem felt equally wrong. He looked back to Joray, who slept on, oblivious to the chaos that mounted around her.

Her skin seemed to have taken on a yellow tinge. McCoy looked up to the monitor, switching the display to a second-level chemistry profile. Sure enough, her bilirubin, ALT, and GGT were elevated. That meant her liver was joining the long list of internal organs that were trying to shut down.

McCoy set up the biofilter to remove the toxins from her bloodstream, then brought a deep-penetration protoplaser to bear on the liver itself. It would heal the damaged tissue, but the metabolic changes necessary to accomplish that would further stress the rest of her system. Something else would almost undoubtedly go wrong as a result. If she didn't stabilize soon, McCoy seriously doubted if he would be able to save her. He could keep her alive for another day or two, probably, just long enough to complicate the hell out of the political situation down below, but her chances of ever resuming her duties as world coordinator didn't look good at all.

It would be so easy to simply let her go. A half hour of neglect would do it. Then Haidar and her allies could force a new vote in the council, and it would be seven to six against the rotation project. They would avert that catastrophe, and by the sounds of it they might avert a war as well. McCoy and Sulu would have time to find the right mutation for the cyclone trees, and they would be able to fix the atmosphere, too.

His hands shook as he continued the treatment. He had made a similar decision once, with his own father. Stricken with a supposedly incurable disease, the elder McCoy had begged for release from his terrible, lingering death, so the young doctor had pulled the plug and let him die with dignity. Then, of course, a cure had been discovered, and McCoy learned that his father could have lived after all. He had vowed then that he would never again make a mistake like that.

But the fate of a planet had never hung in the balance before, either.

McCoy finished the protoplaser treatment and watched the liver functions stabilize. She wouldn't die this time. Nor next time, either, nor the time after that. As Haidar had said, McCoy would work like

184

crazy to build a better cyclone tree that would negate everything Joray had worked to achieve, but at the same time he would work with equal diligence to make sure she lived to see it happen.

And no, dammit, he thought as he put his tools away and turned toward the lab, there was no ethical dilemma. None at all.

The council chamber was the most ornate room that Kirk had seen on Rimillia, or on many other planets either, for that matter. Statuary lined the room all the way around, paintings of past councilors and shelves of historical memorabilia covered the walls, two enormous crystal chandeliers hung from the ceiling, and any space that wasn't already filled with that sort of thing was covered with gold inlay.

Kirk wondered why all this finery hadn't been removed to safety already, but the answer was obvious. Nobody really expected the rotation project to proceed, so there seemed no point in wasting the effort. Kirk hoped he could prove them wrong.

He noted that only three out of the fifty or so portraits on the wall were of men. Evidently the current situation was nothing new here. He wondered how the councilors would react to having a man seated at the head of the table today, but Haidar had asked him to participate, and she wanted him to take the coordinator's chair as a reminder that Joray was still alive on board his ship. And the empty chair beside it would remind them that Councilor Telinga was not, and that an assassin walked among them.

The meeting table was less ornate than the room around it, but it was still elegant in its own right. Oval in shape, made of deep brown wood with swirling grain, and polished until you could look half a light-year into it. Flatscreen data monitors were set unobtrusively into the surface, and tall-backed armchairs stood before each one, waiting for the heads of government to take their places.

As they arrived, each one greeted Kirk with warm words and thanks for his assistance. He nodded and smiled and said "My pleasure" to them all, though he was wondering all the while which one of them was responsible for the assassination. His arrival with Haidar had no doubt lent the impression that he supported her, but he hoped that sitting in Joray's chair would dispel that.

When everyone was seated, the majority party on Kirk's left and Haidar and the minority party on his right, Haidar pressed a spot on her console and a silver bell hanging overhead rang softly. Footmen closed the double doors from the outside, and Haidar said, "The meeting begins. I have invited Captain Kirk to witness the proceedings, and to act as advocate for our absent coordinator. Does anyone object to this?"

There was only the soft rustle of people shifting on their chairs.

"Very well, then. To business. The time we have all been awaiting—some of us with eagerness, some with dread—draws nigh. The Spark and the embers have nearly aligned themselves in their once-in-a-lifetime conjunction. The impulse engines that we have built to give Rimillia a day and a night like other worlds are complete, and the damage to the few that were sabotaged has been repaired. The damage to the control computer has been repaired as well, though with diminished capacity."

Haidar shook her head, then pulled her hair back behind her ears, as if presenting a different appearance would help her present a different idea. "However, the *Enterprise*'s chief medical officer and the ship's resident botanist have taken up the project that the current government abandoned, and their research shows promise that our native vegetation might after all be mutated to grow farther into the hot and cold regions of the world. That would offer a slower, yet less drastic, solution to our atmospheric problems."

She paused again to let that sink in, then said, "The question before us today is to decide whether we should continue on our present course, perhaps destroying our very planet in the attempt to revitalize it, or if we should reconsider, and give the biologists time to find the gentler solution."

The moment she was finished speaking, the councilor across from her said, "They have not yet succeeded, nor proven that they will succeed. Moreover, as I understand it, they would not be able to give us the solution directly unless their Federation approved it. If we were to gamble that either would happen, and lose, then we would be just as dead as if the planet blew to pieces under the impulse engines."

"A generation later, perhaps," said the woman next to Haidar. "Personally, I would prefer that."

Yet another councilor said, "The majority of the people on the planet would not. That is why we're spinning the planet, because most people's lives are little better now than lingering deaths. They need room to expand. We're solving more than just an atmospheric problem with the rotation project."

"If it works," said another on Haidar's side. "Its success was never assured, yet now we are told that the control computer will have diminished capacity. Can we trust it?"

"Can we trust the simulations of the biologists any more?" asked the woman at Kirk's immediate right.

He cleared his throat. He had been reluctant to get involved in their politics, but when one of his officers' abilities was questioned, that was another matter. "You can trust Dr. McCoy's research without question," he told the woman beside him.

"His research, perhaps, but are his opinions as solidly based on fact? Does he *know* that he will be able to produce a more hardy cyclone tree?"

"Of course he doesn't," Kirk said. "But I have never known McCoy's opinion to be based on ungrounded assumptions."

Haidar said, "Nor does Chief Engineer Scott know for certain that his repairs to the engines and computer will work, does he?"

Kirk sighed. "No, that's not assured either. But I will tell you this: Scotty has kept the *Enterprise* together through more tight scrapes than any engineer in Starfleet. He can tune a matter-antimatter reactor by hand, and he has kept my ship running through conditions that should have blown it to bits a dozen times over. I have no doubt that he can hold the planet together as well."

Haidar smiled at him. "You are obviously proud of your officers, and no doubt with good reason. All the same, our situation comes down to a choice: Whose expertise do we trust more, that of the *Enterprise*'s engineer, or its doctor?"

"What of our own engineer?" said the woman next to Kirk. "Professor Kostas designed the system without help from the *Enterprise.* He is back on the job now, and has had a day to assess the situation. No doubt Mr. Scott has provided valuable assistance, but we should not belittle the work that went beforehand. The engineering for the rotation project is our own."

"Just like the engineering that led to the destruction of our homeworld," pointed out the councilor beside Haidar.

And so it went. The debate continued in the same vein for nearly an hour, and Kirk fielded more questions about the capabilities of his officers, but the council never seemed any closer to agreement than when they had started. It looked as if they would continue to argue until someone caved in, but at last the majority party called for a vote.

Haidar touched the console on the table before her again, and the chime once again rang overhead. "The vote has been demanded," she said. "The issue before us, whether to continue with the rotation as scheduled, or to halt the project while we still have the chance and pursue a gentler, biological solution to the atmosphere problem. All those in favor of continuing, raise your left hand."

All the councilors on Kirk's left raised their hands. Six of them. Then the councilor nearest him on that side said, "I believe Coordinator Joray's vote on this issue is already a matter of record," and she nodded pointedly at his hand.

So he raised his hand as well.

Haidar nodded her acceptance of his vote. "All those opposed," she said.

Seven hands went up on her side of the table.

"The council is deadlocked," Haidar said.

"What about Telinga's vote?" asked Kirk. "Isn't that a matter of record as well?"

189

"She is dead, and no longer legally a member of the council," said Haidar. "Her district will elect another representative, but not before this matter is resolved." She rang the bell again, and said, "We lack sufficient votes to change our course of action. Rotation wins by default. May our faith in engineers not be misplaced."

The councilors scooted back their chairs to get up, but the woman at the end of the table on Kirk's left said, "I propose a compromise."

Her companions looked at her as if she'd just grown fangs, but she ignored them as she said, "I voted for rotation before because I saw no other way, and I stuck with that vote now because I still see no better course of action. However, I would put a condition on my vote; namely that if the *Enterprise*'s doctor and botanist do find a viable alternative before the rotation commences, then I will give that my support instead. Without the necessity of calling another meeting."

The other members of her party burst into vocal disapproval, but she ignored them and said loudly, "Vote."

The room fell silent. Haidar rang the silver bell again. "Another vote has been demanded. The issue before us, should the rotation project be halted if a biological solution is found before it begins. All those in favor?"

Eight hands went up: all of Haidar's people, and the one councilor on the end of Joray's side.

"Opposed?"

The other five raised their hands.

"Joray's advocate?" Haidar asked.

It was a politeness only; she had already won the vote. Diplomacy would dictate that Kirk now abstain, but if he was truly voting for Joray, then he would vote for Joray. There was no doubt which way she would choose. Kirk raised his hand.

"Eight to six. The motion passes," said Haidar. "Captain, you are aware of our wishes. Before this council I ask you: Will you carry them out as we request?"

Kirk looked at the empty chair on his left. Telinga's vote wouldn't have mattered any more than Joray's. The legitimate government of the planet had decided their own people's fate; it was not his place to override their ruling. He nodded to Haidar. "The *Enterprise* came here to help you, and that's still our primary objective. We'll do what you ask."

The meeting broke up then, and Kirk found himself invited to thirteen different victory dinners, but he excused himself from them all with the excuse that he had to return to his ship. As he left the meeting hall, he flipped open his communicator and called for beam-up, but he was already thinking ahead to the task at hand. How was he going to break the news to Scotty? For that matter, how was he going to break the news to Bones and Sulu?

Chapter Eighteen

"ONTOGENY recapitulates phylogeny," Sulu said. He was staring into the monitor for the twentieth straight hour after the captain's return from the council meeting, the thirtieth since he'd last slept.

"Huh?" asked McCoy, who had been jumping back and forth between the simulator and Joray's intensive-care bed, wherever his expertise was most needed, for even longer.

Sulu smiled. He wouldn't have pulled a biological term over on the doctor if McCoy wasn't half asleep, but it felt good to surprise him all the same. "Ontogeny, that's the phases an organism goes through in its development," he said. "If you look at the way it grows, you can sometimes see what its genetic ancestors looked like."

McCoy waved his hand dismissively, "Oh, yes, that.

Gill slits in human embryos and so on. Sure. So what?"

Sulu pointed at the screen, upon which another improbable mutation was growing as the computer churned through the billions of calculations necessary to simulate interacting genes. "So I've been watching what comes up here, and I keep seeing the same things time after time. We've gotten them as end results on a couple of runs. The big Christmas tree is one, and the tangle of vines is another. I'd be willing to bet they're actual ancestors of the cyclone tree."

"Maybe the Christmas tree," McCoy said, "but not the vines. They were deciduous, remember? There's no seasonal cycle here to trigger leaf fall or bud growth."

"Then where did the genes for it come from?" Sulu asked.

McCoy stared at him as if he'd just spoken in Klingon.

"Every end product we've come up with that has been even remotely possible has been perfectly viable in a normal class-M environment," Sulu went on. "It's trying to find something that will live in a marginal class-L that's giving us fits. I think that's because this thing never evolved on a class-L world in the first place. Most of its genes code for day/night cycles and seasonal variation and so forth, and that's probably because it evolved in those conditions."

McCoy laughed. "You think we're barking up the wrong tree, is that it?"

"That's right."

"So what do you propose we do? Design something from scratch?"

Sulu leaned back in his chair. "I don't know if that would ever be possible, but it's certainly not going to happen in the, what—" he checked the clock "—the five hours left to us. But neither is what we've been doing, either. We've just about exhausted the possibilities here, and I don't see that we're on the verge of any big breakthrough." He rubbed the stubble on his chin and said, "We've tried the other samples I got from the planet and they weren't any better, but I think that's because I concentrated on trees and bushes. I think we'd be better off trying another sampling mission, and this time look for things that started out different. Look for this world's lichens, or bacteria, or phytoplankton. Those are the big oxygen producers on class-M worlds; maybe they can be altered to do the same job here."

McCoy looked at the screen, which showed a network of straight, slender stalks arranged like an arched bridge, beneath which hung a single fruit like a ball on a rope. He looked at the scale: five centimeters high. Wonderful. Foucault's pendulums for mice.

"What the hell," he said to Sulu. "It sure can't give us any worse results than what we've been getting."

Scotty watched as Professor Kostas and his assistant, Neron, set up the equipment for reprogramming the computer. You couldn't really call it reprogramming with a neural net; it was more like teaching. The information pathways between processors strengthened with use, so the best way to prepare the computer for its job was to give it a similar job to do. After a few dry runs it would perform faster, and its output would be smoother, than the first time around.

Of course, nothing could prepare it for the actual

input it would receive when the thousands of impulse engines all fired at once, and the thousands of seismic monitors and angular accelerometers began sending in data, but the more simulations they ran the better it would function when the time came.

Neron was in charge of the input and output. He was using an analog device that he and Kostas had designed just for the purpose: a matrix of tiny heat sources underlying a fluid convection medium, with a temperature-sensing grid on top. The computer controlled the heaters, and its job was to keep the temperature constant all across the top layer even when the operators introduced random currents in the convection layer. That was supposed to simulate the type of fluctuations they would encounter when the engines put stress on the planet's crust and when their subspace fields interacted to reinforce or cancel each other's effects. It taught the computer pattern analysis rather than rote memory, and flexed its output control circuits as well.

The biggest weakness of the system, in Scotty's opinion, was that it didn't test the entire control chain. The encoded radio links that connected the computer to the engines themselves were too hard to include in the dynamic tests, since that would mean bringing all the engines' local computers on line as well, so Kostas and Neron had settled for hooking up the simulator directly to the computer's input/output ports. The radio links weren't part of the neural-net linkup anyway; as long as they could transmit and receive—and that had already been tested—then they would do their jobs correctly every time.

The trouble was, every type of input had its own particular quirks, and even though the simulator tried to duplicate things like speed-of-light lag in the radio signals and momentary dropouts in the data stream, the computer would be learning the response patterns of the simulator, not the real command links.

And there was one other problem that neither Scotty nor Kostas—nor apparently even Neron, who had designed the simulator—was aware of until it was too late. It was the simple mistakes that always hit the hardest, and this was the simplest of them all: The input connectors and the output connectors were the same shape. They could be cross-plugged. And since the heaters used much more current than the temperature sensors did, the moment the first run started, sparks erupted from the input monitor circuits.

Scotty lunged for the master switch and killed the power, but he was already too late. Smoke rose from dozens of consoles, and the smell of burned electronics filled the air.

Neron stood in the midst of the devastation, a look of horror on his face. "What happened?" he cried, turning around and around as if looking for some part of the computer that hadn't been affected.

It didn't take Scotty long to find the problem. Figuring out the extent of the damage took a bit longer, but within a half hour the grim truth was plain for all to see. Nearly half of the control circuits had been destroyed. It was just luck that it was only half, but since there were so many data lines they had been arranged in two banks, which the computer switched back and forth to, and only one had been engaged when the power surge hit them.

The computer itself was still okay, but it couldn't receive information from half its sensors, nor could it relay its instructions to half the engines scattered all over the planet.

And with only four hours left before the rotation was scheduled to start, there was no time to replace that many circuits.

"I've ruined it!" Neron shrieked, pulling at his hair. "I've killed us all!"

"Calm down, laddie," Scotty told him sternly. "Have ye nae blown a fuse before this? We'll think of something."

Kostas wasn't pulling his hair. He was way beyond that. He simply stood in shock, staring at the melted input stages and muttering, "All gone, all gone." But at Scotty's statement he looked up and said, "You're joking. There's no fixing this. Not in the time left to us."

"There'd better be," Scotty said. "Everyone's counting on us, and I'm not in the habit of letting people down." He squinted into the recesses of a control panel, aiming his logic probe at the charred remains of a circuit board to see if anything could be salvaged, but little could. Only the circuits that hadn't been engaged at the time had been spared.

"Well now," said Scotty, thinking aloud, "there's two ways of looking at this mess. One whole bank is dead, but one whole bank isn't, either. What happens if we fool the computer into thinking it's still got both banks?"

"What good would that do?" Neron asked. "We'd still only be able to control half the engines."

"Half at a *time*," Scotty said patiently. "The computer switches back and forth between banks anyway, so if we can switch the input stages back and forth between engines at the same time, it'll never know there's a difference."

"But the priority interrupts won't function," Kostas said. "The engines will be completely on their own half the time, and we won't know if oscillations are building up until we check them."

"We'll be checkin' every half second," Scotty said. "How much oscillation can build up in that short a time?"

"Plenty," said Neron. "We can't do this. It would be suicide!"

Scotty felt himself getting irritated with this little imp. "If you can't stand the heat, get out of the engine room," he snapped. "It'll work, but it won't if we just stand here jawin' about it all day. We've got four hours to reroute about fifteen thousand data lines and build a switching station for 'em. Now, unless you've got a better idea, let's get to work."

Kostas nodded slowly. "I see no other solution."

Neron's starburst eyes glinted with anger, or perhaps fear, but he said nothing. He just turned toward the nearest control panel and began re-routing circuits.

The atmosphere on the bridge was tense. Kirk knew he was the cause of it, but he didn't care. Time was rapidly running out, and he had no options to choose from. He couldn't bear to just sit in his command chair and wait; he paced back and forth across the bridge, checking the tactical displays, looking over Spock's shoulders at the science monitors, anything to keep himself occupied.

The main viewer showed a compressed-field image of the Rimillian star system, with the curve of

Rimillia itself just visible on the bottom, its Edge making a shadowy arch between day and night. Beyond that the Torch burned bright—though the display peaked out at a level well below its actual brilliance in order to spare the bridge crew's eyes. Beyond the Torch the embers were lining up, the outer ones already nearly in place, and the Spark orbiting beyond them all. Only the last point of light, the one closest to the Torch, still had any angular separation, and that was closing fast.

"Time, Mr. Spock?" Kirk asked.

"Ten minutes to firing window," Spock replied calmly.

Kirk knew that the window of opportunity would last for almost three hours, and only gradually close as the planets drifted out of alignment again, but it would take those three hours and then some to build up enough angular momentum to complete the crucial first quarter of a rotation. Spinning a planet wasn't something you could do in a few minutes.

Uhura turned from her communications board. "Councilor Haidar, sir," she said.

"On screen."

The councilor's face replaced the planets on the main viewer. She was in her own residence, it appeared, and by the boxes scattered on the floor it looked like she had been doing some belated packing of valuables. "Captain," she said. "The moment is at hand. What news do you have for me?"

"None that's good," Kirk replied. "Scotty is still making last-minute repairs on the control computer, and McCoy and Sulu are still running simulations on your native plants. Neither one has succeeded yet."

"Then we are back where we started." Haidar

laughed, but there seemed little mirth in it. "All this time, and all this effort, ultimately comes to naught."

"We're still working on it," Kirk said. "Don't give up hope yet."

Haidar shook her head. "You misunderstand, Captain. This is what I'd hoped for all along. I only regret the waste and the bloodshed that made things unfold this way."

Did she really? Kirk wondered. He still didn't know whether or not she was behind the sabotage and the assassinations. "Don't start the celebration yet," he told her. "We haven't given up even if you have. There's still time."

"The activation window is now open," Spock said.

"It doesn't sound like it to me," said Haidar. She looked away for a moment, then back at Kirk. Someone was no doubt speaking to her from out of the picture. "How is Coordinator Joray?" she asked.

"Out of danger now," Kirk told her, "but still unconscious."

"Can she be revived for an emergency council session?"

"I don't know," Kirk said. "Hold on." He punched the intercom button on his command chair. "Kirk to sickbay. Bones, what's the situation down there?"

McCoy sounded just as harried as Kirk. "We're working as fast as we can, Jim, but we haven't hit the right combination yet. If you'd just give us a little more time, though, I'm sure we—"

"You've got until Scotty fixes the computer," Kirk told him. "How about Joray. Can she be awakened safely?"

"No way," said McCoy. "I've finally got her stabilized, but she's balancing on a knife edge. We can't force her body to do anything more."

Kirk tried not to let himself react to the news, but he felt a great weight lift from him. She would live. He knew he wasn't responsible for her condition, but ever since he had lost the one woman he'd loved the most, he had felt responsible for every woman he'd become involved with, no matter how briefly. There was no way he would order McCoy to revive her if it would put her in more danger. "Very well," he said. "Keep me informed. Kirk out." He turned back to Haidar. "You heard the doctor."

She nodded. "Will you check with your engineer?"

Kirk had been about to do that anyway. He nodded to Uhura, who patched him through. "Scotty," Kirk said. "What's your status?"

A bit testily, Scotty said, "We're rewiring just as fast as we can, Captain, but it'll take another hour before we get it all done."

"Spock?" Kirk asked.

"The window of opportunity closes in thirty-seven minutes. If we do not begin by then, we will not complete the full-power phase of the rotation before the subspace influences become chaotic again."

"You heard Mr. Spock, Scotty. You've got thirty-seven minutes. Time and tide wait for no man."

"Aye, Captain," Scotty said tiredly. "We'll have it for you one way or another."

"Very good. Kirk out."

One of Spock's monitors beeped at him. He looked down at it again, then back up at Kirk. "I believe we have another problem. I detect disruptor fire on the surface."

"Disruptor fire?" Kirk asked. "Where?"

Spock consulted the monitors again. "I see small concentrations of it spreading throughout the Edge. It would appear that the Rimillians have gone to war."

Chapter Nineteen

SCOTTY FOLDED HIS COMMUNICATOR and clipped it back on his belt. "All right," he said to Kostas and Neron. "You heard the captain. We've got thirty-seven minutes to finish, so let's get movin'"

"We can't do it that quickly," Neron said. He was twisting his fingers together nervously, and his eyes darted back and forth from Scotty to Kostas. "It would be foolhardy to try. We'd be better off not starting the rotation at all than to fail partway into it."

Scotty took his arm and steered him toward the input section where he'd been rewiring before the captain called. "It's not our decision to make, and we don't have time to argue. Now, get to work."

Neron looked at the computer console, its insides open to view, then bent down and took a dangling wire and stuck it into the patch connector. Scotty nearly grabbed his hand again, not just because of his

203

poor attitude but because he'd put the wire into the wrong place.

"Not there, lad," he said as calmly as he could manage under the circumstances, "you've put the—"

But Neron suddenly stood up, reached into his pocket, and pulled out a Starfleet phaser, aimed right at Scotty.

"Look out!" Kostas yelled. Neron whirled to cover him, but before he could bring the weapon to bear Scotty kicked out and knocked it from his hand. The phaser clattered to the floor, but Scotty didn't bother going for it; he simply smashed his fist into the side of Neron's head. The Rimillian slumped to the floor, and Scotty grabbed his arms and pinned them behind him in case he wasn't unconscious.

"Get security over here," Scotty told Kostas, but the door guards were already coming on the run. They grabbed Neron and pulled him to his feet, but they had to hold him upright; Scotty had knocked him out cold.

"Well, if that isn't a fine kettle o' fish," Scotty said, rubbing his knuckles. "I guess now we know who our saboteur is."

"Neron?" Kostas asked, incredulous. "Neron was the saboteur?"

"Aye, and a lot more than that, I'd wager," Scott told him. "He had a phaser, and that means he was connected to the people who captured the captain. And who shot Coordinator Joray."

Kostas had to lean against a computer for support. "He was my left-hand man!"

"The best place for a saboteur to be," Scotty told him. "He had access to the entire project." He looked at the unconscious Rimillian, then shook his head sadly. "Lock him up," he told the guards. To Kostas he said, "Come on. He's wasted too much of our time already."

Kostas watched the guards drag Neron away; then he turned his wide eyes back on Scotty. "You can't be serious. We can't do it now. We'll have to check everything he's touched."

"Aye, that we will," Scotty told him. He picked up Kostas's logic probe and handed it to him. "But I'm not going to let that stop me. Not now."

Kostas looked at the instrument in his hand, then wordlessly bent down to the console that Neron had been working on moments earlier.

Scotty would follow him in just a moment, but he had one other job he had to do first. He took his communicator from his belt and flipped it open again. "Scott to *Enterprise*. We've found the saboteur."

Spock kept his eyes on the energy monitors while he listened to Mr. Scott's report. The energy discharges formed two nearly continuous lines about five kilometers apart on either side of the Edge's centerline, and they increased in activity even as he watched.

He heard Kirk ask, "Can you still repair the computer?" and he heard Scotty, clearly disgusted with the whole situation, reply, "No cross-wiring pipsqueak is going to shut *me* down. We'll have it for you. Scott out."

Spock glanced up to the main viewer, where Haidar was looking at the captain with wide-eyed surprise. "Well, it looks like we've caught your saboteur," Kirk told her.

"I assure you, Captain, he was not mine," she said stiffly.

Spock wondered. He had no evidence except her political position, but she had every right to oppose the project as long as her opposition had remained legal. And despite his misgivings, he had no evidence to the contrary.

Evidently the captain didn't either. While Spock looked back to his monitors, he said, "I didn't mean it that way. I only meant that he's been caught, and now maybe we can get on with the project."

"Perhaps not, Captain," Spock said. He had detected definite signs of motion in the line of disruptor fire. He looked to Kirk and said, "The battle lines seem to be advancing inward from either side. I believe it is a squeeze tactic by those living in the outlands, aimed at the inhabitants of the most desirable properties."

"Poor against rich," Kirk said. He looked to Haidar's image on the viewer. "Can you defend yourselves?"

"Not well," she replied. "Most of us have already gone into our underground shelters." She waved at the boxes behind her. "As you can see, I stayed above to pack the last of my belongings, but I was about ready to join the rest of the people below."

"It looks like they may have to come back out and fight instead," Kirk said. "Unless we can stop the outlanders from up here. Spock, do you see any way to head off the attack?"

Spock tried to envision anything the *Enterprise* might do to slow the advance of the fighters, but he could think of nothing. "Negative, Captain," he said.

"Short of giving them a common enemy from orbit, we are powerless to affect the course of their action. They are already engaged in battle along the entire length of the Edge. It appears to be a full-scale revolution."

"Why now?" Kirk asked. "If Scotty gets that computer on line in time, the land they're fighting for will be worthless."

"But Mr. Scott has not," Spock pointed out. "The people of the outlands do not know that he is still attempting repairs. They only know that the time for firing the engines has arrived and nothing has happened. I suspect this was their signal to start the revolution, since they no doubt assume that the rich and powerful have betrayed them."

"Then if we start the engines now," Haidar said, "maybe they'll stop fighting."

Spock admired her swift concession to logic, but Kirk looked at her in openmouthed surprise. "You?" he asked. "You want us to start the engines?"

"I want you to save my life," she replied. "I don't think I'll survive a revolution."

"She has a valid point, Captain," Spock said. "None of the minority party stand much chance. Nor does anyone living within the battle zone."

"You've got to do something," Haidar said, her voice rising in pitch.

Kirk turned to Uhura. "Get me Scotty again."

A moment later the engineer's voice came into the bridge. "Yes, Captain?"

"Scotty, can you give us any power to the engines at all?"

Puzzled, Scott said, "The engines aren't the problem, sir. I can give you full power when I get this computer on line, but not a minute sooner. We're working as fast as we can."

Kirk smiled grimly. "I understand, Scotty, but there's a war going on down there. We need those engines running *now* or there won't be a civilization left on this planet to bother saving."

"A war? What are ye talking about? Since when?"

The computer installation had been heavily guarded since the sabotage, and it wasn't the revolutionaries' primary target anyway; it wasn't surprising that the fight hadn't reached Scotty yet. Kirk told him, "Since the engines didn't start on time. The outsiders evidently think they were betrayed."

"I see." Scotty was silent a moment, then he said, "I can give you quarter impulse. There won't be any fine control at all until we get the computer on line, and even with warp-level generators quarter power won't do more than rock the planet a bit, but at least they'll be working."

"That's better than nothing, Scotty. Do it."

"Aye, sir."

Spock watched his monitors, and less than a minute later thousands of bright sparks showed up on the screens. They were visible only on the nightside at this power level, but sensors in other wavelengths showed them active all over the planet. Energy readings rose, then steadied out as the engines settled into steady firing.

"Engines operating," he said. He watched the stresses build in the planet's crust. Even quarter power would be enough to trigger minor quakes along fault lines, and though the subspace interactions would not be serious at this level, without control they could reinforce one another in feedback loops that could become dangerous in time. This would be an excellent opportunity to analyze their behavior at noncritical levels, and perhaps detect patterns while they could still be corrected.

"Has the fighting stopped?" Kirk asked.

Spock checked the disruptor activity, but it was stronger than ever. "No, Captain, it has not."

"Maybe they haven't noticed yet. Haidar, can you feel anything where you are?"

She held on to the back of a chair for support. "Yes, the whole building is vibrating. I can also feel waves passing through every few seconds. It feels like the whole building is rising and falling."

It was, Spock noted. The entire planet was rippling with long, gentle waves, like the surface of a deep ocean on an almost-calm day.

"They should feel that outside as well, shouldn't they?" asked Kirk. "Why are they still fighting?"

Spock said, "Stopping a conflict is always harder than starting one. Now that the two sides have engaged in battle, I suspect old hatreds will keep them at war despite anything we can do."

Kirk smacked his fist into his palm. "We'll see about that. Scotty, give me half impulse."

"Captain," Scotty said, "we can't do that, not without the computer. The subspace interactions will get out of hand for sure." His voice grew louder as he spoke; evidently he had set his communicator down so he could continue to work.

Kirk said, "At this point, that's just what I want. Half impulse, Mr. Scott."

Scotty was clearly unhappy with the idea even though he was at the pole and least likely to feel its effect, but he nonetheless said, "Aye, Captain," and a moment later Spock saw the power levels rise on the engines below.

Haidar clutched her chair for dear life now. "The whole building is shaking!" she shouted, terrified.

"Transporter room, lock on to Councilor Haidar," Kirk said into his intercom. "Get ready to beam her aboard on my mark."

"Ready," Ensign Vagle said.

"No," Haidar said, pulling herself together. "My place is here with my people. The government cannot flee to safety when the people are in danger."

"Even in the middle of a revolution?" Kirk asked.

"Even so."

"I admire your principles," Kirk told her. "Stay then, for now, but we'll pull you out the moment you're in danger."

"Agreed." She took a deep breath and said, "The vibration is much worse, and the wave motion is—whoa!"

Spock had seen that one from orbit. "Scale-seven quake," he reported. "Epicenter only one hundred kilometers from government headquarters."

"That ought to slow down the revolution," Kirk said with satisfaction.

"To which revolution do you refer?" Spock asked. "Sensors indicate that the Edge has moved one hundred and three meters westward since the thrust started. The *planet's* revolution has in fact just begun."

"Thank you, Spock," Kirk said, grinning, as Spock had known he would.

But a moment later he had to spoil that grin with the news from his energy monitor. "The fighting has not stopped."

"Three-quarters impulse, Scotty," Kirk said immediately.

"Captain, we can't! Give me ten minutes to patch in this computer first."

Kirk shook his head. "A smooth ride isn't the point," he said. "I want to knock every person on the planet to his knees. Let's see if they can fight then."

"All right," Scotty said dubiously, "but I'm going to shut 'em down again the moment there's trouble."

"Fine," said Kirk. "Three-quarters impulse."

Spock could see the increase in power on visual now. The bright points of light from the plasma jets stretched out into tongues of flame now, their brilliance visible even on the planet's dayside.

The stresses multiplied geometrically. Along the equator, where the thrust was strongest, Spock saw force ten and eleven quakes rattle the crust. The wave motion formed nodal points now where rock exploded upward as if bombs had been placed there.

Haidar screamed as a tile fell from the ceiling, narrowly missing her. "Let us beam you out of there!" Kirk said.

"No. Not until I'm sure everyone is safe." Behind her, Kirk could see other people running for cover, presumably into the underground shelter.

"Then at least get under an archway," Kirk told her, and she moved to stand in a doorway just within video range.

Spock looked at the energy monitor. "Disruptor fire still continuing," he reported.

"Damn it, what's it going to take?" Kirk demanded. "Scotty, how much longer on that computer?"

"Another five minutes at least," Scott said. "But even then it's anybody's guess if it'll work. We've had no time for any tests."

"Hook it up anyway," Kirk told him. "We don't have any other choice."

The entire bridge crew waited tensely as the minutes ticked by. Haidar, barely in view now, kept up a running commentary as the building bucked and heaved around her, but it held together. Spock watched the stresses mount elsewhere on the planet, though, and saw that the current situation would not last much longer. The subspace oscillations were becoming critical, and would soon burst forth into real-space forces beyond anything that had hit the planet so far.

They were even reaching out into orbit. The *Enterprise* lurched as a particularly strong fluctuation momentarily overpowered its inertial dampers.

"Mr. Scott," Spock said, "I am monitoring harmonic buildup. Prepare to throttle back."

"If she'll just hold another minute, I don't think we'll need to," Scotty said. "We've just about got 'er done here; if we get the computer on line then we can keep right on going with the rotation."

"I can see them outside in the courtyard now!" Haidar shouted. "They're storming the building!" The sound of breaking glass and the *zip-bang* of disruptor fire came through clearly.

"Beam her up," Kirk said. "Beam up everyone in the building."

The viewer image showed Haidar shimmering out

of existence just seconds before the right-side wall burst inward and dozens of heavily armed revolutionaries rushed through the gap. "Not the newcomers, Mr. Vagle," Kirk said.

"Roger," Vagle replied. "Late arrivals have missed the launch."

Scotty said, "We're almost there . . . one more connection . . . the computer is on line!"

"Full power!" Kirk ordered immediately.

Spock watched the power levels rise again on the surface as Mr. Scott complied with the order. This time they didn't rise smoothly; some engines thrust harder than others and the pattern changed constantly. The computer appeared to be working, adjusting their output to smooth the subspace interactions and the loads on the planet's crust. Harmonic resonance levels began to drop, and nodal point explosions ceased.

No amount of finesse in the engine's thrust patterns could eliminate the stress entirely, however, and now that the engines were running under full power that stress began to show in greater and greater quakes. The viewer had been left on in Haidar's quarters in the councilors' mansion; the *Enterprise's* bridge crew watched through it as the building shook. Ceiling tiles and blocks from the breached wall fell to the floor. The outlanders had pressed on into the inner offices, leaving the room empty, the gap in its wall showing the battle that still raged beyond. Outside, another building twisted sideways and fell to the ground. The rumble of destruction coming through the comm link was like continuous thunder. Uhura turned down the level, then turned it down again a minute later.

Spock saw a violent flare of seismic energy release on his monitors. "Force-ten quake two kilometers from government headquarters," he reported. "Well within the Edge."

For a moment the viewer filled with a rain of stone as the roof over Haidar's quarters caved in; then it went blank.

Chapter Twenty

THE SUDDEN SILENCE startled Chekov even more than the rumble of falling debris. He was tense as a Klingon at a peace conference, and anything unexpected made him flinch now. He was waiting for the photon torpedoes he knew would be coming any moment, and wondering if he would spot them in time in the midst of all the other chaos going on below.

Energy readings were clear off the scale. Thirty thousand impulse engines operating under warp-power loads looked to the navigation displays like a major space battle confined in one tiny volume hardly big enough to maneuver a single ship in. Even maintaining orbit was a trick with all the subspace activity going on. The oscillations were subsiding now that Scotty had got the computer on line, but not quickly enough to suit Chekov; the *Enterprise* bucked again as another fluctuation reached out from the planet.

215

The turbolift doors swished open, and Councilor Haidar stepped onto the bridge. Chekov barely spared her a glance, but he heard Kirk say, "Welcome aboard," and he heard her ask anxiously, "Has the fighting stopped?"

Chekov looked to his board, but any disruptor fire it could have detected was buried beneath the much stronger signal coming from the engines.

Spock, however, had more sensitive detectors in his science station. He said, "Much of the activity has stopped. I still see sporadic outbursts, but I believe we have stemmed the tide."

"Good." The captain sounded satisfied with himself, as indeed he might. It looked like he was going to pull off another last-minute rescue.

But the moment he had that thought, Chekov knew he'd been premature. The bright spark he'd been dreading burst free of the planet, streaking tangentially outward from a point just on the horizon—straight at the *Enterprise*.

"Incoming!" Chekov shouted.

"Shields up," ordered Kirk.

Chekov hit the shields, and while they were building he made sure the phasers were on line. He was getting tired of being fired upon.

But the torpedo arched over in the planet's gravity, its course missing the *Enterprise* by thousands of kilometers. "What are they shooting at?" Chekov asked aloud, but then he noticed the plasma trail streaming out behind it.

Spock saw it as well. "It is one of the impulse engines," he said. "It apparently sheared loose from its mount. The power core failed upon breakout, and

is venting plasma as it follows a ballistic traj⏷⏷⏷
back to the surface."

"Where is it going to hit?" asked Kirk.

Chekov looked at his tracking instruments, but
their readings kept changing. He said, "Unable to
calculate, Captain. The subspace fluctuations are tossing it around too much."

"Then vaporize it," Kirk ordered.

Glad for the chance to shoot back at something,
Chekov aimed the ship's phasers at the tumbling
impulse engine and fired. Two brilliant beams of
energy reached out to the engine, which burst into a
cloud of ionized gas at their touch.

"Like shooting fish in a barrel," Chekov said.

"Fish in a—?" Spock began, but another brilliant
spark shot upward from the surface.

"There's another one!" Chekov said. "And another!"

"Shoot them down," Kirk said calmly.

Chekov fired twice more, and two more ionized
clouds drifted across the face of the planet.

Spock said, "The violent shaking before the computer went on line evidently shattered their foundations. We should expect more."

"How many more?" asked Haidar. She seemed just
as afraid now that the engines would fail as she had
been earlier that they would work.

Spock said, "Impossible to predict without close
structural analysis, but based on the wave patterns I
observed, I would estimate about eighty engines were
near nodal points, and thus susceptible to damaging
vibration. We will know soon; those with structural
damage will undoubtedly fail within the next few
minutes."

Sure enough, seventy-one more engines broke free in the next two minutes, but they were easy enough to vaporize, and their numbers dropped after that. Their contribution to the total energy output of the engines was small, and the installations weren't manned, so there was no loss of life to worry about, either. In fact, Chekov thought as he blasted another one, they made a festive fireworks display for a great occasion in Rimillian history.

Two more engines blew up on the ground, their warp cores going critical before they could be shut down, but the sites weren't near the Edge so that didn't matter either. The planet was beginning to move now, gaining angular momentum at a phenomenal rate. It was already moving at nearly a kilometer an hour at the equator. Not yet fast enough to push the tidal bulge past the halfway point, but it was a start.

Then the *Enterprise* shook as if it had just hit a meteor head-on. Chekov looked to his monitors and saw a huge ripple in the subspace fields surrounding the planet. What they had just hit had been nothing compared to what was coming. "Brace for impact!" he said, gripping his navigation console.

The great starship plowed straight through it, its energy fields reacting with the subspace fluctuation and tossing the crew from side to side. Chekov fell to the deck, and Haidar, standing beside Kirk's command chair, nearly wound up on his lap. Chekov helped her to her feet, then turned back to his navigation controls. The ship had been knocked off course—no surprise.

He awaited the command to take them higher, but Kirk remained silent. Only Spock said anything, and that was just to observe calmly, "Subspace fluctuations are increasing, Mr. Scott."

"You can say that again," muttered Chekov as he fed the helm the coordinates to get them back to their original orbit.

Scotty knew about the fluctuations even before the *Enterprise* did. Alarms were flashing all over the computer control consoles and on the overhead situation map of the world as engine after engine stopped responding, and to top that off the shock waves had reached all the way up to the north pole now and the whole building was shaking like a shuttlecraft in an engine-out descent. The makeshift circuits they had installed were pulling loose right and left, and some of the permanent ones blinked off and on as well.

The computer had never been trained to deal with sudden interruptions in its data stream—of course not, since Neron had been in charge of that—so it wasn't handling the situation well at all. It kept trying to reestablish the links instead of continuing fine control of the ones that remained, which meant the subspace interactions began to grow again.

"I see it," Scotty said when Spock gave him the report from orbit. "I don't know how much we'll be able to do about it, but we'll try."

He had left his communicator on top of the main control console so he didn't have to waste a hand to hold it. Uhura could turn up the gain if his voice didn't come through well; he was busy. Too busy, in fact, to wait around for a response. He stuck his head in through the access hatch to the primary input circuits, a penlight in his mouth so he could see in the dim interior, and checked for damage. Kostas worked in the output bank beside him.

Fortunately, they didn't have thirty thousand separate lines to worry about. Kostas had at least multiplexed the signals so a single line could monitor a hundred separate inputs. The trouble with that, of course, was that when one of the lines disconnected they lost touch with a hundred engines at once, and when it came back on line the computer had a hundred new inputs to deal with just as suddenly. The oscillations going on in subspace were nothing compared to what was going on in the circuitry right there next to Scotty's head.

Another quake rattled the complex. Scotty rode it out where he was, then probed for open circuits the moment he could move again. Seven lines were loose. Seven hundred engines without guidance for at least three seconds. He hastily locked them down again and checked for more.

An aftershock bumped things sideways, and Scotty heard his communicator fall to floor.

"Scotty, are you still there? Mr. Scott?" came Kirk's voice.

"Aye," he said, scooting out from within the console again and picking up the communicator. "I'm here, for all the good it's doing. This computer's coming apart at the seams, Captain."

"Hold her together, Scotty. We just need . . ." Kirk paused, no doubt realizing that they weren't halfway there, or even a quarter of the way. Not even a tenth.

Scotty sighed. "Now you see what I mean. We've got to keep it going for *weeks*. At this rate we'll be lucky if we get another ten minutes out of it before something blows."

"We can't stop now, Scotty. The planet's already moving."

"Aye, and we'll do our best to keep it that way, but it doesn't look good." Another alarm rang, and Scotty set the communicator down again. "Hold on." He checked the telltales for the source of the trouble, then ducked down inside one of the processor consoles to trace another open circuit. At least nothing had actually blown out since Neron had misconnected the testing device.

Scott had to take a deep breath when he thought about Neron. How could someone work so closely with a project like this, actually help build the engines and the control computer, and then sabotage it at the last moment? Had he intended to do it all along, or had he gotten cold feet when the time came and tried to prevent what he thought would be a catastrophe? Whatever his motives, he had nearly caused that very catastrophe, and it might happen yet if Scotty and Kostas couldn't keep ahead of the malfunctions in their jury-rigged repairs.

The guards had presumably taken Neron to a cell somewhere. Scotty hoped he would have a chance to ask him a few questions when this was all over, though he supposed it would be a moot point by then no matter which way things worked out.

It wasn't a moot point to Kostas. It had been a heavy blow to him to realize that his second-in-command was a Denialist. He was working now on sheer momentum, but Scotty knew that the moment things calmed down the scientist would probably go to pieces, leaving him in charge of the entire operation.

Provided the operation didn't go to pieces first. Another quake shook the building, and the new repairs in the roof and walls creaked ominously. The construction crew had reinforced everything with steel beams, but too big a quake would bring even that framework down, probably right on top of the computer.

If that happened, there would be no fixing it. The rotation project would be dead, and so would everyone on the planet, because Rimillia was already moving too fast to stop now. Even if the tidal bulge didn't make it beyond the halfway point, it would rock slowly back and forth for millennia, giving the Edge scorching hot days and freezing nights all the while, before it settled back into its former position.

That might be preferable to ripping the planet apart at the seams, though, Scotty thought as another shock wave passed through. At least people could survive for a while in their shelters if all they had to worry about was heat and cold, but if the crust ripped open and exposed the molten hot mantle beneath it would be all over in a matter of hours.

It looked as if that very thing was about to happen, too. On the overhead map, seismic monitors were going wild in dozens of places across the planet. The engines in those areas had already ceased to exist, either blown up when their warp cores breached or ripped free into space when their foundations collapsed. Scotty looked at the total lost now: nearly two hundred. Over half a percent. That was becoming significant. Given their budget constraints, the Rimillians hadn't built any more engines than were absolutely necessary. If they lost many more, they would never be able to push the tidal bulge past the halfway point, no matter how long the remaining engines fired.

Kostas pulled his head out of the output section and stood up. "It's like weaving wet tissue paper," he shouted over the roar of the quakes. "Everything I touch falls apart."

"I know the feeling," Scotty told him. Another quake nearly knocked his communicator to the floor again. He rescued it before it went over the edge, and while he was holding it Kirk said, "It's getting pretty rough up here, Scotty."

"I'd gladly trade you places," Scotty told him. "We're up to our—"

A sudden violent shock threw him to the floor. Sparks flew from one of the I/O banks. Kostas crawled on his hands and knees toward it and pulled open the access panel, but he didn't see the component rack beside it teeter on edge and tip forward.

"Look out!" Scotty yelled. He grabbed Kostas's feet and pulled him aside just as the rack crashed to the floor right where the scientist's head had been.

Kostas looked at the fallen equipment in horror. "That was one of the main processors," he said.

Scotty shared his anguish, but there was nothing to do about it now except reroute its data to another processor. At least that could be done through the keyboard controls. As he worked on it, Scotty said, "I know. We'll just have to hope the others can compensate for the loss."

"It was never meant to take this kind of damage," Kostas said. "There's no way it can keep up now."

Scotty hoped he was wrong, but unfortunately the professor knew his computer. Too few circuits were left to monitor all the engines and calculate their interactions. The subspace oscillations grew stronger with every passing minute, and the quakes grew with them. The seismic monitors were completely off the scale in some places now. On the overhead map, a string of quakes rocked a great arc over a thousand kilometers long, triggering one another in sequence.

"Volcanic activity in three sites now," Spock said over the communicator. "Tectonic rifts are forming."

Scotty looked around the computer room. Every monitor was ablaze with warning lights, and smoke rose from two of the consoles. The place had the look of a ship that had lost a major space battle, just moments before the warp core went critical and blew it to atoms.

Another aftershock rattled the entire building, but it was tiny compared to what was happening elsewhere. Seismic warning lights blinked on all across the map.

Scotty shouted into his communicator, "Captain, the planet canna take any more of this! She's breaking up!"

"We can't stop now," Kirk said grimly. "Hold it together, Scotty."

Kostas looked at the communicator in disbelief. Scotty shook his head and grabbed hold of a control panel for support. "We've tried everything we can, sir. There's nothing else we can do. We've got to shut down the engines."

"We can't do that!" said Kirk. "We have to finish the rotation."

"The only thing that'll be rotatin' if we keep this up

will be the fragments," Scotty insisted. "We've got to shut 'em down."

He heard Spock say, "I agree with his assessment, Captain. The stresses have mounted well beyond the planet's structural tolerances, and harmonic vibrations continue to mount. If we do not shut the engines down within the next three-point-two minutes, the planet will be destroyed."

Scotty mopped his forehead with his sleeve while he waited for the captain to make up his mind. Kirk always thought he could bull his way through situations like this, and sometimes he was right, but this wasn't one of those times. If he tried to play hero now it wouldn't be just the *Enterprise* and its crew of 430 at stake; this time a whole planet would die, and millions of people with it.

Scotty couldn't let that happen. He had never disobeyed an order before in his life, and he didn't want to start now, but he didn't see any other choice. If the captain wouldn't give the order, then—

He was reaching for the cutoff switch when Kirk let out a deep sigh and said, "Disengage all engines, Scotty."

Scotty slapped the switch. The computer went into shutdown mode, lowering the thrust in each engine carefully so that it didn't cause more shock waves as the planet's crust rebounded. Blinking alarm lights winked out one by one as engine after engine went off line, but plenty of them stayed lit. The computer was still a mess, and now that more data lines were opening up it received error messages from the less-vital peripherals as well. Several engines had experienced thrust decays that would take them out of service soon, some of the transceivers had been damaged in the quakes, and so on. Scotty noted wryly that the palmprint reader at the gate had blown out during a voltage spike.

None of that mattered anymore. The project was over. They'd given it their best shot, but it hadn't been enough. They had failed.

Chapter Twenty-one

KIRK SLUMPED BACK in his command chair, hardly able to believe the order he'd just given. Shut off the engines. Never mind that the Edge was moving westward now on a relentless first foray into the inhospitable regions, or that the rest of the planet had been shaken to pieces apparently for nothing; it was time to cut their losses.

At least the revolutionaries would be off the streets now, running for shelter as the Edge slid into sunlight or shadow, depending on which side of the world they were on. The fighting could continue underground, of course, but Kirk bet it wouldn't. These people had bigger problems now.

What was it Spock had said? *Short of giving them a common enemy from orbit . . .* Well, the *Enterprise* had certainly done that.

He looked to Haidar. She stood beside his command chair like a lost child, her arms held tight to her chest, her whole body shaking as she gazed at her world below. It still looked serene from this altitude; only a few dark plumes of dust and smoke marked the new volcanoes.

Kirk stood up and guided her into his chair. She needed to sit; he needed to pace.

"What——" she began, but her voice broke and she had to swallow. "What can we do now?"

Kirk took a deep breath. The burn on his chest tightened uncomfortably, reminding him that he wasn't completely healed yet from his own adventure on the surface. He thought about the thousands of other people who were wounded down there, either from the war or the collapsed buildings. They would need help. But what good would the *Enterprise*'s rescue efforts do if the planet itself became uninhabitable? No, only one kind of assistance would mean anything in the long run. Kirk turned to Haidar and said, "We repair the engines and try it again. There's no other option."

Spock said, "The full-power activation window is rapidly closing. It is unlikely that Mr. Scott can effect repairs before the opportunity is past."

"He's right about that," Scotty said over the communicator. "It'll take at least a day just to——hold on!" A deep rumble drowned out his voice, and the sizzle of an electrical short followed close on its tail. The planet was obviously still ringing with the vibrations they had induced. "Make that a day and a half," said Scotty.

"There seems little point," said Haidar. "What about evacuation?"

Spock said, "To effect it within a reasonable

timescale would involve most of the starships in Federation space. That seems unlikely. Even if it were possible to redirect nearly all of our fleet to one evacuation project, it would be strategically unwise."

"So it's shelters for the rest of our lives?" Haidar asked.

"No," Kirk said. He looked from her to Spock to the rest of the bridge crew. Gripping the handrail that separated his command chair from the rest of the bridge, he said, "I won't let it end like this. There has to be something we can do. Redesign the engines, or redesign the control computer, or use tractor beams instead of impulse engines. I don't care what they are, but I want some options."

Spock looked at him with a peculiar expression, surprise or disbelief or something else entirely, Kirk couldn't tell which. He was about to ask when the intercom whistled for attention and McCoy said, "McCoy to the bridge. Are y'all through throwing us around for a while now?"

"Yes, Bones."

"Well that's just fine." McCoy's voice was oozing Southern politeness—not a good sign. "I just thought I'd let you know that we've found a variant that might work. It's not the best thing in the world; it's ugly as a mud fence and it'll only withstand a fifteen-degree hike in average temperature, but it's a start. Was a start, anyway. But I guess that doesn't matter now, does it?"

Kirk felt like jumping down his throat for his attitude, and if it had been anyone else he would have, but this was Bones so he let it slide. "I don't know," he said. "Maybe it will. Hold on. Spock?"

He looked hopefully to the science officer, but after

consulting the computer for a moment Spock shook his head and said, "There is too much motion. The planet will not rotate, but it will rock back and forth. No place along the Edge, except near the poles, will receive less than a ninety-seven-degree average increase in daytime temperature. And a corresponding drop at night, of course."

"Of course," McCoy drawled. "Sorry we didn't catch you before it got so far out of hand. Course, it might have been nice if you'd at least checked with us one last time before you started things spinning."

"We didn't have a choice," Kirk said. "Dammit, Bones, you know as well as I do that you can't always wait for the best solution to come along; sometimes you have to take what's offered. We had a war to stop as well as a planet to spin, and we did what we had to." The words rang hollow even as he spoke them. He was trying to convince himself as well as McCoy, and not doing a good job in either case.

But McCoy backed off just the same. "Sorry," he said. "I know you did the best you could. I guess we all just missed the mark this time."

"Well, let's turn right back around and hit it," Kirk said. "There has to be something else we haven't thought of."

McCoy didn't reply for a moment, and when he did it was only to say, "I don't know, Jim. Maybe someone back at Starfleet might have an idea, but I'm fresh out."

Kirk pounded on the handrail. "Starfleet? We weren't sent out here to scuttle back home with our tails between our legs the first time we ran into trouble. *We're* Starfleet out here. We're the finest the

Federation has to offer, and if we can't do the job ourselves then it can't be done. I want some ideas, and I want them *now*. Think, people. What can we do to save Rimillia?"

Haidar laughed softly. "Maybe the Nihilists are right. Maybe we've done just exactly enough already. You didn't cause this; we did, with our relentless expansion and our technological recklessness. We've had two chances to build ourselves a paradise, and we've blown them both. Why deny the obvious? Maybe it's time to admit that we're a dying race and accept our fate."

Kirk examined her expression for a hint of the fanaticism that usually went with such statements, but he didn't see it there. "You don't really believe that, do you?" he asked.

She shrugged. "Captain, right now I don't know what to believe."

Kirk followed her gaze to the forward viewer and the planet below. He wasn't sure if he did either.

Spock felt uncomfortable. It bothered him that he felt anything at all, but his human half would not be denied, and the prospect of failure and all that it implied—for the *Enterprise* and its crew as well as for the people on the planet—weighed heavy on him. With the exception of the engineer, Neron, everyone involved had done everything they could to prevent catastrophe, yet it had still occurred. Spock knew that some things were inevitable, and that he should not waste time agonizing over his regrets, yet he couldn't help feeling that something else could still be done.

But then again, perhaps it was just the captain's

emotional plea that swayed his logic. Kirk had done that to him before, deliberately to influence his behavior. Could that be his plan now as well?

It didn't matter. He and Spock both wanted the same thing: a way to salvage the situation. Spock would do everything in his power to do so, emotions or no.

Not that such a thing was necessarily possible. Much as it pained him to admit it, Spock shared the doctor's sentiment on that. If a solution existed, it certainly was not apparent to him.

Everyone on the bridge seemed tense. The captain obviously expected a miracle, and he expected it fast. He'd trained his crew to deliver when he asked for something, and it didn't seem to matter to him that what he wanted now was beyond anything he'd ever demanded of them before.

He was waiting impatiently even now. Chekov, Uhura, and the others on the bridge fidgeted under his stare. Spock turned to his computer and science displays.

The first step in solving a problem was to identify it. So what exactly was the problem here? They needed to finish spinning the planet, or failing that cancel the rotation they had already imparted and return it to its previous state. The problem with that was the narrow window of opportunity, which was rapidly closing on them.

Why did that window exist? Because of the subspace influence of the other planetary bodies in the star system.

That suggested one solution: eliminate the other bodies, and there would be no timetable to worry about. Mr. Scott would have all the time he needed to repair the engines and the control computer, and the rotation could proceed on its own schedule.

Of course that was ridiculous. A thought experiment, nothing more. The *Enterprise* didn't have enough power to destroy a whole planet, much less six of them. But the notion did bring up a possible solution: If the subspace influence of the planets could be eliminated, that would be just as good as eliminating the planets themselves.

But planets were huge compared to the scale of a starship. They were far away and moving slowly, but their influence was still stronger than any shield or standing wave the *Enterprise* could generate to block it.

The next syzygy alignment wouldn't happen for 1,217 years, so waiting for that wasn't an option, either.

Could they fire the engines at less than full power? They had done so once already with no computer control at all, and the harmonic vibrations had not become overwhelming. But the Rimillians had not built an excess of engines; it would require full power to push the tidal bulge past the libration point. After that they could throttle down, but not until then.

Could they install more engines? Possibly, given time and a healthy economy, neither of which Rimillia had at this point.

Perhaps the existing hardware could be modified somehow. Warp engines were more efficient than impulse engines . . . but they interacted with subspace even more directly, so using them would be even worse.

Spock ran down the list of possibilities, shooting down each one nearly as quickly as he came up with it, but something Kirk had said still echoed in his mind. What was it? He'd said, *I don't care what they are, but I want some options.* No, before that. *There has to be something we can do. Redesign the engines, or redesign the control computer, or use tractor beams instead of impulse engines.* Yes, that was it. Tractor beams. Pitifully inadequate for influencing an entire planet, of course, but something had connected for Spock when he'd heard that. Then the interchange with Dr. McCoy immediately afterward had driven it from his mind.

Most irritating.

He closed his eyes and concentrated. Tractor beams. What could they do with tractor beams that would influence their ability to rotate the planet? Keep the control computer from shaking so badly, for one. They should have thought of that earlier. All right, then, that was one thing they could do. It wouldn't be enough, but it was a step in the right direction. What else had they overlooked?

The intercom whistled again. He tried to ignore it, but when he heard McCoy say excitedly "Jim, she's awake!" he found that he couldn't. He opened his eyes and turned to see Kirk and Haidar both standing beside the captain's chair.

"Who is?" Haidar asked. "Joray?"

"That's right. She's out of danger, and she's asking for both of you."

"On our way," Kirk said. He took Haidar's arm and led her toward the turbolift. Almost as an afterthought, he turned back at the doors and said, "You have the conn, Spock."

"Acknowledged, Captain," Spock said.

The turbolift doors swished closed behind Kirk and

Haidar. Spock looked around the bridge and noted that the crew seemed greatly relieved to have the captain gone. That would ordinarily not be a good sign, but in this case it seemed appropriate.

Spock bent back to his task, glad to have less chance for interruption now. Tractor beams. What could they do with tractor beams? Dampen the seismic motion near the control computer, and presumably a few other places as well, but not the whole planet at once. Yet something had suggested itself to him in that fleeting moment when the captain had mentioned it.

Back to the problem. Subspace interactions caused harmonic vibrations, which built up over time to dangerous levels. How could tractor beams affect that?

Well, he certainly had enough data to run simulations on. He had recorded the entire spin attempt, from the moment the captain had ordered the engines started to the moment he had ordered them stopped. If a tractor beam could affect anything, he could soon find out how.

Spock bent to the task, setting up the computer to calculate just how much the *Enterprise* could influence the planet.

The answer, when it came, made the hair stand up on the back of his neck.

Chapter Twenty-two

McCoy STOOD like a stern father at the head of the intensive-care bed while the captain and Haidar spoke with Joray. He wasn't about to let them overtax his patient now that she'd finally regained consciousness. He would let them talk for a minute or two—it would let him take some measurements while her body reacted to normal stimulus for a change—but then he would kick them out again and put her back to sleep to continue healing.

Of course the shock she'd felt at learning that Councilor Telinga had died messed with her readings right from the start, so McCoy wasn't sure what good any more might do. Why did people always tell a freshly awakened patient the worst news first?

Then she asked, "What about the rotation project? Has that started yet?" and McCoy realized maybe they hadn't.

"It has begun," Haidar told her.

"And I missed it! Oh, the universe is so unfair." Then she blushed and said, "I'm sorry. I'm sure you're much less excited than I am. But I would like to go forward now with no hard feelings if we could."

Haidar took Joray's hand in hers. "I have no room for hard feelings. So much else has happened. I hardly know where to begin."

Joray's face fell. "What? What's wrong?"

Kirk said, "There was more sabotage to the main control computer. It took us a while to repair, so we had to start late, but evidently—"

Joray gasped, and her pulse rate jumped to 110. "You missed the start-up window? Then the outsiders . . . did they . . . ?"

"You knew there was going to be a revolution?" Haidar asked.

Joray smiled wanly. "Revolution. One way or another, the outsiders were determined."

"And you did nothing to stop it."

Joray shook her head. "I am an outsider, too. Besides, what could I have done? Warn the police that the citizens were arming themselves? They would have gone to war immediately. The best I could do was make sure the spin project went ahead as planned. I never considered that it would merely be late." She leaned back. "I assume they stopped fighting when they realized their mistake."

"You assume wrong," Kirk said. "We had to, ah, shake some sense into them, you might say."

McCoy was growing alarmed at Joray's vital signs. Heartbeat was 120 now, adrenaline levels were rising, and her temperature was going up as well. "The revolution stopped," he told her. "And you're getting

237

a little too excited." He turned to Jim and Haidar.
"There's plenty of time to tell her the news when she's
feeling stronger. In the meantime, I want you to relax,
and—"

Joray tried to sit up. "No. There's more, isn't there?
I want to know. Is it working? Were there quakes?"

Haidar said, "Uh, yes, there were, but—"

"Tell me! How much damage was there? Who was
killed?"

"We don't know that yet," Kirk said.

McCoy nearly laughed. That was an understate-
ment. It would take hours for the casualty lists to
come in. He would help where he could, now that he
could do more good on the ground than here on the
ship, but he knew there must have been thousands of
people killed in the quakes.

He didn't want Joray to know that now, not with
her condition as fragile as it was. "I'm going to have to
insist," he said. "You're getting too excited. Visiting
hours are over."

The intercom chose that moment to interrupt, and
McCoy breathed a silent thank-you—until he heard
Spock say, "Spock to Captain Kirk. I think I have
discovered a possibility, but in order for it to succeed
we will have to resume thrust within eighteen minutes. Preferably sooner."

"Resume thrust!" Joray exclaimed. "What happened?"

"We had some trouble," Kirk said quickly, "but
now it looks like it's over." He stepped back from the
bed. "I'm needed on the bridge."

"Of course," Joray said. Haidar looked toward the
departing captain, but Joray didn't let go her hand.

"No, stay with me," she said. "Tell me what happened."

"Doctor?" asked Haidar.

McCoy looked to the monitors. Joray's vital signs were still elevated, but the promise of good news had actually brought them down a bit. Best to leave well enough alone.

"I think later would be better," he said. To Joray he said, "You should sleep."

"Are you kidding? With thrust resuming in eighteen minutes? I want to see it. Can you get visuals on this thing?" She pointed at the computer terminal beside the bed.

"Yes," McCoy said reluctantly, realizing he would have to knock her out if he wanted to keep her from learning everything all at once. She hadn't worked her way up to the head of the government by being submissive.

Neither had Haidar. "Look," she said to Joray, "your health comes first. Once we get the planet up to speed, we're going to need a pro-spinner in power to keep things going. If you die of exhaustion now, *I* inherit the job, and frankly I don't want it."

Joray laughed. "That's such a strange thing to hear you say, after all these years of fighting for supremacy."

Haidar looked away. For a moment her eyes met McCoy's, and despite her tough attitude he saw in her face an expression of loss so deep that he reached out instinctively to comfort her. She smiled and said softly to Joray, "I was fighting to preserve the life I knew. That no longer exists."

Joray squeezed her hand and said, "We'll bring it

back. The only difference in the new world will be that we'll bring your lifestyle to *everyone.*"

Sure, McCoy thought. And the Klingons will join the Federation, too. But he was much too polite to say that.

"What have you got for me, Spock?" Kirk asked as he stepped from the turbolift onto the bridge. He noticed that Chekov and Uhura were even more nervous now than they had been when he left. Evidently Spock had spooked them with his Vulcan candor again.

Spock seemed completely unaware of his effect on the crew. "I have analyzed the subspace vibration patterns induced by the Rimillian impulse engines," he said, "and I have determined that the *Enterprise* could, in fact, influence those patterns to a significant degree."

"How?" Kirk asked. He walked over to the science station and looked at the screens that Spock had displayed. Graphs of tractor-beam effectiveness over distance, a Vukcevich projection of Rimillia with all the engines and all the major nodal points marked, and a headache-inducing pattern of counter-rotating black lines that could only be a subspace detector of some sort.

Spock confirmed his guess. "I have keyed this subspace field monitor to the harmonic patterns I recorded during our abortive attempt to control the engines. When I replay them through the ship's computer, adding in a new component to simulate the dampening effect of the *Enterprise*'s tractor beam in certain key areas, I am able to reduce the synergistic buildup of vibrations by eighty-three percent."

Kirk tried to imagine what Spock was getting at. "You want to use the tractor beam to stop the *planet* from shaking?"

"That is correct."

No wonder the bridge crew were nervous. Spock had gone crazy. "What will that do to the *Enterprise* if we try it?" Kirk asked him gently. "For every action there's an opposite and equal reaction, you know."

"I am aware of Newton's laws," Spock said.

"Then you can't seriously expect to stop an earthquake with a tractor beam. We'd be shaken to pieces."

Spock nodded. "If we attempted to do it directly, yes we would. However, if we use the beam to induce countervibrations of the proper frequency, we can dampen the natural oscillation of the planet's crust before the wave motion becomes too strong for our onboard inertial dampers to compensate."

"Oh," Kirk said. He saw it now. "Sort of like spreading oil on troubled waters," he said, searching for the right image.

"'Sort of,'" Spock repeated dryly. "However, 'antiphase wave cancellation' would be a more exact description of the process."

Kirk sighed. "I'm sure it would, Spock. Now, tell me why we have to do it in eighteen minutes."

"Fourteen minutes, six seconds now, Captain. The reason for that is the growing complexity of the subspace influence exerted by the other planets. Our ability to compensate for it decreases as their alignment grows wider. Even if we tap into the warp core for power, the energy required will surpass our capabilities if we do not begin within that time." Spock looked back to his computer monitors. "As it is, we

241

will have to push the limits of our inertial dampers, and the longer we wait the worse it will get."

Kirk didn't like the sound of that. If the inertial dampers failed, the crew could wind up looking like raspberry jam. "So what's the good news?" he asked.

Spock raised an eyebrow. "The good news is that the planet is unusually stable now after all the quakes. Every fault that was under stress has broken free already, and the aftershocks are subsiding as well. This time there should be no seismic activity beyond what we will generate with the engines. And we can compensate for that near the computer installation, so we will avoid repeating the damage that occurred there last time."

"I'm sure Scotty will be glad to hear that," Kirk said.

"He was," said Spock. "Given the time constraint, as soon as I realized we had a chance I took the liberty of ordering him to redouble his efforts to stabilize the computer. He is currently at work on it, and promises at least partial success within the deadline."

Kirk looked around the bridge. It was only a tiny part of the ship, but it was the control center for all 190,000 tons of precision machinery and its crew of 430. With a simple command the helmsman could send them off into space at hundreds of times the speed of light. The communications officer could scan every wavelength of the electromagnetic and subspace spectrums for meaningful signals, and the computer could translate whatever she found into English. The science officer could probe anything they encountered with sensors of nearly magical capability. And if the ship were attacked, the crew could defend it with weapons the equal of any in the galaxy. The *Enterprise* was the culmination of centuries of progress in science and engineering, the finest starship humanity had yet built.

All to be used as ballast.

Spock, sensing his mood, said, "It was the only solution I could come up with in the short time allowed."

Kirk nodded. "Well, I did ask for it, didn't I? I guess I shouldn't complain when you deliver." He turned to Uhura and said, "Get me Scotty."

"Already on line, sir," she said.

"Scotty, how about it? Are you ready for another go at this?"

The engineer sounded harried, as well he might. "We're gettin' her there, sir. Just another few minutes."

Kirk sighed. To the entire bridge, he said, "Well, people, it looks like once more into the breach."

Chapter Twenty-three

SCOTTY WINCED WHEN he saw Neron reach into the damaged processor rack. He hated allowing the saboteur near the machinery again, but he agreed with Kostas that the two of them could never finish the repairs in time by themselves. They had to have another hand, and unlikely as it seemed, Neron's was the best hand they could get on short notice. He had helped design the computer, after all; he would know as well as anyone how to repair it.

Provided he wanted to. He'd sworn that he did now, that he had only been trying to prevent the project from starting before, and that now that his worst fears had come true he would do his best to salvage the situation however he could; but Scotty still didn't trust him as far as he could throw him. Anybody who could sabotage a perfectly good computer was capable of anything, in his book.

All the same, he didn't have time to check his every move. That would negate the advantage of using him in the first place. So Scotty got to work on the tangled mess of the output stage and settled for just keeping his eye on him from time to time.

Neron did know his computer, that much was clear. He had the processor that had tipped over back up and running in no time, and he got the input section straightened out shortly after that. Then, as if sensing Scotty's unease and trying to fix that as well, he moved over to work beside Scotty in the output bank.

"I know you don't think much of me," Neron said as they traced the bad circuits and rerouted data lines, "but I did what I did because I honestly thought it was the best."

"It wasn't," Scotty told him bluntly. "You damned near killed us all. And if what we're trying now doesn't work, a lot more people will die."

Neron's hands shook as he held his logic probe over the multiplexer. "Believe me, that's the last thing I want. I was trying to *save* lives."

"I've heard people say that before."

Neron tapped a command into the computer and tried the probe again. As he worked, he said, "I believed in this project when we first started it. I really did. It offered the first real promise of a better life for all of us. And in the more immediate term it offered thousands of jobs, too. But the closer we got to actually doing it, the less sure I became about it. In the first few years the political climate flip-flopped back and forth with every election, so our budget kept getting cut and reinstated. We ran out of money long before we finished all the engines. We had to cut corners, trim our safety margins, redesign crucial systems at the last minute. By the time Joray and her people regained power this last time, we were committed to doing it with inadequate equipment, and I knew we would fail. So I decided to stop it before we could hurt anyone." He looked up at Scotty. "I didn't figure on you showing up and trying it anyway."

"I didn't have much choice," Scotty told him. "You seem to forget why you were doin' all this in the first place, laddie. Your world was dyin' already."

Neron nodded. "Yes, but it was a slow death. It's easier to accept something that won't happen for years. Especially when you're staring a much more immediate death straight in the face."

"Maybe," Scotty said. He wasn't sure about that, but he supposed different people might feel differently about it. He had always preferred a situation he had some control over, no matter how risky it was, to one in which he merely waited for the inevitable.

But he understood now why Neron had done what he did. He'd lost his nerve. Scotty hoped he wouldn't do it again when things started to shake a second time.

They would find out soon enough. The moment was rapidly approaching when they would have to fire the engines and hope their second round of repairs would hold together better than the first. It was frustrating to not be able to fix the computer right, but as Scotty had discovered many times in the past, a tight deadline helped wonderfully to prioritize things. It didn't have to be pretty; it just had to work.

They were rerouting the last of the circuits when his communicator beeped for attention and the captain said, "So how about it, Scotty. Are you ready down there?"

"Aye, Captain," Scotty told him. "We're just locking down the last of it now. We'll be ready when you are."

"Spock says the sooner the better. Full power as soon as you go on line."

"Actually," said Spock, "a gradual buildup would allow me to better compensate for vibration patterns as they develop."

"Copy that. A slow start, going to full." Scotty looked at Kostas, then to Neron. "Ready here?"

"As ready as we can get in such short time," Kostas said nervously.

Neron just nodded and said, "Ready."

"All right, then, here we go. Starting engines." Scotty tapped the command into the master console. Indicator lights in the overhead map blinked on, and power readings began to rise.

"Engines at one-quarter." Scotty ran them up a notch; then, when no warning lights blinked, he ran them up again. "Half impulse," he said.

The ground remained stable. "Whatever you're doing up there, it seems to be working. Going to three-quarters."

"Three-quarters," Kirk replied. His voice sounded a bit ragged, as if he were getting a bumpy ride.

The north polar computer complex, for a change, wasn't even vibrating. Scotty wouldn't have known anything was happening if it weren't for the indicator lights. Even the seismic monitors on the situation map showed everything in the green, all over the globe. "Going to full power," he said.

The engines throttled up smoothly. One of them— just one, out of 29,713 left!—triggered an alarm at full power, and that was amber rather than red. Its internal diagnostics had detected a fuel-flow imbalance that would become critical in another six hours. Scotty left it running; they would need every engine they could get to compensate for the ones they had lost.

Kostas looked disbelievingly at the monitors, then slowly began to relax. A big grin spread across his face. "This is the way it's supposed to work," he said.

"Don't jinx it," Scotty told him, but he was smiling, too. Even Neron looked around in wonder.

"Angular velocity increasing," Scotty said. "Thrust is ninety-nine-point-six percent of nominal. Captain, the way it's looking down here I could probably coax a wee bit more out o' those engines and bring it all the way up to specs if you want."

"That won't be necessary, Mr. Scott." Kirk's voice over the communicator seemed even rougher than before, and Scotty could hear loud rumbling in the background.

"Captain," he said, suddenly alarmed. "Is everything all right up there?"

Kirk wished he knew the answer to Scotty's question. The *Enterprise* was shaking like a box falling down stairs. With the tractor beam tying it to the planet, every vibration in the crust was transmitted directly to its hull. That was exactly what they wanted to happen, but staying inside that hull at the time was exciting to say the least. And to top things off, they had to fly a high-speed forced orbit so they could cover the entire planet, and that meant they hit every subspace fluctuation at ten times their normal speed.

The inertial dampers that normally kept them from feeling forces from the engines' thrust were working hard to account for the unusual new motion. It was a vibration, not a simple vector, and the gravity generators were having trouble compensating fast enough. The bridge crew were all hanging on to their workstations, and Kirk kept both hands firmly clenched on the armrests of his command chair.

"We're still in one piece, if that's what you mean," he said to Scotty. "But I'm afraid you're going to have a few loose bolts to tighten when you get back."

"Don't let her go to pieces on you while I'm away, now," Scotty admonished him.

"We'll do our best," Kirk replied. The ship lurched hard enough to rattle teeth, and he looked to Spock and said, "Do you hear that, Spock? Mr. Scott will be very upset if you shake us apart without him."

Spock was busy monitoring the tractor-beam deployment. Without looking up, he said, "He is welcome to beam aboard at any time."

Kirk laughed. As if anyone would want to beam into this carnival ride. Then he remembered who he was talking to. Scotty would definitely rather be here, especially now, than wonder about his ship's fate while he rode it out safely on the ground. Kirk couldn't very well order him aboard, though. He was needed too badly down there.

Another shudder ran through the ship. The superstructure groaned under the unusual load, and a loud *crack* rang out as something broke free inside one of the walls.

Then again, Kirk thought, maybe Scotty would be able to do more good up here.

* * *

Spock was thinking the same thing, but for a different reason. The tractor beam's dampening effect on the ground motion was not as efficient as his simulations had indicated it should be. Natural processes seldom matched predictions exactly, but this was a much larger deviation than he had expected, and it was getting worse.

The effect was too small to be noticed yet on the ground, but the *Enterprise* was taking a much stronger beating than it should have. Even with his Vulcan strength, Spock could hardly keep himself seated at his science station, and he had twice miskeyed commands into the computer because the keypad had moved unexpectedly beneath his fingers. The squeaks and groans of fatigued metal were an ominous reminder that they were already exceeding design loads, and if he couldn't discover what was wrong with his calculations soon then the mounting tensions could rip the hull into scrap.

He examined the data as it came in. Seismic activity was responding as predicted, just not as rapidly as the model had shown. It was almost as if the rock were more dense than his remote measurements had indicated. If it was more massive, the tractor beam would have less effect on it, but the vibrational frequency would also be different from the predictions and that was not the case.

No, something else was at work here. Perhaps the subspace interactions were more complex than he had anticipated. If they were reinforcing one another more energetically than his model had suggested, then it would take more power from the tractor beam to dampen the motion they induced. Yet if that was happening, then the vibrational nodes would not be where he had predicted, and that, too, was exactly as the model had shown.

The only thing that wasn't right was the dampening effect itself. The tractor beam had to flick from site to site hundreds of times per second, staying ahead of the harmonic buildup in thousands of sites at once; perhaps it was inducing some sort of oscillation of its own due to a carryover effect.

It took less than a minute to disprove that theory as well. It was a minute of bone-jarring jolts and heavy shaking, and damage reports coming in from all over the ship, but the sensors read no oscillation within the beam.

But he had exhausted all the other possibilities. If it wasn't rock density, inaccurate modeling, or carryover effect, then that led to one inescapable conclusion: Something was wrong with the tractor beam itself.

He paused the beam's motion long enough for a complete diagnostic of the system. The starship quit shaking for the three seconds that took, and people sat up in their seats; then it jolted again as Spock released the beam and a collective groan went up from everyone on the bridge. Spock looked at the readout, where the problem was clear to see: There had been a phase shift in the graviton collimator, which was sapping the beam's effectiveness.

"Captain," Spock said over the thunder of shuddering starship. "We have a problem."

The ship's careening motion was bouncing Kirk half out of his command chair. He shifted his grip so he could look over to Spock without falling free and said, "I would never have guessed. What now?"

"The graviton collimator is drifting out of phase. The beam is losing its focus."

"How bad is it?"

"A twelve-percent drop in power delivered to the surface, but the effect is growing worse. I will attempt repairs, but that will mean leaving the dampening program to run by itself, and it cannot compensate for varying efficiency in the beam. Someone will have to monitor it and shut it down if the shaking grows any worse."

Scotty had been listening in. He said, "No, Mr. Spock. Let me do it. I know just what's wrong with that bloody thing. I was workin' on it when we diverted course for here, and I thought I'd got it fixed, but the resonators're obviously drifting out of alignment again."

"Mr. Scott, are you not needed on the ground?" Spock asked him.

"Not now I'm not. And if we keep the *Enterprise* doin' what it's doin' I won't be. Kostas and Neron can certainly handle whatever comes up."

"Neron?" Kirk asked. Spock also felt surprise at the mention of the saboteur, but he immediately realized what had to have happened. He approved of Scott's use of available talent in a crisis; it was a logical decision.

"It's a long story," Scotty said to Kirk, "but the gist of it is that everything is under control down here for the moment. Let me beam back up and fix those resonators and maybe we can keep it that way."

"Very well," said Kirk. "Transporter room, beam Mr. Scott aboard."

Spock turned back to his station. Tractor-beam phasing had drifted another three percent. Coupling efficiency with the ground was correspondingly weaker, but that didn't mean the ship got any respite from the shaking. Without the tractor beam's dampening effect, the planetary harmonic buildup had increased, which in turn was transmitting even more vibration to the ship than before.

A severe jolt brought an automatic alarm from the computer. "Structural integrity breached on deck twelve," it said in its feminine voice. "Pressure containment fields on in sections one and two."

That was no surprise. Deck twelve was where the inertial dampers were located. Those and the tractor-beam mounts at the bottom of the ship would naturally be the points of most stress. But if the hull was actually buckling there, then the ship was in serious trouble.

Kirk shouted to be heard over the noise, "Spock, we've got to cut back on that tractor beam!"

That seemed the obvious course of action, but Spock knew the true situation was counterintuitive. He had to raise his voice as well to be heard over the vibration as he said, "Actually, Captain, we must *increase* power to the beam and dampen the seismic activity if we wish to decrease our motion. Otherwise we will have to shut off the beam entirely and throttle down the engines below as well."

"Can we pick up where we left off if we do that?" Kirk asked.

"I am afraid not, Captain. The subspace influence of the other planets will grow beyond our ability to compensate. We have to do this now or not at all."

The ship shuddered again. Kirk punched the intercom controls in his chair and said, "Bridge to engineering. How soon can you give us full power, Scotty?"

"I just got here, Captain," Scotty said. "Give me a second to hang up my hat."

"You'll have to do it with your hat on," Kirk told him. "We're out of time."

Chapter Twenty-four

SULU HAD GIVEN UP his genetics simulations. It was obvious that the Rimillians weren't going to need a hardier cyclone tree anyway. By the way the *Enterprise* was shaking, the planet must be spinning like a gyroscope by now.

Not that he could tell. He'd been stuck in front of the simulator for days now, without even a peek at the stars or the planet below. He supposed he could get outside video on the monitor, but he was too busy hanging on with both hands to try it.

He heard a crash from the intensive-care room, and McCoy's irritated drawl: "I thought I'd seen everything, but now we've got spacequakes. I always knew Spock had a sense of humor."

Sulu laughed, but it was short-lived. The entire ship groaned as if it was about to split open at the seams, and four sharp jolts in a row knocked him to the floor.

Then the internal gravity quit entirely for a second, and he would have rebounded all the way to the ceiling if he hadn't clutched the countertop and pushed himself back down. He had just gotten his feet under him when the gravity came back on, and he found himself crouching like a cat, waiting to see which way to jump.

He heard Haidar say to Joray, "I can't believe it. I just *left* this!"

"I always wanted to go into space," Joray replied, "but now I don't know."

"Tell me about it," said McCoy. He said something else, too, but it was drowned out in the rumble of another beam-transmitted quake.

When the voices from the other room could be heard again, Sulu heard Joray saying, "—want to just settle in under a tree with a good book and watch the sunset."

That wasn't likely to happen quite the way she wanted it, either, thought Sulu. By the time Rimillia had a normal enough rotation period to give her a decent sunset, every tree on the planet would be long dead. New forests might be planted by then, but unless they grew incredibly fast, Joray would be an old woman by the time they were big enough to sit under.

Sulu considered going into the next room to join her and the others while the decks seemed relatively stable, but the thought about trees made him pause and settle back into his chair before the genetic simulator again. He had seen plenty of trees in the last few days, but one of them stuck in his mind. If he could just find it among the thousands of possibilities he'd generated . . .

If he could just reach the controls, he thought as

another tremor rattled the lab. The simulator screen flickered, but it had been doing that when the ship was rock-steady, so that didn't mean anything. Sulu braced himself with one hand and steadied his other near the controls, and began to page through the mutations he'd recorded.

It didn't take long. The image leaped out at him the moment he saw it: an enormous pillar of rough brown trunk with a conical canopy of green boughs. A phenomenal oxygen producer, and fast-growing. Seven meters a year for the first decade, and not much slower after that. It would peak out at just under two hundred meters, and a single mature tree would produce enough lumber for a small town. Considering how much rebuilding the Rimillians were going to have to do, a forest of these things would make a great asset.

Sulu rode out another shock wave; then, when he got the chance, he sent a copy of the file to the monitor next to Joray's bed in the convalescent ward.

"What's this?" he heard her say.

He got up and staggered to the doorway. Joray sat in her bed, its patient-restraint field holding her in place. Haidar and McCoy didn't have that luxury; they clung to the sides of the bed and rode out the shock waves like sailors at sea. Clutching the doorframe for support, Sulu told them, "That's what your new forests will look like, if you want them to. I think I can make trees like that for you, provided we aren't killed in the earthquakes first."

The problem with the tractor beam, thought Scotty as he pulled open the access panel that led into the control circuitry, was that the resonator was worn out.

257

Jerry Oltion

It had been giving him fits for the last three months, requiring delicate adjustment and then never staying tuned once he'd gotten it right. It should have been replaced months ago, and it would have been if the *Enterprise* had made any of its last three supply rendezvous, but in the meantime Scotty had nursed it along as best he could and hoped that he wouldn't have to count on it for anything important.

Now, of course, his very life hung in the balance, and the fate of the entire ship as well. That was the trouble with machinery; you never knew which part you'd need most. Except of course when something wasn't working right; then you could count on needing that.

He steadied himself against the control console, then reached inside with the circuit analyzer. Sure enough, the resonator was misaligned, so instead of sending out a coherent graviton beam of just one frequency, the emitter was generating a wideband signal that interfered with itself and canceled some of its own effectiveness.

Fortunately it could be realigned remotely from here. If he'd had to suit up and go outside to the actual emitter to do it, they would have had to shut down the tractor beam while he worked on it. As it was, he just had to hang on long enough to make the adjustment without knocking anything *else* out.

That was going to be tough enough. It wasn't simply a dial that needed to be twisted; this was one of those damnable "factory adjustments" that the designers intentionally made as difficult as possible so people wouldn't be tempted to fool with it. It had to be done through an induced signal in the data line. Not normally a problem, but then this wasn't a normal

258

situation. Every time Scotty reached into the tangle of circuitry, the ship would lurch and he would over-shoot the mark. The system had never been designed to be worked on in motion; evidently the factory where these adjustments were normally made didn't shake like this. Scotty wondered fleetingly if they might have an opening for another engineer.

He wedged his elbow against the hatch frame, held the analyzer up to the proper data line, and triggered the signal inducer. The circuit analyzer's tiny screen displayed a graph of the graviton-beam collimation. It dropped at first, so Scotty reversed the polarity and watched it climb back toward nominal, but the ship was vibrating too badly to let him read the screen closely.

He couldn't reach the intercom from where he was, so he flipped open his communicator and said, "Scott to bridge. How does it look now, Mr. Spock?"

"Efficiency has risen to ninety-two percent," Spock replied.

"I'll see if I can get that last eight percent out of her," Scotty told him, "but I don't know how much success I'll have. This thing is just plain worn out."

Cheap piece of junk, he thought as he bent back to the task. On the other hand, he had the feeling they were probably violating the manufacturer's warranty by using the beam to tug on an entire planet.

He triggered the inducer again, and a moment later Spock said, "Ninety-six percent. No, now it is down again to ninety-four. Ninety." Scotty ran it the other way until Spock started counting up again, but ninety-seven was the highest it would go.

"I believe that will be sufficient," Spock said. "If we can hold this level for another fourteen minutes, the planet will have picked up enough momentum to rotate past the libration point at three-quarters power."

That would be good. At the lower power level the engines wouldn't generate so much resonant vibration, and in another fifteen minutes the neural-net control computer would probably learn enough from experience to handle the job on its own.

That was, if the ship could survive that long. It bucked savagely as Spock used the strengthened tractor beams to dampen the vibrations that had grown worse below. Scotty banged his head on the access cover, then cursed as an alarm sounded elsewhere in engineering. It sounded like the warp core. Wonderful. If that went off line then they couldn't get full power to the tractor beam no matter how well the resonator was aligned. Scotty got up from the tractor-beam controls and staggered off to the warp core to see what needed to be done there.

Kirk had ridden horses that felt like this. Usually a good heel in the ribs would break them out of a trot into a smooth gallop, but he got the feeling that trying the same tactic here would only make things worse. If that was possible. He'd almost forgotten what it felt like to sit calmly it his command chair and watch the stars go by on the viewer. He could hardly *see* the viewer now; the constant vibration jostled his body enough to blur his vision. Chekov and Brady at the navigation and helm controls in front of him were blurs as well, and Uhura kept making little "oof" sounds as her chair slammed into her.

"Damage reports are coming in from all over the ship," she said. "Decks nine and ten are open to space, dorsal interconnects on deck thirteen are buckling, life-support is on auxiliary power . . ." She tilted her head, listening hard to hear over the roar the ship made; then she burst out laughing. "And we have a broken conduit in the clothing recyclers."

"Don't laugh," Kirk said, suppressing a grin himself. But at this point it was either laugh or cry, so he said, "The air on a starship can get ripe in a hurry if we lose recycling." He turned to Spock. "Any improvement now that the tractor beam is back up to specs?" he asked.

Spock consulted his board, then said, "Stress levels are within design tolerance again; however the ship's structural integrity has been compromised enough to make those figures questionable. Fortunately, the effect of the improved tractor beam is beginning to be felt on the planet, and quake activity will soon be decreasing."

"Good," Kirk said. It was high time something went right for a change. The sooner they could stop shaking his ship to pieces, the better he'd feel about the whole situation. Maybe, if Spock's estimate of the time was accurate, that would be soon.

Or maybe not. The intercom whistled for attention, and Scotty said, "Engineering to bridge. All this shakin' has damaged the warp core. It's going to go critical on us in about ten minutes if we don't cut power consumption."

Spock looked up from his station. "Can you be more precise, Mr. Scott? We need full power for another eleven minutes, fifteen seconds."

"No, I can't be more precise," Scotty said. "The antimatter stream is diffusing before it reaches the dilithium crystal. It's eatin' the articulation frame, and it's anybody's guess how long that'll hold out, but when that goes the whole reactor goes."

Kirk gripped the arms of his chair hard enough to leave dents in the padding. Not now. Not this close to success. "You'll have to coax more time out of it, Scotty," he said. "We're not shutting down until we get the job done."

"We'll shut down when it burns through, and that's a fact," Scotty replied, "but I'll see if I can't coax eleven minutes and fifteen seconds out of 'er before she does."

"Eleven minutes will be sufficient now," Spock said helpfully. "Even ten minutes fifty seconds will probably do."

"Well, that's a relief," Scotty said.

At least the rough ride was smoothing out now that the tractor beam was once again dampening the harmonic vibration on the planet. The inertial compensators arrested the ship's motion for seconds at a time now, allowing everyone to let go and flex fingers that had gone white from holding on to support for so long.

"Whatever you've done, keep it up," Kirk told Spock.

Spock said, "I cannot take full credit for the smoother ride. The Rimillian control computer is becoming more efficient as well."

"How long before we can turn the entire job over to them?" Kirk asked.

"Their engines must remain at full power for eight more minutes, twelve seconds. After that they will have imparted sufficient angular momentum to overcome tidal braking, and they may throttle down to three-quarters. We may disengage at that time."

"Scotty, do we have eight minutes left?"

"It'll be nip and tuck, Captain," said Scott, "but now that we're not shaking so badly I can tighten the antimatter stream a bit and improve the odds."

"Do that," Kirk said. He almost stood up to pace the bridge, but another shock reminded him that they weren't out of danger yet. He settled back in his command chair instead.

The minutes ticked by like hours. Each time the ship lurched, Kirk was sure it was the warp core going, but Scotty kept it on line and Spock kept the tractor beam playing across the planet, smoothing the harmonic vibrations before they could build up to dangerous levels again. Uhura eventually stopped calling out damage reports, and Chekov was able to use both hands to stabilize their orbit.

Kirk turned to Uhura. "Get me Professor Kostas."

"On line," she reported a moment later.

"What's your status?" Kirk asked him.

"Smooth as can be," he replied. "We're ready to throttle down on your mark."

"Coming up in one minute, forty seconds," Spock said.

"Scotty, are we going to make it?" Kirk asked.

"I think so," he replied. "Power levels are fluctuating, and I'll have to completely replace the articulation frame, but it looks like we—"

The ship lurched, and there came a loud *bang* over the intercom. Kirk winced, expecting to be blown into atoms any second, but a moment later Scotty came back and said, "Sorry about that. The hatch cover slipped out o' my hand."

Chekov was breathing heavily. "After all this, I nearly die of a heart attack," he muttered to Brady.

The last minute and a half ticked slowly by, the ship bouncing less and less, until at last Spock said, "Sufficient angular momentum has been attained. You may throttle back to three-quarters impulse power."

"Three-quarters power," Kostas replied.

"Ease off on that tractor beam," Kirk ordered immediately after. "Scotty, you can shut down the warp core now."

"Aye, Captain."

The rumbling and the shaking diminished as the tractor beam weakened, and the *Enterprise* glided on in a smooth orbit again. Kirk leaned back in his chair and let out a deep breath. On the forward viewer the planet below was a glittering hemisphere, the bright sparks of its engines still firing, the shadow line dividing it in half between day and night. And already a few degrees out into the bright side, visible even from orbit, the straight line of city that had once been the Edge, and was now just a meridian, crept away from the shadow.

Chapter Twenty-five

THE OBSERVATION DECK was a mess, since it shared space with the inertial dampers, but the going-away party was held there all the same. No place else on the ship offered a naked-eye view of space like this one, and the world coordinator and her second-in-command wanted a good look at their new home before they departed.

McCoy thought the party was a lousy idea, at least in medical terms. Joray was still in no shape to be on her feet. She had insisted, however, and Kirk had leaned on him to let her do it, so here she was. And here was McCoy with a hypospray at the ready in case she wasn't as strong as she thought she was.

In the meantime, it was a beautiful view. The planet was covered with storms as the frozen gases on the nightside boiled off into the atmosphere and redistributed themselves around the globe. There wasn't enough Coriolis force to curve them into cyclones yet, but that wouldn't be long in coming. Beneath the cloud cover, the Edge had made nearly half its first transit already, and the engines were still working fine. They would have to keep working for months to build the planet's speed up to anything like a normal day, but they could do that at three-quarters power, well below the critical level. The tough part was past.

The technological tough part, at any rate. Now came the long job of rebuilding what the rotation project had destroyed. And what the Rimillians had destroyed before that. McCoy couldn't help thinking that the whole situation could have been avoided if they had just taken a little better care of their habitable zone to begin with. The Edge wasn't big, but it would have been big enough if they hadn't overrun it and cut down all the trees.

Of course, that was a fine thing for someone from Earth to say. Earth people had made the same mistakes, and they had a whole planet to work with. It had just taken them longer to ruin it, that was all. But the Rimillians had gone through the same stages, the same political wrangling over what to do, jobs versus the environment and progress versus conservation, until it was nearly too late. Like Earth, they hadn't moved to fix anything until the last moment, and now they would be paying for that procrastination for generations to come.

It was a damned lousy way to do things, in McCoy's opinion. But then, nobody had asked him. Not in time to do any good, anyway. But maybe he could do some good now.

"Councilor, I believe I owe you an apology," he heard Kirk say to Haidar. "I mistook Neron's actions for yours, and allowed that to influence my judgment."

McCoy turned away from the window and saw Joray nodding. She and Haidar and Kirk, plus Scotty and Kostas, who had beamed up from the surface, were all in a tight group near the end of the hors d'oeuvre table. "I, too, apologize," Joray said. "I falsely accused you of treason. When we return, I will understand if you press for disciplinary action."

Haidar waved a hand dismissively. "I accept your apology, both of you, but it's hardly necessary. Until Neron revealed himself, I was the most likely suspect. And you—" she smiled at Joray "—are going to have a hard enough time without me adding to it. I believe we should put this behind us and work together for Rimillia."

"Agreed," Joray said.

"I propose a toast," Kirk said, picking up a wine goblet from the table. Haidar and Joray took goblets as well, and Scotty and Kostas refilled the ones they had already been drinking from. McCoy shuddered to think what the alcohol would do to Joray on top of all the other insults her body had endured, but he supposed it wouldn't kill her. Kostas—and the guards who had kept him and Kirk captive—had already proven that Rimillians could drink alcohol without any more than the usual penalties. McCoy wondered if that would become a custom now on the planet, but if it did they would have to buy their booze from passing traders, because McCoy had beamed up and sterilized all the yeast-infected canisters of Romulan root beer that Kirk and Ensign Turner had brewed. He wasn't about to let a major breach of the Prime Directive occur on his watch.

Of course, what he carried in his pocket could be construed as an even bigger breach, but he figured he had a pretty good defense if anyone ever confronted him about it. After all, what he planned to introduce to the native culture had already been part of the biosphere for millions of years. It was all through the fossil record, and still existed in the genetic code of the most prevalent species on the planet. So what if he and Sulu had tweaked a few genes here and there to reactivate that code; it wasn't as if they'd made anything up out of whole cloth, or even used techniques the Rimillians themselves didn't have. They'd just sped things along a little. Reintroduced them to a piece of their heritage they didn't even know they had.

Sulu was grazing among the hors d'oeuvres. His cold was finally over, and he was hungrily trying to replenish the energy he'd lost to that and to lack of sleep over the last week. McCoy caught his eye and nodded toward the captain and the two councilors, and Sulu met him halfway there.

"Shall we give them our going-away present?" McCoy asked him.

"Now looks like as good a time as ever," Sulu replied. He wiped rumaki oil on a napkin and made sure he hadn't gotten anything on his dress uniform.

As they approached, Kirk said, "Bones, Joray was just telling me how well she likes your bedside manner." Both women giggled, and McCoy blushed. Hah, he thought. Get 'em drunk and tell thousand-year-old jokes. I'll have to remember that next time I have to entertain two beautiful women.

He smiled and said to Joray, "I always aim to please." He nodded to Haidar as well and added, "But now that you're both about to head back home, I thought this might be a good time to give you a little present that Sulu and I cooked up for you in the genetics lab."

"Oh, yes," Joray said. "The trees! I was hoping you hadn't forgotten."

McCoy could hardly hold back his grin. Sulu couldn't. "Well," he said, "while we were working on that we saw a few other things that might be useful, and we had samples from quite a few different native plants, too, so we cloned a few other variants for you as well."

"A few other variants?" Haidar asked. "Like what?"

"Let me show you," said McCoy. He reached into his pocket and pulled out a clear plastic bag of dark brown, wrinkled seeds. "These will produce what I immodestly call Leonard trees. They grow about three meters high—just overhead—put out bright orange flowers in the springtime, and bear fruits about the size of your fist about two months later. We didn't force-grow a whole fruit, but from the analysis we made it looks like they should be good to eat." McCoy held out the seeds to Haidar.

"Fruit trees! Thank you," she said.

Sulu pulled a bag of seeds from his pocket. "These are Hikaru orchids," he said. "Not edible, but pretty. They have big purple blossoms, and a very delicate fragrance that I *did* synthesize just to make sure you liked it." He opened the packet and held it out. A honeylike aroma immediately wafted out into the room, and both Joray and Haidar said, "Mmmm, yes."

Sulu handed the seeds to Joray, and McCoy pulled out another packet. "Orangemelon," he said. "A small bush. Not much for flowers in the spring, but it puts out four or five vines with two or three big melons each on them. Also edible, of course."

"That sounds wonderful," Joray said, taking the packet of seeds.

Sulu was ready with another. "Fern," he said. "One of nature's simplest and most beautiful plants. There are variants on almost every planet we've encountered, and I didn't want you to be left out. Rimillia's should be especially nice, because its leaves are soft and velvety."

While the women were thanking him for that, McCoy brought out his next offering. "Carroot," he said. "Like carrot—" he picked up one from the hors d'oeuvre tray to show them "—but the roots grow horizontally for meters. They sprout new tops every few centimeters, and those make good salad greens."

And so it went, back and forth until the women couldn't hold any more seed packets and had to set them on the table. McCoy felt like Santa Claus, handing out treat after treat to delighted children. Flowers, berries, fruits, grasses—the list went on and on.

At last, when both his and Sulu's pockets had been exhausted, Kirk laughed and said, "I've noticed a definite pattern here. Every one of McCoy's offerings have been edible or medicinal. And every one of Sulu's has been aromatic or tactile or provides shade or some other comfort. Did you divide up your labor that way intentionally or is that just the way it came out?"

McCoy felt himself blush. He looked over at Sulu and saw the same reaction there, because it hadn't been planned that way at all. They had both just created the best plants they could come up with. Evidently their definition of "best" was a little different.

Joray laughed good-naturedly at their embarrassment, then quickly changed the subject. "You keep mentioning springtime," she said. "What's that?"

McCoy laughed with her. "Plant these and see."

As Chekov settled into his navigation chair, he felt his pulse rate begin to rise. It always did when they broke orbit. Not because it was such a tough or dangerous task—in fact it was one of the easiest parts of his job—but because of what it represented. Their business here was done, and they were about to step off into the unknown again. In just a few hours they would be back in deep space, heading for uncharted territory and who knew what strange new wonders.

To be sure, their first stop would be a long-delayed resupply break and a week of R&R on Coleman's Planet, provided Starfleet didn't redirect them before they got there, but after that it would be anybody's guess. By this time next month they could be halfway across the sector.

He checked his control board for anomalies, but all the indicators were green. It had taken quite a bit of repair work, but the *Enterprise* was spaceworthy again. It might not do warp nine anytime soon, but it would get them to their next stop.

He looked around at the rest of the bridge. Sulu was once again at the helm beside him, Mr. Scott was at the engineering board, Spock at his science station, Uhura at comm—and the captain sat in his raised command chair, McCoy standing at his side.

Kirk was looking at the forward viewer, upon which

Rimillia glowed with bright sunlight. Its cloud cover was beginning to look like a normal class-M planet's now, the long arcs of storm fronts advancing across it, clockwise in the northern hemisphere and counter-clockwise in the south. Through gaps in the cloud, the Edge could still be seen, now nearly meeting the terminator again after its first revolution. It would be centuries before that great circle faded into the landscape, but Chekov had no doubt that it would.

He looked back to Kirk. "Course, Captain?"

Kirk rubbed his chin, thinking it over. "How about," he said, narrowing his brow and pursing his lips momentarily, "how about one low pass just out of the atmosphere, west to east, for about a quarter of an orbit, then heading one-seventy, mark forty-six."

One-seventy by forty-six was correct for Coleman's Planet, but the initial pass over Rimillia seemed needlessly complex. Puzzled, Chekov asked, "Why the low quarter-orbit, sir?"

"Yeah," said McCoy. "Aren't you a little old to be buzzing planets?"

Smiling wryly, Kirk said, "As a matter of fact, no, I'm not. Besides, my course will take us through the terminator against the direction of rotation. I just thought, considering all the trouble we've gone through to create it, that we ought to at least fly off into the sunset."

THE ART OF
STAR TREK®

THE never-ending multimedia phenomenon that is STAR TREK has treated generations of viewers to a dazzling barrage of unforgettable images of the future. Bizarre alien beings, breathtaking extraterrestrial landscapes, exotic costumes, state-of-the-art special effects, and remarkably convincing futuristic sets and props have brought Gene Roddenberry's inspiring vision to life before the public's awestruck eyes.

- Over 1000 photos and illustrations
- Hundreds never before seen

By Judith and Garfield Reeves-Stevens

POCKET
B O O K S

A Pocket Books Hardcover

1160